COSPLAYED

TO

DEATH

COSPLAYED

TO

DEATH

A SUDDENLY FRENCH MYSTERY

ELLE JAUFFRET

To Grand-Mère.

To those who have the courage to be themselves, in a world that often asks them to be something else.

Contents

Praise for the Suddenly French Mysteries   iv

A Note from the Author   vii

Chapter One   1

Chapter Two   5

Chapter Three   9

Chapter Four   14

Chapter Five   18

Chapter Six   24

Chapter Seven   29

Chapter Eight   33

Chapter Nine   37

Chapter Ten   40

Chapter Eleven   43

Chapter Twelve   50

Chapter Thirteen   54

Chapter Fourteen   57

Chapter Fifteen   62

Chapter Sixteen   66

Chapter Seventeen   73

Chapter Eighteen   77

Chapter Nineteen   80

Chapter Twenty   84

Chapter Twenty-One   87

Chapter Twenty-Two   92

Chapter Twenty-Three   94

Chapter Twenty-Four   97

Chapter Twenty-Five 100

Chapter Twenty-Six 103

Chapter Twenty-Seven 105

Chapter Twenty-Eight 107

Chapter Twenty-Nine 111

Chapter Thirty 113

Chapter Thirty-One 119

Chapter Thirty-Two 123

Chapter Thirty-Three 127

Chapter Thirty-Four 130

Chapter Thirty-Five 134

Chapter Thirty-Six 139

Chapter Thirty-Seven 144

Chapter Thirty-Eight 149

Chapter Thirty-Nine 155

Chapter Forty 159

Chapter Forty-One 165

Chapter Forty-Two 170

Chapter Forty-Three 172

Chapter Forty-Four 179

Chapter Forty-Five 181

Chapter Forty-Six 184

Chapter Forty-Seven 187

Chapter Forty-Eight 191

Chapter Forty-Nine 195

Chapter Fifty 200

Chapter Fifty-One 203

Chapter Fifty-Two 208

Chapter Fifty-Three 210

Chapter Fifty-Four 214

Chapter Fifty-Five 217

Chapter Fifty-Six 219

Chapter Fifty-Seven 223

Chapter Fifty-Eight 226
Chapter Fifty-Nine 229
Chapter Sixty 233
Chapter Sixty-One 236
Chapter Sixty-Two 239
Chapter Sixty-Three 243
Acknowledgments 248
About the Author 249
Also by Elle Jauffret 251

Praise for the Suddenly French Mysteries

PRAISE FOR *COSPLAYED TO DEATH*

"Extreme cosplayers, champion surfers, and professional rivals abound in *Cosplayed to Death.* This cozy mystery brims with quirky charm, clever plotting, and a heroine you can't help but root for. A fun, modern take on citizen detectives, this tale will keep you guessing who's settling scores until the last chapter."—M.C. Vaughan, author of *Romancing Miss Stone* and *Code Name Gorgeous*

"Full of surfside vibes and delicious food drama, *Cosplayed to Death* kept me guessing until the end! A perfect summer read."—M.K. England, author of *All Fired Up*

"Jauffret delivers an absolute riptide of a mystery in *Cosplayed to Death*! A clever plot, charming heroine, and sparkling humor take center stage as Claire plunges headfirst into the equally fascinating worlds of cosplay and professional surfing along with her delightful best friend Suggie and her annoyingly handsome roommate Torres. I can't wait to see what other mysteries await us in Caper Cove!"—Jenny Adams, Agatha Award-nominated author of the Deadly Twenties Mysteries

"I was immediately immersed in this cleverly written drama that I could not put down until all was said and done. A solidly crafty multi-plot storyline where the mystery was skillfully accomplished with the right amount of intrigue, tension, suspense, and apprehension."—Dru Ann Love, winner of the Agatha, Anthony, Macavity, and Raven Awards

"If you're looking for a cozy murder mystery that will feed your curiosity and your appetite, look no further. *Cosplayed to Death* has it al—a quirky lead, lovable sidekicks, delicious food descriptions, and a setting you'll wish you could visit in real life. Looking forward to book 3."—Janina Scarlet, author of *Superhero Therapy* and *Dark Agents*

PRAISE FOR *THREADS OF DECEPTION*

"Elle Jauffret spins a powerful, complex, and compelling mystery! THREADS OF DECEPTION dives deep into the human experience and does so with elegance and insight. Highly recommended!"—Jonathan Maberry, *NY Times* bestselling author of *NecroTek* and *The Dragon in Winter*

"A charming traditional mystery with a unique French twist—and a captivating mix of fashion, food, and fascinating characters! Elle Jauffret is a smart and fresh new voice, and this chic, cinematic, and unpredictable story, revealed in a gorgeous setting, will keep you turning the pages as fast as you can."—Hank Phillippi Ryan, *USA Today* bestselling author of *One Wrong Word*

"*Threads of Deception* is a fast-paced mystery with unique characters, refreshing humor, and unexpected adventures that will keep you turning pages. Jauffret's use of an unusual medical condition, fascinating backstory, and vivid setting add to the intrigue and interest, but her descriptions of scrumptious food will have you planning a visit to the nearest French bakery. By the last page, she's left just enough breadcrumbs to draw you forward into what will no doubt be a delightful series you'll enjoy with a book in one hand and *pain au chocolat* in the other."—Annette Lyon, *USA Today* bestselling author of *Just One More*

"Elle Jauffret's *Threads of Deception* is a delectable debut novel in which Jauffret stitches together a mouth-watering mystery that will leave readers hungry for more!"—Daphne Silver, Agatha Award-winning author of *Crime and Parchment*

"With a charming and confident heroine, a sexy police detective, and dripping with Hollywood intrigue, *Threads of Deception* is a must-read for mystery lovers, a fierce debut for author Elle Jauffret!"—Gretchen McNeil, author of *Ten* and the #murdertrending series

"When it comes to serving up an intriguing, unique and satisfying mystery, Jauffret is the crème de la crème."—Wendy Toliver, bestselling author of *Regina Rising* and *Red's Untold Tale*

"Death and deception in the cut-throat world of fashion? Yes, please! *Threads of Deception* was such a delicious ride. Claire Fontaine is a smart and likeable protagonist in the vein of Finlay Donovan and Aurora Teagarden. Highly recommend!"—Lorien Lawrence, author of the Fright Watch series and *The Many Hauntings of the Manning Family*

A Note from the Author

Dear Readers,

Five quotes have inspired this book:

"This above all: to thine own self be true,
And it must follow, as the night the day,
Thou canst not then be false to any man."
— *Hamlet*, Act I, Scene III

"Metamorphosis is the most profound of all acts."
— Catherynne M. Valente, *In the Night Garden*

"Always be yourself, express yourself, have faith in yourself, do not go out and look for a successful personality and duplicate it."
—Bruce Lee

"Don't bend; don't water it down; don't try to make it logical; don't edit your own soul according to the fashion. Rather, follow your most intense obsessions mercilessly."
— Anne Rice,
Foreword to the 1995 Schocken Books edition of Kafka's short stories

"The only normal people are the ones you don't know very well."
—Alfred Adler

* * *

In writing Claire's story, I wanted to explore how identity and privilege shape our experiences during crisis. When Claire faces targeting by ICE agents, her terror is genuine—but so is the immediate support she receives from her white privilege, her community connections, her documented professional status, and her father's position in law enforcement. This protection isn't available to everyone who faces similar harassment or accusations.

Claire's race and background create a safety net that many others don't have. While her fear and trauma are real, I hope readers will also consider the broader questions: whose voices are believed? Whose documentation is accepted? Who receives community protection when they need it most? How might this encounter have ended differently for someone without Claire's advantages?

* * *

To schedule a talk with your book club (online or in person), comment or ask a question about my book(s), please, visit https://ellejauffret.com/Contact. I look forward to hearing from you!

Chapter One

Claire's lungs burned as she sprinted through the coastal fog, her bare feet pounding against wet sand. The morning mist wasn't the gentle cotton candy most beach-goers romanticized—it was more like running through soup while blindfolded, if the soup was made of salt water and poor life choices. At 5:30 AM, this wasn't exactly how she'd planned to test her post-explosion recovery, but her best friend Suggie had insisted that early morning beach runs were the only cure for both physical therapy and sexual frustration.

"Come on, slowpoke!" Suggie called from somewhere in the grey void ahead. "Nothing beats running in a swimsuit! The ocean is Nature's perfect exfoliator!"

"Yeah, and hypothermia is nature's perfect weight loss program," Claire muttered, adjusting her too-tiny bikini bottom for the hundredth time. The top at least did its job containing her assets, but the bottom seemed determined to make a break for it. Still, running nearly naked was oddly liberating—when there weren't any witnesses to her scars or her pathetic attempts to keep her swimsuit in place.

The fog thickened around them like a living thing, muffling even their footsteps. The fishermen were out there somewhere, their boats mere shadows in the murk, probably laughing at the two crazy women running through what felt like a horror movie set.

"This beats your twelve-cookie solution!" Suggie shouted back, splashing through the breaking waves.

"Don't you dare disparage my Earl Grey and anise biscotti therapy!" Claire yelled, finally catching up. "Those cookies got me through my entire law career without committing a single justifiable homicide!"

They had pushed further than usual today, past the "Natural reserve. Fishing prohibited" sign that was barely visible in the murky air. Every step was a mystery—would it be solid sand, a hidden shell, or perhaps a portal to another dimension? With Claire's luck lately, probably the portal.

Suggie slowed down to a manageable pace. "How far are you from your pre-explosion shape?"

"I don't know. Ninety-five percent there, I guess." She had to admit: running on an empty beach wrapped with the surrounding sound of the sea was incredibly soothing. The explosion that destroyed her D.C. law firm and killed its entire staff felt like another lifetime now. Her back and tailbone no longer ached after long shifts catering, and the steady rhythm of morning jogs with Suggie had become her salvation.

"That's fantastic. So no more physical therapy."

"No, but I'm thinking about resuming speech therapy soon." She might have survived a deadly explosion, but the head trauma had gifted her with Foreign Accent syndrome—an accent so thick that strangers assumed she was a French tourist on vacation instead of an American-born attorney-turned-caterer.

Suggie slowed down. "Why? Your French accent is beautiful."

"Thanks. I don't really mind it anymore." Nothing says 'trust your caterer' quite like suddenly sounding like Julia Child's long-lost French cousin. "It's just that there's this new chef in town who's been spreading rumors about me."

"You mean Kerant Weber? The sandwich guy who's called you a French imitation?"

"Yes," Claire groaned. "The man who's convinced I'm a French impostor. Because the most logical explanation for my accent isn't a neurological condition, but that I'm running an elaborate catering con while secretly plotting to overthrow the local culinary scene with my superior baguette technique."

Claire's smartwatch beeped, and she jumped like she'd stepped on broken glass. "I have to go. I have to get to the fish market before all the good seafood's gone."

"I thought you didn't do early mornings," Suggie smirked.

"I don't. I was so busy helping my dad with the café's inventory, I completely forgot to place my order. The town's expecting over ten thousand visitors this weekend for the surfing festival, and the fishing co-operative can't guarantee last-minute pre-orders," Claire said, leading the way.

As they turned back, the marine layer started to recede. To the south, the Caper Cove lighthouse emerged from the dense shroud of mist, its lantern room catching the sun's first rays. To the north, the cliffs' shadows appeared like giants in the dissipating fog. The tide was coming in strong now, waves crashing against the shore with increasing aggression.

"Maybe one of those ten thousand visitors could be your future weekend boyfriend?" Suggie waggled her eyebrows.

"The last thing I need is—" Claire's retort was cut short by Suggie's scream as a wave knocked her friend down.

"Help! I think a seal just tried to make me its breakfast date!"

Claire rushed forward, grabbing what she thought was Suggie's hand in the foam. "Since when did you get man hands? And holy protein shakes, what have you been lifting?"

Suggie laughed from somewhere behind her. "That's not me you're pulling, genius! Must be driftwood."

Claire looked down at her catch and immediately wished she hadn't. The thing in her grip was definitely not driftwood. The corpse had cold, gray skin and hadn't been doing early morning cardio—unless you counted becoming fish food as exercise. A tattoo of the World Surf logo on his shoulder identified him as one of the pro surfers in town for the competition, though his current condition suggested his wave-riding days were over.

"Well," Claire said, her old criminal attorney instincts kicking in as she checked for a pulse she knew wouldn't be there, "I guess this beats finding another negative Yelp review from Weber."

Suggie, now a safe distance away, was frantically trying to decontaminate herself in the waves as if death cooties were a thing.

"You think it could be something more than an accident?" Suggie whispered. Though an accountant by trade, Suggie freelanced for the San Diego News and published The Caper Cove Whisperer, a weekly blog covering the resort town. She was always on the lookout for the next big story, especially since her coverage of the double murder two months ago had quadrupled her subscriber count.

Claire's stomach clenched. "You mean murder?"

Suggie recoiled at the word and nodded.

With the Olympic qualifying event in town, competition was fiercer than a rush for the last pack of toilet paper during the pandemic. Testosterone ran high among contestants of all genders. In a competitive setting, as in murder trials, some people would kill to win.

"With the stakes this high, murder is definitely not off the table, but I surely hope not."

It was the third body she had discovered since returning to Caper Cove, and she had zero interest in being dubbed a "serial body finder" or being compared to a truffle-sniffing pig for corpses. She could picture the headlines: LOCAL CATERER UNCOVERS DEAD BODY—AGAIN. "She needed to figure out who this surfer was and how he'd died before the rumor mill started grinding out theories about her being cursed—or worse, involved.

Chapter Two

I t was the first time Claire regretted not getting her smartwatch a data plan or taking her phone on a run. The disconnection from the world Suggie and she enjoyed by leaving all electronics behind while jogging was now an impediment. Stumbling on the corpse hadn't been on the list of foreseeable events, and they needed to alert the authorities fast. Since Claire had a stronger stomach and more blasé attitude when it came to corpses and death in general, she stayed with the dead body to preserve evidence while Suggie sprinted away.

Fifteen minutes later, Detective Ben Torres arrived at the scene aboard the lifeguards' red beach buggy he must have commandeered. He wore his wetsuit half-on and half-off, the top casually hanging around his waist like most surfers after their morning surfing. His sleeves dangling by his sides and the saltwater droplets clinging to his chest hair and Marine haircut conjured the image of a sexy cowboy straddling a mechanical bull.

"Backup's on the way," he said sternly as he dismounted the buggy. "Where did you find the guy?"

"I didn't find him. Suggie got slammed by a wave carrying him," Claire explained. She wanted to make it clear that she hadn't personally stumbled on it on her own.

Torres inspected the corpse and took a few pictures. "Did you touch him?"

"Yes, I pulled him out of the water, thinking it was Suggie, took him to the dry sand, and took his pulse. Other than that, no." She knew better than to touch evidence.

"And you're good?" he asked as he gave her a concerned look, followed by a languorous once-over. His corner smile and the way his gaze lingered on her mid-riff made her suddenly aware that she had nothing more than a tiny bikini on.

She folded in on herself, suddenly self-conscious of her scars striping her back and thighs; of her butt-cheeks and small fat rolls bulging out of her swimsuit as if trying to escape the too-tight fabric.

"Yes. I'm good," she said, tucking her belly in. Besides the discovery's initial shock, she was fine. Her past life as a criminal attorney handling felonies and going through gruesome pictures of murder cases had prepared her well to handle corpses with cold, professional detachment—but nothing had prepared her for being ogled in a tiny bikini. Turns out, the dead are much less judgmental or objectifying. She suddenly found herself wishing the corpse was the only one staring.

It's not that she wanted to seduce him—she would never consider any personal relationship with her father's protégé— but standing half-naked in front of her concerned roommate was sure to make their living arrangement more awkward. The unacknowledged sexual tension that already existed between them was plenty enough.

The detective smiled and spoke into the buggy's radio. "Call the coroner and keep the ambulance."

The two-way radio crackled, and a voice replied, "Copy that."

"Can I go now?" Claire asked, bent over on herself to hide as much of her body as she could. "I promise to drop by the station later to give you my statement." The medical examiner's and Caper Cove Police Department's trucks were approaching the area, and she wasn't looking forward to finding herself in a sea of first responders, considering her skimpy attire.

"Why, do you have a date?" Torres flashed her a sweet smile, reached into the buggy, and handed her an emergency blanket.

"I need to go to the fish market," she said, hastily wrapping the metallic cloth around herself. "I have a bouillabaisse and seafood buffet to prepare for a party tonight." Though challenging, sizable catering jobs were financially rewarding. A year of them would allow her to save enough to put a down payment on a small apartment—or at least to secure its rent. She wouldn't be forced to share a communal apartment and bathroom with Torres, and she would soon entertain the idea of a boyfriend without having Torres breathing down her neck—or outright scaring her guests. No matter what her detective-roommate said, leaving his police uniform hanging at the front door, whenever she invited a man over, wasn't a coincidence.

It was her first gig of the week. With the surfing festival and competition in town, her schedule was booked, and that's not even counting her helping out at The Osprey, her father's taco bar. With the thousands of visitors flocking to the shores for the two-week-long event, he would need all the hands on deck he could get.

"Why go to the market when you could simply plant a couple of fishing lines along the shore?"

"I don't think so!" a man in a tan uniform exclaimed as he stopped by their side. "She can't fish here. If she wants to fish in town, she must purchase a license. Only local residents can fish for free. Second, no one can fish here."

Torres stared at the newcomer with a frown. "And you are?"

"Fish and Wildlife, here to investigate." He ignored Torres's presence and focused his attention on Claire. "What were you doing here?" he asked loudly, over-enunciating as if Claire was hard of hearing.

"Hey, buddy. You can't question her. I'm Caper Cove Police, this is my jurisdiction, and she's my witness."

The wildlife officer stared down at Torres's neoprene suit, dismissing the detective's legitimacy with raised eyebrows. "Can you prove it?"

Claire stepped forward, the Mylar blanket tightly wrapped around her. "He is a detective with Caper Cover PD. I can vouch for him."

"*You* can vouch for him?" The man snickered. "You found the body. You're the first suspect."

Claire swallowed hard, trying to clear her throat from the ball that had just formed. Not again, she thought. Through her years as a criminal defense attorney, she had met her share of investigators whose boorishness and greed for power sent innocents to jail. So she chewed on her inner cheek and remained silent.

Torres shook his head, sighed loudly, and left to meet the newly arrived responders. "I'll be right back."

A few yards away, uniformed police officers scattered orange sawhorses along the shore and strung do-not-cross tape to secure the scene. One of them handed Torres a bag of clothes. On the ocean side, a coast guard response boat had stopped close to the shore.

Multiple agencies could claim pieces of the investigation based on location and circumstances, though local police had primary jurisdiction over the body.

"You better confess now," the Wildlife deputy said. "Why did you kill him?"

Claire jerked back, wondering whether to be offended or amused. "How can I be a suspect? I literally stumbled upon this hours-old corpse by accident."

"You can fool people, but not me, missy," he over-mouthed his words. "Tourists don't go walking on the beach this early unless they've got something to hide."

Claire rubbed her temples and forehead with her hands, wishing she had been dressed and had her wallet with her. Her driver's license or state bar card would have come in handy to shut the man up. "I'm not a tourist, I live here, and I was jogging. Nothing illegal about that."

"Actually, you committed a crime. The reserve is off access," he wiggled his finger at Claire as if scolding a child, and chin-nodded at Torres, who had reappeared in Caper Cove PD athletic wear. "These foreign tourists, I tell you, they should learn to read English and respect the law, am I right?"

Claire mentally gasped. Though she understood that her speech disorder could easily confuse people, that didn't give the man the right to dub her a "foreign tourist who couldn't read English." She inhaled deeply, held her breath a few seconds to keep calm, and released it slowly.

The man had accused her of being a tourist and a killer in the same breath. If Torres wouldn't chase down the real killer, she would.

Chapter Three

"You're wrong. Most state reserves are open to the public for recreational and educational activities unless specifically stated. So you may want to reread the law. Also, the reserve only starts at the boulder over there, the one tagged with a yellow X. Far from the place where the body was found," Claire pointed at the State Marine Reserve sign. "You have no jurisdiction over this case."

Torres listened to her, grinning, and turned to the Wildlife deputy. "Which means, you're standing on a free public beach, under Caper Cove Police Department's jurisdiction. My jurisdiction. So you need to stop badgering my witness and return behind the police tape, or I'll have to arrest you."

The Wildlife guy's face flushed red. His jaw clenched as he adjusted his ranger hat with a sharp tug. "This is absurd! I've been working these beaches for three years. I know exactly where." He swiveled on himself, like a dog chasing its tail, searching for a sign of his right to be here. His confident demeanor crumbled as his eyes landed on the yellow X marker clearly visible on the distant boulder. "That's…that can't be right," he muttered, pulling out a worn jurisdiction map from his back pocket and squinting at it in confusion until a uniformed officer escorted him behind the police tape.

Torres laughed. "You sure you want to leave the law behind? I sort of enjoyed watching you throw this guy back to his lane."

"Yes, I'm sure. At least for now." The neurologist and the FBI had been firm: to recover and protect herself from a deadly threat, she needed to stay out of the spotlight and keep stress at bay. The practice of law was too strenuous for her healing brain. The high levels of cognitive function required for the job, long hours, and the pressure to meet deadlines could potentially hinder her recovery—and worsen her accent. She was fine catering meals for the vacationing out-of-towners for now. "I've got to go. I'll drop by the station on my way back from the fish market if you don't mind."

"Sure. You need a ride?"

"I'm okay, thanks." Suggie was supposed to pick her up at the boat launch, which was fifty yards away. But if her friend wasn't there, a fifteen-minute jog back to her apartment might be the best thing for her to process the event.

"Okay, just make sure to let the paramedics check your vitals before leaving."

Claire glanced apprehensively at the EMT, a bodybuilding buff with a leering gaze. "Do I have to?"

"Yes, it's standard procedure for any crime scene witness."

"But I didn't witness a crime. The man was already dead."

"If you have a problem with EMT Quincy, just say so. You wouldn't be the first one." Torres cracked a side smile. "Wait…is he the flop blind date you went on?"

"I prefer not to talk about it, alright?" She didn't feel like sharing the details of her disastrous first date, a blind rendezvous she went on at Suggie's insistence. And she had no desire to drop her emergency blanket and have her pulse taken by a man she had no interest in seeing again up close.

Torres laughed. "No worry." He placed two fingers in his mouth and whistled in the direction of the corpse. "Hey, Vic, you mind coming here to check on Claire?" he shouted at the forensic pathologist examining the corpse.

Dr. Vikram Thomas, the local pathologist, rose to his feet and rushed to Claire's side. Like many locals, Vic surfed every morning before going to work and was still wearing his wetsuit—a tight red neoprene layer that outlined his lean, muscular frame. His curly hair was slicked back with ocean water.

"Hey, you okay?" he asked Claire, his eyes wide with concern.

"I'm fine. Torres's exaggerating. As if he weren't pesky enough as a flatmate," she said. "You mind checking my pulse and telling him I'm fine, so I can leave?"

"Sure, but I need you to sit or lie down." Vic guided her to the lifeguard buggy while Torres got updated by two police officers on the scene.

Claire settled on the driver's seat sideways, her feet dangling, and extended her arm. Standing by her side, Vic pressed his index and middle fingers on the inside her wrist, just below the base of the thumb, and stared at his analogue watch for fifteen seconds. A light red spread across his warm complexion, making Claire wonder if it was just sun kisses or a temporary blush.

"Seventy beats per minute. You're good to go."

"Thanks. Since you're here, what can you tell me about the corpse?"

"It's too early to say, but the victim seemed to have drowned. He also has a contused head and a wound on his back. Looks like he snapped his spine. Which suggests he was thrown against a rock, more likely by a wave."

"While surfing?" The high wind of the past night could have generated massive waves and turned the ocean into a lethal playground, more likely to involve drowning—not a spine breaking incident.

"That's the theory," Vic said, glancing at the ocean. The gale had subsided, but the air speed still reached a six on the Beaufort wind scale—about thirty-three miles per hour. The ocean churned with towering waves, which streaked the water white as they broke. Navigation was difficult and surfing perilous, especially on this rocky side of the beach.

"We're searching for the board." With a missing foot, they could assume the leash—the rope that keeps the surfers connected to their surfboards to prevent the boards from drifting away when they fall or wipe out—was responsible for severing the surfer's limb. "Only a full autopsy will be able to confirm it."

"Claire!" The familiar silhouette of Frank Fontaine grew against the rising sun. "You alright? I heard about the dead body over the radio. Everything's alright?" Her father asked between gasps.

"Yes, Dad, I'm fine. Suggie just caught a dead body. Her biggest catch to date," Claire said, trying to lighten the mood.

"I didn't catch it; it attacked me. A wave threw it at me." Suggie appeared from behind Frank and handed Claire a bag of clothes. She was all dressed up and had her phone out, recording the scene—a video she would likely post to her popular news blog or try to sell to the *San Diego County News,* which had vetted her as a freelancer a month before.

"Where? Who is it?" Frank asked.

Torres stirred Frank away by the arm. "Sorry, Frank, you can't be here."

"What do you mean I can't be here? My daughter and her friend just found a body."

"I know, but I don't want you to be contaminating the scene," Torres explained. The DNA found on and around the body was crucial evidence in establishing a list of suspects if the death was determined felonious and not accidental.

Frank shot an incredulous gaze at Torres. "Why, it's not like I know the guy."

Torres stared at Frank. "Actually, you do. It's Ricky Bingle."

"What? The jerk who fought me the other day?"

"Yes, that one."

Claire tensed up. The day before, Richard "Ricky" Bingle had hired a party taco food truck to illegally park right next to Frank's taco bistro, specifically to serve food to him and his friends. When Frank Fontaine called a tow truck to remove the food truck from his private parking lot, Bingle had punched him in the jaw. Frank hadn't retaliated against the pro-surfer. As a former cop trained in de-escalation techniques, he had simply warned the man that "he'll regret this" and that karma would get him one day. A statement that could be easily interpreted as a threat.

"What? You think the guy was murdered?" Frank asked.

Torres looked unusually stern. "We don't know yet. Just in case, you need to stay away."

Claire cleared her throat and took a step forward. "What are you talking about? If it turns out to be a homicide, you think my dad's a suspect?"

"I'm sorry, Claire. I'm just following protocol."

Claire shook her head, trying to shake the oddness of the day away. First, a Wildlife Deputy accused her of murder, and now her roommate is calling her dad a suspect? Nothing made sense. She'd find out what really happened, especially if it meant clearing her father's name. She had ten days before the festival ended, and half the suspects flew back to their home countries.

Chapter Four

The fish market was easy to spot. Located along the docks, its blue weathered wooden façade was ornate with fishing nets and shells, and squawking seagulls circled overhead, hoping for some discarded fish, during its operating hours.

Claire parked her scooter, a turquoise blue refurbished Vespa, at the back of the building and rushed to the fish stalls, her head reeling with questions. Vikram had promised to share the autopsy's preliminary findings with her as soon as he got them, hopefully determining the cause of death to be accidental. Claire's father didn't need the scrutiny and reputation-shredding consequence of a full-blown homicide investigation, especially during an international competition.

"Morning," local restaurateurs greeted Claire on their way out as they pulled seafood-filled carts behind them. "Better hurry up if you want the best products before the tourists sweep in," they reminded her.

"Good morning," she greeted back as she passed the old barn's double doors.

She navigated swiftly through the sea of haggling customers and stalls of fishermen shouting out their prices. The boisterous atmosphere reminded her of the hustle and bustle of Washington, D.C.'s courthouses where she had spent over ten years representing wrongly accused defendants. She missed fighting to make a difference in the world, but she also loved being back home in Caper Cove, where the scent of the briny ocean air and the warmth of camaraderie permeated every activity, including townsfolk gathering early to select the day's catch.

A man in a wheelchair left her favorite fish stall with a cooler full of fish. His movements were practiced, efficient, like someone who'd mastered the art of navigating crowded spaces.

"Who's that guy taking all your catch?" Claire asked as she reached the fish stand. "Should I worry about the competition?"

"That's Lance Foster. Former surfing champion, runs the adaptive surfing program in Orange County now. Lost his legs in a drunk driving accident years back, but you'd never know it slowed him down. Trains athletes for the Paralympics. He's only cooking tonight, raising funds for surf classes for disabled vets with a beach BBQ tonight."

Claire inspected the bare display. She mentally scolded herself for not having planned better, but no one could have predicted a dead body would have delayed her morning shopping.

"I guess I've arrived too late."

"Don't worry, sweetie, we've got plenty for you to choose from," Alma, the fishmonger, a silver-streaked woman with weathered pale blue eyes and a warm smile, said.

"Oh yes, we do." Her husband, Harvey, a wiry man with calloused fisherman's hands and a missing thumb, retrieved a large cooler hidden beneath the stand and grinned. He removed the top, dug through the ice with his bare hands, and pulled out the largest rockfish Claire had seen. "We've kept these beauties for you. Perfect for a bouillabaisse, if you ask me."

"For me?" Claire's fear of botching her catered evening due to her lack of quality food vanished at the sight of the orange fish. They were the size of a bodybuilder's forearms.

The woman smiled. "We knew you'd be late. We heard about the body washed up on the shore. We figured we'd hold onto something special for your seafood feast."

"It's so thoughtful of you. Thank you so much!"

The wife swatted the air with her hand as if brushing away Claire's gratitude, downplaying the favor. "Don't mention it. Your father's been one of our best customers for years. And now you. We couldn't let you down." She said, weighing each item and jotting the price down on a small calculator. "By the way, how are you and Suggie doing? Finding a corpse on the beach isn't part of anyone's morning routine."

Claire nodded. "No, it's not. But we are both fine. Thank you for your concern."

"What about that body? Is it true it's one of the competition's surfers? Do you know what happened?" the wife asked as her husband carefully wrapped each item with waxed paper.

"We're not sure of anything yet, but it's probably an accident," she added. Such a determination would spare her father from any suspicion.

"Must be a guy from the Blue Crush team," a passerby butted in. Claire recognized him as a local surfer, a twenty-something man named Ted who worked at the local aquarium. "I heard them fighting the day before, got all riled up, and teamed up against one of their own. Money surfers like them forget about the ethics and beauty of the sport."

"Do you remember what they were talking about?"

"Yeah, one of them paid for his place to be on the team. He didn't have the best skills and was jeopardizing the team's chance at winning."

"Do you remember who they were talking about?"

Ted nodded. "Richie or Ricky Rich, something like that. It's that surfer-influencer that's all about money and forgets about the true spirituality of the sport. Karma, am I right?"

"Good riddance if you ask me," an old man in a Vietnam Veteran cap said as he walked past the booth. "All these visitors invading our town and blocking the streets. All vermin."

The fishmonger shook her head and slapped the air in dismissal. "Don't mind Henry. He's just a grumpy old man who doesn't like the tourists," she said. "Been grumpy since he fell down the stairs last year."

"Harvey and Alma, I can't thank you enough for your help. I'll drop two large servings of bouillabaisse at your house later on." Claire quickly threw her purchased food into her insulated bag. She needed to let Torres know about this lead. If the tragedy was indeed a homicide, they needed to investigate the victim's teammates. The sooner she could clear or at least take the heat off her dad, the better.

"Not a problem at all. Enjoy your meal, and take care now. And if you ever need more fish or just want to chat, you know where to find us…"

Claire dashed to the back exit, the one reserved for the vendors, unable to hear the end of the fishmongers' sentence. She dropped her insulated bag in the trailer of her scooter and called Suggie.

"What can you find on the Blue Crush surfing team? Any inside information you heard or secrets you can unearth?" she asked her best friend. As the accountant for Spa OhLaLa, the resort luxury spa owned by her mother, Mrs. Oh, Suggie had front seat and ear to the local gossip.

"Does that have something to do with the dead body?" Suggie's voice boomed through the Bluetooth speakers of her motorcycle helmet, drowning out the roar of the engine.

"Yes, it could be a lead. There was some tension in Ricky Bingle's team. Maybe one of his fellow surfers killed him. But please, keep it on the down-low. I'd rather avoid Torres's wrath should he discover we're investigating on the side."

"You can count on me. But aren't you going to tell him?"

Torres could be irritably territorial when it came to investigations.

"I will, later this morning. I have fish and mollusks to clean and marinate first. Then, I'll stop by the morgue to check if Vic got the autopsy results."

Chapter Five

Claire flew through the door of the Medical Examiner's office and down its greyish hallway, her eyes on her wristwatch. With meringues baking in her oven, at home, she had only an hour before her French cookies turned brown—just enough time to get the autopsy's preliminary results and share with Torres what she heard at the fish market. If the medical examiner ruled the death a homicide, the police should direct their investigation on the Blue Crush surfing team for a suspect and spare her father from further scrutiny. Her heart hammered against her ribs as the terrifying thought crashed over her—what if they didn't, and her father became their prime suspect?

"Good morning, I'm here to see Doctor Vikram Thomas," Claire asked between breaths.

The clerk, a middle-aged woman with a wide face and droopy eyelids, grimaced at her. "We're closed for lunch, come back at one p.m."

Claire glanced at the schedule hours sign posted next to the desk window, which clearly stated 'Open 8-12 and 1-5'. "It's only eleven forty and my visit won't last more than ten minutes."

The clerk shrugged. "Your watch must be off. Different time zones between here and France."

Claire forced a smile and pointed at the wall. "My time is the same as yours."

The woman glanced at the wall clock slowly, then at Claire, then back at the wall clock. "Name and ID."

"Claire Fontaine." She presented her driver's license for the twentieth time in the past two months.

The woman took the small card and studied it meticulously, frowning as if suspecting a fake. "Purpose of your visit?"

"Thanks, Debbie, I'll take it from here," Vikram's soothing voice echoed from behind Claire, instantly melting away the tension. He wrapped his arm protectively around Claire's shoulders and walked her through the large swinging metal doors separating the lobby from the lab.

Claire paused as Vic grabbed the handle to the Doctors' Lounge. "Wait, we aren't going to the autopsy room?"

"We can't. Torres is in the viewing room with the dead guy's fiancée. I thought it would be better to wait here until they leave." It was a smart move. Claire didn't want Torres to catch her prying into the investigation. A ridiculous rivalry also existed between both men, and Vikram purposefully avoided Torres as much as he could, for reasons that still remained a mystery to Claire.

"Wait? For how long?" Claire checked her watch. She only had fifty minutes left before her meringues turned brown. Worst-case scenario, she could still dip each meringue in ganache to cover the burn.

"Shouldn't be long. Identifying a body doesn't take more than a few minutes."

Claire followed Vic into the lounge, leaving the door ajar behind her. She forwent the seat at one of the blue tables that Vic offered her and stood still by the door. Vivid paintings of various organs contrasted sharply with the blinding white walls, artfully reminding visitors that they were at the morgue—a fact even the watermelon-coconut scent from the diffuser couldn't entirely obscure.

"Is the fiancée the only next of kin?" she asked.

"His parents are on their way back from Australia on a business trip. Coffee? We've got a new espresso machine." He smiled as he inserted a small aluminum pod into the designed slot on the machine and pressed the START button.

"No, thanks. I already had my dose of stimulant for the day." Learning that her father was a possible murder suspect while having to cater a thirty-person seafood fest that evening was stressful enough without adding the jolt of caffeine.

"I was wondering…" Vic cleared his throat and inched toward Claire with soft eyes, a light blush spreading across his face. "Are you seeing anyone?"

Claire took a step back and glanced through the blinds of the windowed walls. They were half-open, allowing her to see the coming and going of the Medical Examiner's Office staff.

"Not yet and not for a while. I've crossed dating off my to-do list. I'm focusing on building my catering business and clearing my dad's name right now," she said. She might have taken the best cooking classes there were, but she was still an amateur when it came to mass-cooking, and the transition from criminal attorney to a private chef wasn't easy or smooth.

Claire noticed his hopeful expression falter slightly. This wasn't the first time—the coffee invitations, his offers to "taste test" her new recipes, the way his eyes lingered when he thought she wasn't looking. The signs were getting hard to ignore.

It wasn't that she wasn't interested in dating. She had thought about it, a lot, as she missed the comforting warmth of another being in her bed. She was also constantly teased by Torres, her roommate, who roamed their shared apartment shirtless. But since the destruction of her firm, her post-coma rehabilitation, and her return to Caper Cove, Claire was more interested in settling into a new normal than gallivanting around town. When ready to date again, Vic would still remain in the 'absolutely undatable' zone. No matter how handsome he became, Claire could only see him as the little boy she once babysat.

"I see, but what if—"

"Here they come!" Claire whisper-shouted as she caught sight of Detective Torres accompanied by a young woman with pink-streaked blond French braids. The two of them were conversing in what appeared to be a serious but relaxed atmosphere—chatting about the police's fundraising gala. "Is that the fiancée?"

Vic nodded. "Her name's Amy Walsh. She used to surf too, excelled in her category, but quit to become Ricky's manager."

"She doesn't look very distraught by her fiancé's death. How long had they been engaged?"

"Over two years. Hadn't set a date for the big day yet. Why?"

"That's a long time to be engaged without a concrete wedding plan. That couple either didn't really want to get married or fell out of love." It wouldn't be the first pretend-relationship Claire had encountered. Fake relationships could bring or keep people in the media spotlight. They were also the quickest way to reshape one's public image—to create a narrative, appeal to a specific fan demographic, or deflect attention from their personal lives.

Claire approached the ajar door and stretched her ear.

The woman's face was cold with no trace of tears—no running mascara or shiny salty tracks on her cheeks. "He was a great swimmer. He can't have drowned," she said, oblivious that even the toughest of men could lose against the treacherous grip of riptides. "We had dinner after his afternoon training session."

"And you didn't notice anything out of the ordinary? A change in attitude, maybe, or a fight he might have had with people?" Torres asked as he guided her down the hallway.

"Ricky wasn't the easiest of people and could be boorish at times. He always wanted to prove he could make a name for himself without his parents' money. But I can't see why people would want to kill him now."

"Again, I'm sorry for your loss. If you have any information or recall any detail about his last whereabouts, let us know." The detective handed her his business card and exited the building with the woman in tow.

"Let's go," Claire pulled Vikram out of the lounge as soon as Torres and the fiancée disappeared behind the swinging metal doors. She speed-walked to the autopsy room along with Vikram, who struggled to keep up without having to enter into a full jog or spilling his coffee. "What can you tell me about the deceased?"

"Time of death was last night between ten p.m. and midnight," he said, entering the formaldehyde and disinfectant-scented room. The body had been wheeled by an assistant for further examination. Vic logged in on the computer located on a standing desk near the door. "And it was no accident."

Claire approached the corpse. A white cloth covered it, except for its right toes, from which a tag hung. In her criminal defense career, she had seen enough dead bodies not to be affected by the hard reality of death, yet she shuddered. She preferred the sight of naked, decomposing bodies, where death was undeniable. A white sheet, on the other hand, could conceal a body still clinging to life, ready to spring up in a last claim for life.

"It was ruled a homicide?"

"Yep. He was struck with a blunt object before he died." With one swift tug, Vic pulled the sheet away and rolled the corpse onto its side, exposing a dark, purplish bruise shaped like a thin baseball bat across its back. The area around it was swollen and scraped. "The bruises suggest he was struck by a metal rod, then hit by a sharp object, hard enough to break his spine. We also found water in his lungs."

"What could the steel pipe be? Could he have gotten into a fight?"

"That's the assumption, but we aren't sure yet. We sent the lung water sample to the lab to get a definitive answer. We also found particles embedded in the wound that can tell us more about where he was hit. We sent them for analysis. We should know more in a couple of days if people stay on their game despite the festival." His jaw tightened. "Though with the new evidence protocols requiring three signatures for every report, it could take longer."

A throat clearing interrupted Vic and Claire's exchange, calling their attention. Torres stood by the door, his arms crossed against his chest. "Don't you have a seafood feast to prepare?" he snarked.

"Seafood's marinating as we speak," Claire force-cheered, uncomfortable at having been caught investigating red-handed. She was also confused by Torres's knowledge of her seafood fest. Had she told him about it? Was he cyber-stalking her or being a foodie genuinely interested in her culinary posts? Unless she smelled like fish. Did she smell like fish? Maybe she should have taken a shower after she scaled and gutted her morning purchases.

"Talking about food, I've got meringues calling my name," she said, checking her watch. "Thanks, Vic. Please, keep me updated."

Torres blocked her way out with his body. "Wait a second. I've got a couple of questions for you," he said, thrusting his chest forward, his Oxford shirt stretching taut across his chest. "How well do you know that beach where you found the body?"

Claire shrugged. "Like any local, I suppose. Suggie and I run there when the tide's low." She didn't share with him the tragic history of that beautiful beach. How it had been her missing sister Aurora's favorite place, and how she used to check the tidepools and read books hidden in the small promontory above. It was also the last place her sister was seen before she disappeared twenty years ago.

"Why? Do you have a lead or a list of suspects?" she asked.

"Not yet. Do you know your father's whereabouts last night between ten p.m. and midnight?"

Claire jerked back, startled by the question. "You're joking, right? You can't seriously think my father has anything to do with this! After everything he's done for you. That's how you thank him for the cheap rent and free food?"

"I know that, but—"

"There's no BUT. How dare you ask me that?" She could feel the tension tightening her body and jaws, vibrating through her bones. "You may want to add Walsh to the suspect list. Her relationship with the victim was hitting a rough patch."

Claire didn't know if this was true or not—the two-year engagement without a concrete wedding plan wasn't exactly the sign of a healthy relationship. But if Torres wanted to throw around baseless accusations, she could play that game too.

She left the room fueled with anger, hoping her meringues baking in her oven wouldn't be as burnt as she felt inside. Then she'd check out the surf team herself and share her findings with Torres *only if needed.*

Chapter Six

Claire packed her meringues into a pink dessert carrier, pushing the thought of canceling the evening's catering gig from her mind. She'd been paid for it. She had to do it. But all she could think about was investigating the surfer's murder to clear her dad's name.

She joined Suggie on the terrace. The second-floor balcony overlooked the beach and ocean, the perfect spot to snap photos of public events. Today, it was the upcoming surfing festival, and her friend had been watching the surfers below like a hawk, vibrating with excitement. Among the athletes warming up, Vandstam performing surfers stood out in their elaborate Nordic folklore-inspired wetsuits—silver and blue designs flowing like water across neoprene, their movements as graceful as the mythical warriors they embodied. Claire set down a charcuterie board, the plates glinting under the seagulls' watchful gaze.

She flopped back into the chair, the hums and chatter from the Osprey customers below filling the air. A few yards away, sponsors were setting up booths under the rhythmic tapping of hammers, ready to peddle their brands to anyone who'd listen.

"Are you covering the festival for your blog or the newspaper?" Claire asked.

Suggie grinned, her eyes gleaming with excitement. "The paper. With the traffic my article's going to generate, they may offer me front page for the entire week."

"This is great! And front page?" In her years in Washington, D.C., Claire had only seen political commentaries and world events grace the newspapers.

Sports were usually limited to the sports section—except, of course, when the local teams won a championship or to announce the upcoming Army-Navy game.

"Of course! I'm talking about athletic prowess and men in Speedos. I like to call it the Sports Illustrated Swimsuit edition for the ladies, Caper Cove style. When I covered it on my blog, I got close to a million reposts. The most popular are of the Vandstam, the Nordic water tribe from the TV show."

Claire chuckled, shaking her head, remembering how Suggie had always loved watching surfers after school and during their summer breaks as teenagers. "I understand the appeal."

Aesthetically speaking, surfers were beautiful, human machines of muscles, skills, and grace. Surfing was not that different from interpretative dance in that a deep connection existed between the performers and their environment. Their movements were spontaneous and fluid, responding intuitively to external forces—waves for surfers, music or emotion for dancers.

"What about you? I heard Torres barred your dad from checking out the scene, citing the possibility of his involvement. Is that true?"

"I know, right? It's hard to imagine him mixed up in all of this." Claire swirled her glass of Perrier and watched the bubbles rise to the surface and disappear. The tension from her earlier interaction with Torres still hung in the air like a heavy cloud. But as frustrating as it was, she couldn't fault the detective entirely. Torres was only doing his job. These days, too many well-connected criminals flew under the radar because of misplaced allegiances and returns of favor. "My dad's involvement is just absurd!"

Suggie nodded in agreement as she reached for a slice of Prosciutto, its paper-thin edges catching the breeze. "Especially since there's enough tension in the victim's surf team for someone to have a motive to kill. Rumor is that Ricky got Axel Briggs booted off the team."

Claire straightened in her chair. "Who?"

"Axel Briggs, the former team captain."

"Where did you hear that?"

"At the spa. The entire surfing team came to get waxed before the competition, and I got all the juicy tea. Did you know that one of their best surfers lost her sponsorship because she showed armpit hair and refused to shave? How sexist is that! I'm writing an article about it and told her that you could review her contract to see if they had the right to terminate her like that."

"C'mon, Suggie. I've already told you. I don't practice law anymore, and sports law is a beast on its own. Her agent should deal with that."

"Her agent dumped her. Said she should shave, that she's the one breaking the contract. Now the media's calling her Chewbacca."

"Fine. I'll help…. About Ricky, the victim. Did they say anything about him?"

"Yes. The men's team has become chaotic and divided since Briggs left and Ricky joined the team. But they couldn't do much about it because Ricky got Speederoo, the swimsuit brand, to endorse the team. Without the sponsorship and Ricky's money, the Blue Crush team wouldn't have had the budget to attend surfing competitions. But without their former captain, the team's chance of winning plummeted. Ricky isn't half as skilled as Briggs."

"That's sure to create factions within the team. Did they say why Briggs was kicked off the team?"

"Something to do with Ricky paying his way into the team captain position."

"Is that a thing?"

"Not sure, but I can see how a coach could choose an athlete over another. Surfing competitively can get really expensive with all the travel, accommodation, and equipment expenses to travel to the qualifying series or world championship tour. Getting funding is often what floats or sinks a team. Ricky's beyond wealthy; any financially struggling team would have welcomed him."

"Any teammate had problems with that?"

"No, but Ricky had a fight with both his coach and Briggs. Nobody knows what it was about. But I may have an idea." Suggie placed her phone on the table; its screen displayed a picture showing Walsh, Rick's fiancée, with another surfer.

"That's Walsh. Who's that with her?"

"Axel Briggs, the surfer who got kicked off the team because of Ricky."

"They're standing unusually close." Claire zoomed in on the picture with her index and thumb. After years of trials, questioning prisoners and observing witnesses, she could tell when people were close. From this picture, Claire could deduce a certain level of intimacy and comfort from their open body language.

"Walsh. Briggs. The coach. Anyone who had a conflict with Ricky or had something to gain." Claire swiped through the pictures. "When did you get these?"

"This morning, right after you left for the market. I'm thinking a love affair gone wrong, maybe. I shot every beach visitor for three hours following our discovery. If it's murder, the culprit should be in these pictures. They always return to the scene of the crime, don't they?"

"They often do. But three hours? Doesn't your mom mind you missing work?"

"She initially did, but she knows accounting can be done after hours. She also loves seeing my name in the paper, especially since my byline mentions the spa. That's free publicity for Umma and Spa OhLaLa."

From their vantage point, Claire and Suggie observed the line of customers getting longer. International competitions were different beasts from national events. Since travelers were from around the world, with bodies and stomachs used to different time zones, there were hungry customers around the clock—which meant a never-ending queue at the restaurant.

"Isn't that the Blue Crush team coach?" Claire motioned at a frowning man in the line below.

"You're not thinking of asking him questions, are you? Torres won't like you investigating behind his back, and with that line, he might be hangry."

"That's what I'm counting on." Claire rose from her seat, the chair scraping against the wooden deck. "The meringues on the blue plate are all for you. Just pull the door shut behind you on your way out."

If Ricky stole Briggs's spot, and Walsh was closer to Briggs than she let on, this wasn't just about money. It was personal.

Chapter Seven

Claire rushed down the stairs barefoot and approached Coach Kovac with a smile. The sun-warmed wood planks creaked beneath her feet.

"Interested in bypassing the line?" Claire asked the man.

"Of course, but is this going to cost me double?"

"No, just the answer to a few of my questions about Ricky Bingle."

The man studied her for a few seconds and said, "A quid pro quo? Why not? I've already talked to the cops. Are you with the French press?"

"Why, does that make a difference?"

"It does not. But I like to know who I'm talking to."

Claire extended her hand. "Claire Fontaine, private chef."

The man shook it gently. "Virgil Kovac, but you can call me Coach."

"Nice to meet you, Coach. What about a Caper Cove special number two?" she proposed, knowing it would take seconds to prepare.

Coach glanced at the board and smiled at the description. "Sounds perfect."

A few minutes later, Coach was biting loudly into his order of beer-battered fish tacos under Claire's eyes.

"What'd you want to ask me about?" He asked before pushing a fork of coleslaw into his mouth.

"When did you last see Ricky?"

"At the Clubhouse, last night. He was with all the other boys, celebrating the first night of the festival with the team. They do everything together from training to hating me," he laughed. "They don't like it when I raid their quarters and get rid of their booze and lovers."

"I heard you had an argument with Ricky. Can you tell me what it was about?"

Coach took a gulp of his beer, condensation dripping down the glass. "Ricky was a tough kid. Self-entitled kid with an easy life who never heard the word 'no.' I needed to rein him in. Competing isn't for the lazy. He needed to step up with his training schedule and cut down his social life if he wanted to make his mark in the competition. Today's youth thinks it's easy to make it: pretty faces and tiny Speedos may work for marketing, but the waves require skills."

"What can you tell me about Amy Walsh and Axel Briggs?"

"There's nothing to say. Amy's friendly with everyone and tends to care more about underdogs."

"Briggs was the team's captain before Ricky joined the team. Why the sudden change?"

"You tell me. Briggs came to see me one morning and told me he was quitting the team. No notice, no explanation."

In her decade as a criminal attorney in Washington, D.C., Claire learned that no man ever gave up fame and fortune of his own volition. Coercion took many forms: physical threats were obvious, but blackmail, economic pressure, and reputation damage could be just as compelling and just as illegal. The only reason a surfer rising to stardom, like Briggs, would renounce his position on the team had to be blackmail. "Who was blackmailing Briggs, and with what information?" was the key to solving this murder? To find that out, she would have to interview every member of the Blue Crush team.

Claire grimaced. "Nobody knows why?"

"Nope. Nobody knows why," a voice interrupted as a shadow loomed over the table.

Claire turned around and found Torres standing right behind her. He was wearing navy blue bike shorts and a tight top, the bike patrol officer uniform that a third of the Caper Cove police department adopted during event season—including detectives if any event attracted over one hundred thousand visitors. Bikes were easier to maneuver around traffic and busy roads than cars, and were faster than being on foot.

"Are you following me?" Though Torres and she were roommates, Claire wasn't accustomed to bumping into the detective outside of the police station and their shared apartment.

"Just keeping an eye on you. We wouldn't want your side-investigating to end up in a repeat kerfuffle of last time." Torres referred to her most recent encounter with death, when a killer chased her and misguided border agents took her for a terrorist smuggling illegal drugs into the US.

Claire forced a grin. "A kerfuffle that sent a killer behind bars isn't that bad," she said, reminding him that it was her superior investigating skills that had solved a double murder and led to the arrest of the killer. "But don't worry, I don't intend on venturing outside of Caper Cove this time around."

Torres nodded, his jaw tight. "Don't waste your time questioning the rest of the Blue Crush. I've already interviewed them. The victim was probably windsurfing, got hit by the boom," he said, blaming the horizontal bar attached to the sail, which the rider gripped to control the sail's angle and power while maneuvering. "We'll probably find the remains of his board and sail down the current."

"Windsurfing booms aren't as hard as steel pipes. They are typically made from aluminum or carbon fiber, which are strong yet lightweight. It would take an incredible force to be knocked out by your own boom. Plus, getting hit in the back by one while windsurfing seems improbable."

Coach wiped his mouth with the back of his hand and nodded. "She's right. It's pretty unlikely for a windsurfer to get knocked out by the boom during tacking or jibing since those moves are controlled, and anyone with a bit of experience knows to dodge the sail as it swings across. Plus, windsurfing's a big no-no during a surfing competition; no one wants to deal with a sail out there when they're trying to catch a wave! So yeah, the chances of Ricky getting clocked like that are pretty slim."

"I wouldn't talk so fast if I were you," Torres told the man. Then he bent forward and whispered in Claire's ear, his breath warm against her skin. "Listen, you don't want to assume murder and spread panic around, especially since your father is the only person with a motive."

Claire's stomach dropped. Her father? She pulled back to see Torres's face, searching for any sign he was baiting her. But his expression was deadpan, almost smug. How dare he? Heat rushed to her cheeks as her mind raced through what this meant. The police couldn't have already settled on her father as a suspect. Could they?

"Winds were strong last night; anything is possible. So why don't you drop it, huh?" Torres added.

Drop it?! There was nothing that made Claire investigate faster than a man telling her to look away. Especially when the "request" was made with a controlling, almost threatening tone. No matter how limited the police's resources were, an inquiry into every case with potential foul play should be made without delay. When a death is left uninvestigated, the suspects face public suspicion, gossip, or unwarranted blame—all of which could affect her father's reputation. In the eyes of the public, it wouldn't be the first time the police would protect one of their own. Retired or not. Without a proper investigation and formal exoneration clearing her father, suspicion could follow him forever. She had seen too many lives ruined by unresolved allegations.

If Ricky Bingle had been murdered, she would find the culprit. Which she could guarantee was not her father.

She checked her watch. She had just over an hour before switching into full catering mode. She stopped first by The Osprey's kitchen, crafted twelve Pan Bagnats—the sandwich of choice for athletes, made with a hearty blend of tuna, olives, tomatoes, and olive oil, all packed into a fresh, crusty bun— and grabbed two packs of beer from the fridge. Though not reliable as a truth serum, good food and alcohol were the magic formula to lower inhibitions and make people talk, which she shamelessly counted on using on the Blue Crush team.

Chapter Eight

The surfing competition tents, proudly emblazoned with each team's name, lined up the shore, turning the beach into a vibrant hub. A mix of coconut sunscreen and grilled food wafted through the air as surfers strategized and geared up amidst a sea of colorful surfboards. Vendors hustled to ready their booths, their voices carrying over the constant rhythm of waves breaking against the shore. If Ricky had enemies on the team, someone here knew. She needed to find out who hated Rick enough to kill him.

Claire made her way to the Blue Crush's bright orange tent, the fabric snapping in the ocean breeze. The men's team had gathered underneath, their hair tousled by the salty wind, debating about who would stand in line to get everybody's lunch. None of them appeared grief-stricken by the morning tragedy.

"I have sandwiches and beers on the house if you're interested!" She cheered as she approached them with a grin, holding the beers in one hand and a bag of sandwiches in the other, the paper crinkling in the breeze.

"No way!" "For reals?" they said with relief on their faces.

"Yes. I just need to ask you a few questions in exchange," Claire said as she placed the glistening drinks and paper-wrapped food on the table. Condensation beaded on the cold bottles, leaving wet rings on the weathered wood.

The surfers exchanged knowing glances, their expressions turning serious until six of them rose from their beach chairs to grab their share and tear into their sandwiches. The scent of fresh bread, tuna, and herbs mixed with the salty air.

"You're with Justine?" a teammate with the name Jared Jones printed on his rashguard asked.

"Who?"

Jared frowned. "Justine Dupont, France's premier female big-wave surfer in the world. You're not into surfing?"

"Only superficially. I'm more into investigating." Claire knew her way around a surfboard and how to approach the waves. She had learned the sport with her dad at the tender age of four, but had given up the beach the day her sister disappeared, focusing her every waking moment on finding clues about Aurora's disappearance.

"Ahhh, a French detective like Hercule Poirot. I'm Tony Ramos." A surfer in a red competition jersey approached her slowly, appraising her seductively with his eyes. Salt crystals sparkled in his raven hair. "You're investigating Ricky's death?"

"Yes. Do you know what Ricky and your coach were fighting about?"

Ramos took a loud gulp of his beer, the bottle clinking against his teeth before answering. "Coach was too hard on us. With him, it's always no alcohol, no junk food, and no girlfriends. Which isn't fair."

"Yeah, how can we enjoy competing when we can't enjoy a little fame and flirt with the fans? And beer helps us relax. It's not like we're downing a fifth of Tequila," another added.

Claire nodded in agreement. A strict schedule and diet were required for peak performance, but too many restrictions usually led to mutiny. "Can you tell me where you all were last night?"

"We were all celebrating our new sponsorship at the Swim and Racquet Club. Ricky was with us until about ten p.m. when he left to go on a date."

"With Amy Walsh?" Claire asked.

The surfers laughed, the sound carrying over the crash of waves. The breeze picked up, rustling the tent fabric overhead.

"What's so funny?"

"Ricky was a dog."

"Yeah, the kind that can't be tamed. The guy didn't even care about the sanctity of marriage. It's like he dated married women on purpose. Like there aren't enough single girls around," Ramos explained, wiping beer foam from his salt-chapped lips.

"I see. Do you have the name of his date by chance?"

"Nope. But it's probably a girl he met on social media. His DMs are overflowing with flirty texts from fans."

"Do you know of anyone who hated him or wanted to hurt him?" Claire continued, noting how the team's dynamic shifted at the question, shoulders tensing beneath their sun-tanned skin.

"Ricky was easy to hate," Ramos said. "Maybe start with the husbands and boyfriends of the girls he dated."

"And of course, Briggs. They both hated each other," Jones added, kicking at the sand beneath his feet.

Ramos shook his head. "Ricky should never have been allowed to take Briggs's place. Didn't even deserve to be on the team. Now that he's gone, maybe we've got a chance to place as a team."

"C'mon, Tony. The guy's dead, show some respect," a teammate said.

"I don't see why. Ricky never showed me any. The only reason Coach got him on the team is because his mom's company is covering our championships' travel expenses and fees. And now we've got to wear their stupid logo!" Ramos pinched his jersey where an embroidered shark was biting into a board—not the most surfer-friendly design a team could get.

Behind him, another teammate thrust his hips forward, exposing a larger logo of the shark biting right into the board that covered the man's bulge. "We call it shark love."

Half of the team laughed while the second half kept angry faces, the tension palpable in the small space beneath the fluttering tent.

"Where's Briggs now?" she asked, redirecting the conversation.

"Probably at the Swim and Racquet Club. He used to work there before joining the team, and I heard he got his old cabana boy job back. He's working the night shift, though."

The wind picked up again, sending grains of sand dancing across their feet and making the tent poles creak. Claire left the gathering, mind already racing with new leads to follow. The country club would be her next stop—after her catering gig was done. She'd talk to Briggs herself. Whatever made him leave the team might explain what got Ricky killed.

Chapter Nine

The bitter taste of her interaction with Torres lingered on Claire's tongue, even hours later. How dare the detective tell her what to do? How could he assume the drowning victim was merely an accident or suspect her father? The circumstances surrounding the man's death were highly suspicious. Ricky Bingle had been hit before drowning, and before his death, he had fractured the Blue Crush's team chemistry and possibly caused the supposedly voluntary departure of Axel Briggs, the team captain he replaced. She would have to dig deeper into the team's politics. A visit to Briggs was in order.

The gentle clink of crystal against crystal echoed as Claire focused on filling cups with crème anglaise. Even with a small pitcher, she needed a steady hand to avoid spills. The rich vanilla scent wafted up as she topped each with a small meringue, its surface crackling like delicate ice under her spoon. Hired staff cleared trays and plates of seafood from the patio's dining table, the scrape of silverware against porcelain marking their progress as they readied for dessert.

The house where she catered that evening was a sprawling, ultra-modern mansion, one of the latest additions to a neighborhood of quaint, aging cottages. The cool evening breeze ruffled the crisp white tablecloths on the patio dining corner, where candles and hurricane lamps flickered gently against a pink and orange-streaked sky. Salt air mingled with the day's lingering warmth. The view was so pretty that Claire almost forgot that from the outside, the blockish, sterile lines of the new construction loomed over the oldest, modest homes, drowning out the history and character that once defined Caper Cove.

"The vol-au-vents and fish soufflés were incredible, Claire. The whole meal was spectacular. I couldn't imagine a seafood feast more perfect than what you created tonight. Thank you. You're free to go," the hostess said, her designer perfume overwhelming the subtle aromas of Claire's cooking as she handed over a check. "Let's hope your father gets cleared so I can refer you to my friends and hire you again."

Claire's fingers crumpled the check as she slipped it in her pocket with a frown. How could the woman know her father's situation? Was the entire town suspecting her father because of the fight he had with Ricky two nights ago? "I don't see what my father has to do with your decision to hire me again."

"Well, you know…since your father's a suspect…." The woman sported a constipated smile, the type people give when they realize they've blundered into something indiscreet and inappropriate. What the French call *mettre les pieds dans le plat*—to step in a dish with both feet. "We can't hire a killer's daughter in good conscience."

Tension knotted Claire's brow like a wire pulled taut. "My father hasn't killed anyone."

The woman's head bobbed, pearls gleaming in the dying light. "That's what we all hope for. But with your father's past, we can't be too prudent. These dinners I'm throwing are networking events. I wouldn't want to appear to be endorsing his behavior."

Her jaw clenched until it ached, Claire piled her bowls and pans into her large bag, the metal clanking a harsh counterpoint to the gentle evening breeze. "My father's past?"

"Yes. Wasn't he placed on administrative leave for excessive use of force twenty or so years ago?"

"I wouldn't know. I was a child back then." At the time, she was a teenager with more pressing concerns than her parents' employment status.

The copper taste of anxiety flooded her mouth as memories surfaced. Her father had taken a leave of absence when her sister went missing. Claire had always assumed it was to better concentrate on finding Aurora. Her parents were fighting so much then, she must have repressed most of those memories, buried them like shells beneath sand. All she remembered was that it was at that time her mom decided to leave Caper Cove for New York.

She could hardly envision her father as an aggressor and the sole cause of their departure. But then again, humans were fallible, and her legal experiences had taught Claire that anyone could be prone to violence given the right triggers and circumstances. Still, when it came to her dad, that hypothesis was dubious at best.

"That must be when you moved to France," the woman said as if having a revelation, her voice dripping with false sympathy. "Well, it's a good thing you've got yourself a lovely French accent. People won't realize you're connected to him."

Claire jerked back, the motion sharp as a slap. "I'll never hide my connection to my dad, and people are innocent until proven guilty."

Her hands trembled with anger as she shoved the rest of her utensils, clean and dirty, in her bag. The metal implements clattered against each other as she stacked all her belongings on her small utility cart, its wheels squeaking slightly as she headed to the door.

"Thank you for the opportunity to cook for you. Have a good evening," she said, each word brittle as sugar glass. Then she stomped out of the luxurious villa without looking back, her footsteps echoing on the marble floor. No one could disparage her father without concrete evidence. Not in her presence or under her watch. Not even her paying clients. If she were to lose a gig over this, so be it.

Chapter Ten

Claire's phone buzzed. A text from Suggie appeared on the screen.

SUGGIE: <Is the coast clear?>

CLAIRE: <Torres just got in the shower. Why?>

SUGGIE: <The shower at 9 PM?>

CLAIRE: <He's going out>

SUGGIE: <Smart. Good looking and clean. He'll find plenty of dates this weekend.>

CLAIRE: <DateS—plural?!>

SUGGIE: <Yes, why? Never pegged him as the settling type. What have you heard?>

CLAIRE: <Nothing. Why do you need him gone?>

SUGGIE: <Just open the front door. I'm right outside>

Claire tiptoed down the wooden hallway to find Suggie standing barefoot, shoes dangling from her pinky fingers, clutching a craft store bag and an easel whiteboard.

"Quick!" Suggie darted inside and rushed to Claire's bedroom, glancing over her shoulders like a skittish mouse.

Claire followed, eyeing the plastic bag. "What's all this?"

"Everything you need for a new murder board! Since your old one's still evidence in the Vee Brooks case, I thought you could start a new one. This one is not only clean and dry-erase, it's magnetized." Suggie set up the tripod in the corner of her bedroom, near the window.

"When did you have time? Didn't you have to go to work?"

"I ordered it online during break, picked it up after work. The craft store is open till midnight during competition season—they make a killing on plain shirts, markers, and body paint. I know Torres warned you off, but you're investigating anyway, right?"

"Obviously, but why not keep the board at your place?"

"Seriously? Umma would flip if she found murder documents in the house. She says it's bad energy for the house and the spa business." Despite being a newlywed, Suggie lived at her mother's while her Marine husband was deployed, saving to buy a house upon his return.

"What about bad energy here, in my place?"

Suggie punched her shoulder. "Please. You've spent ten years defending wrongfully convicted clients—you might as well have wallpapered your apartment with autopsy photos."

Claire laughed. As a D.C. criminal attorney, work always followed her home—who wouldn't when the life of an innocent was at stake? Though she never decorated her walls with evidence, she had often passed out from exhaustion on case files. "Not quite, but I get your point."

As soon as she conceded the point, Suggie dumped her supplies onto Claire's bed—colorful ribbons, notecards, tacks, and magnets. "The bright colors will cheer us up as we investigate. You know, keep our mood up while we rummage through the autopsy pictures and murder theories."

Bedazzling a murder board wasn't a bad idea. "Good thinking."

Claire grabbed a black marker and wrote "Who killed Ricky Bingle?" across the top.

"Hey Suggie, craft emergency?" Torres passed by, fresh from his shower, leaving a trail of fragrance.

"Hey, Torres." Suggie sniffed before whispering to Claire, "Don't you love that fresh-man scent?"

"Never noticed," Claire lied. "Wish he would wear more than that tiny towel."

"I don't mind." Suggie grinned. "That scent though—flowery but sophisticated. Unusual for a man, but nice. Might get the same for Daniel when he returns. What do you think?"

Claire leaned into the doorway and inhaled. "Wait...that's jasmine verbena.

That's *my* soap!" She stormed to the kitchen. "Did you use my soap? I can't wait for the second bathroom to be finished."

Torres just smiled, flexing his arms and abs, water glistening on his skin. "Oh yeah, I ran out. Thought you wouldn't mind. Do you?"

"It's a bit late now, isn't it?"

"You know what the French call defined abs?" Suggie chimed in.

"Not now, Suggie."

Torres grinned. "No, what?"

"A chocolate bar. So yummy, don't you think?"

Chapter Eleven

The next morning, Claire rose up before Suggie's text pulled her out of bed and through the door for their morning run. She reached the crime scene as the rising sun bleached the thick marine layer suffocating the coast. The tide was low, revealing a faint path that had been carved in the cliff. The narrow walkway led to a secluded beach, known only to the locals who had dubbed it Lovers Beach. The unstable cliff made its access challenging from dry land, and the sharp underwater rocks rendered the water unsuitable for surfing. The place was a haven of privacy and unbreakable peace when the high tide sealed its access. The police had excluded the area as a potential crime scene, but something told Claire to go check it out.

Claire combed the shore in search of evidence. If he wasn't trying to prove himself by surfing in dangerous waters, the victim might have brought a date here. Many couples who hung out at the beach unknowingly left items behind: a set of keys, candy wrappers, or tissue that fell out of their pockets as they embraced on the sand. The force of the incoming tides sometimes embedded lost items in the rock surfaces' cracks—small costume jewelry or a forgotten bikini top. Maybe something to clue her in as to the identity of Ricky's last date.

"Anything?" a voice asked, startling Claire.

"Suggie! What are you doing here?"

Her friend smiled wide, teeth flashing white against her sun-kissed skin. She was wearing a bright pink swimsuit—a high-cut one-piece with a crotch so narrow it screamed 1980s aerobic fashion and required serious landscaping—more personal maintenance than a Zen garden.

"Same as you: investigating. You shouldn't come here alone."

"I couldn't sleep and didn't want to wake you up or distract you from your work." Covering the competition and investigating with Claire would take Suggie away from her job, eating many accounting and reporting hours away. "How did you know I was here? Are you spying on me?" Claire asked.

Suggie shot her a crooked smile and waved her phone, its screen shining with the "Find My" app, the blue dot pulsing steadily. They had both enabled the tracking of each other's locations after Claire's near-death experience at the Mexico-United States Border a few weeks ago.

"I just wanted to make sure you were okay. It was Aurora's favorite place, wasn't it?" Suggie glanced at the cliff wall. Claire's sister's name had been carved into the rock many times. After the final search efforts to find her were called off, the high school held a memorial there, and each of her classmates had engraved her name in the stone.

Claire nodded in silence as the first wave of the rising tide licked her feet, remembering how Aurora used to race her to the water's edge, always laughing as the cold foam caught them by surprise. How could such a beautiful, serene place be the source of so much pain and turmoil?

"Let's go before the tide gets us," she said, pulling her friend by the hand. The rising tide could be exceptionally fast with strong current, especially on days approaching the full moon.

"What's with the new swimsuit? I thought you hated pink, that it reminded you too much of work."

"It was Umma's idea. She thought I could advertise the spa while jogging. Since we made the news in our swimsuits, she wanted to be prepared if it were to happen again. She added her own swimsuit line to the spa shop."

"But there isn't anyone on the beach to see it."

"That's what I told her, but she insisted. You know how she is."

Claire laughed. Mrs. Oh's business acumen was sharp.

"Oh, you can laugh. She had a swimsuit made for you, too!"

Claire and Suggie accelerated their pace to exit the secluded beach before the water could strand them. Getting wet wasn't a concern as much as the danger of getting swept away by the riptide, especially when the morning mist obscured landmarks and navigating back to shore was impossible. They sprinted for half a mile and collapsed on the dry sand.

The beach was empty but for one surfer riding the waves through the fog.

"Who's that?" Claire squinted through the spray. An idiot was actually out there in these conditions. She shook her head. Everyone knew you never surfed alone, especially when the waves were this angry. She'd seen enough accidents to know how quickly things could go wrong.

"Probably a local getting his early training in, or someone really stupid. Also, don't they know that sharks often feed at dawn?" Suggie shuddered.

"I don't think it matters. Sharks are like criminals; they are opportunistic predators and may feed at any time of day or night, depending on their hunting habits and the availability of prey. That guy could be the killer."

Suggie laughed. "Your criminal lawyer's showing."

"And your mother was right! Early morning jogs are swimsuit modeling opportunities," Claire said as she spotted a photographer on the boardwalk, her camera lens glinting in the strengthening sunlight.

"What?" Suggie swiveled on herself and stared at the camera woman. "Wait, isn't that Ricky's fiancée?"

Claire grabbed her cellphone from her armband, took a few shots of the photographer and the surfer, and zoomed in on the surfer's face.

Suggie gasped. "That's Briggs! The guy who was kicked out of the Blue Crush team."

The surfer didn't wear a wetsuit but an orange rash-guard with the Blue Crush's logo, the bright color a beacon against the misty backdrop. "Looks like he's back on the team. Ricky's death benefited him. His departure might not have been voluntary after all."

"And Ricky's manager-fiancée now has a new client to represent," Suggie added.

"Two very strong motives for murder. But why isn't he training on the main beach with the others?"

"To avoid the paparazzi or the crowds? The beach started to get busy when I parked at your place." The distant sound of car doors slamming and early morning chatter drifted down from the parking lot.

"Busy at this time?" Claire checked her watch and sprang to her feet. "Six a.m. already? My shift's about to start!"

"You aren't going to wait to interview him?"

"I can't. My dad's counting on me with the morning crowd. Plus, a hungry surfer isn't very approachable. He'll be easier to question when he stops at The Osprey to get a bite, like most early surfers do. What about you?"

"Same. I'm filling in at the spa. Umma had started an early yoga class for the jet-lagged East Coast and international visitors and couldn't find anyone to take the early shift. The last temp cashier she hired let her friends in for free, so I'll be the cashier until nine every morning for the duration of the competition, then back to regular accounting until four, and then on to cover the Gidget competition for my blog.

"What's a gidget?"

"Gidget's the name of the iconic 1959 movie that celebrated California surf culture. The competition holds an all-gender look-alike contest. The cast of Vandstam will be there. The show was renewed for another season, and the Vandstam Queen is one of the judges. Their cosplay is incredible. It's going to be fun."

Claire imagined a beach full of minimally clad surfers in vintage swimwear and actors with prosthetic shark fins and scales, and gills painted on their bodies to resemble the Nordic water tribe members they embodied on TV. Cosplaying was hard enough indoors—doing it on a beach was next-level commitment.

"I take it you'll be photographing more men in their Speedos."

Suggie giggled. "Yes, I know, my life's tough."

* * *

The number of customers lining up at the counter of the Osprey was double the estimate. Luckily, the two most popular breakfast menu items were easy to assemble: the Surfer's Quesadilla, a protein-packed quesadilla filled with chicken, black beans, cheese, and spinach, and the Surfer's Choice with quinoa, scrambled eggs, fresh spinach, and avocado wrapped in a spinach tortilla.

When the morning rush ended, two hours later, Claire's hands were hurting. She was also parched. Using the pizza oven to accommodate the lack of an extra griddle had been smart, but had caused her to lose at least a pound of body water. Taking a break from the law had been good for her brain, but not for her body's hydration level. After all, each working environment had its own challenges. However, cooking with an ocean view and perfect seventy-degree temperature year-round was what she called a paradisiac workplace, hands down—even if some customers acted like they'd rather eat their surfboards than wait five extra minutes for their tacos.

"Why don't you take a two-hour break?" her father suggested as he handed her a matcha strawberry smoothie, her favorite. "Jimmy's cousin just got into town and will help with the lunch prep."

"Thanks, Dad." She took the drink, grabbed a Surfer's Choice on her way out, intent on questioning Briggs and maybe bribing him for answers, and paused. "Before I go, can you promise me something?"

Her father's forehead creased with concern. "What is it?"

"Don't talk to the police without me. If they want to ask you any questions, call me first."

Frank Fontaine laughed. "I don't need an attorney, sweetie. You know better than anyone how this works—both as my daughter and as a former criminal attorney. They already brought me in because they have to check every box. Former cop with connections to the case? Standard protocol. If they had anything on me, I wouldn't be standing here talking to you right now. Trust me, it was just procedure."

"I know that. Please, promise me," she asked, withholding the hundreds of questions she wanted to ask him about his past suspension. She had defended enough innocents to know that becoming a prime suspect didn't require a wrongful act or guilty behavior. Her father's recent confrontation with the victim and his past seemed enough for people to question Frank's involvement.

"I promise, but only if you start dating."

The question startled her, leaving her breathless for a moment. "Where does that come from, you or Suggie?"

"Both. We really care about you. We understand you're still healing from the explosion. Losing your colleagues and friends and relocating here must not have been easy, but you need some levity in your life. You need daily joy and to be more social."

"I appreciate your concern, but I can't date if there aren't any viable men for me." She pulled her father aside to keep her love life, or lack thereof, private. And whispered, "I'm not going to date the first passerby."

A dubious frown appeared on Frank's forehead. "But if the right guy presents himself, you will?"

"I guess. "

"Wonderful, that's just what I wanted to hear." He hugged her, kissed her on the cheek, and handed her a bag. "You mind delivering this order to booth 27, VersaFit Adaptive Performance Gear? It's two tents before the Blue Crush's, so it's on your way."

"How do you know it's on my way?"

Frank Fontaine laughed and pointed at Axel Briggs, the surfer Claire was about to question. "I saw you ogling the guy."

"I wasn't ogling." She refuted his suggestive remark, unwilling to share the true nature of her interest in Briggs. If her father knew she was investigating, he would probably attempt to stop her or convince her to let the police handle matters. Police officers and detectives, retired or not, could be so territorial about active cases. It was one thing to want to control information, protect their reputation, and avoid competition or interference from rival units or agencies. It was another to be so proud as not to want your daughter to clear your name, or in Torres's case, to have a private chef share, or take, the credit for solving the case.

"I'm not judging. Every woman your age has needs and desires.

Claire's eyes widened in horror. "Dad, please—"

"And before you run away, I have a whole PowerPoint presentation about work-life balance and the importance of—"

Claire slapped her hands over her ears. "Oh my god, stop talking!" Her face flushed crimson as she snatched the bag from his hands. "I'm leaving now, and we're never having this conversation again."

Frank grinned. "It's forty-two slides with animations and—"

But Claire was already sprinting across the sand, moving faster than she had during any morning jog, her father's laughter chasing her all the way to booth 27.

Chapter Twelve

The VersaFit Adaptive Performance Gear tent showcased state-of-the-art water sports equipment designed for adaptive athletes. Smooth, sand-colored tiles mimicked the beach, welcoming wheelchair users who would otherwise be stranded in the sand. Sleek racks displayed adaptive surfboards, custom wave skis, and tandem paddleboards. Each item was engineered to accommodate various mobility needs, with adjustable grips, specialized foot straps, and reinforced buoyancy systems, so athletes with disabilities could experience the thrill of surfing.

Lance Foster, the booth's owner, demonstrated a specialized surfboard to a young amputee who seemed eager to learn how to surf, his patience evident as he explained the equipment modifications.

"The key is finding your new center of gravity," Lance was saying, his weathered hands steady on the adaptive board. "It's not about what you've lost, it's about discovering what you can still do. You can either use a prone paddleboard if you prefer to lie on your stomach or a wave ski if you prefer to stay seated. All our boards are custom and are designed based on your specific requirements," he said as he handed the customer a brochure. "And if you're interested in flying, we've got a whole line of kiteboards and adaptive hang gliding equipment. Feel free to look around." Then he pivoted his wheelchair toward Claire and rolled toward her.

"Is this my Osprey order?"

Claire read the receipt stapled to the bag. "Are you Lance Foster at booth 27, who ordered two Surfer Choices and two green drinks?"

"That's me. Merci," he replied with a soft smile, the French word falling naturally from his lips. Claire felt grateful he hadn't asked if she was French—she was tired of explaining that her connection to the language went no further than her accent. He turned his head sharply to the right and signaled a Blue Crush surfer to come as he shouted, "Briggs! Breakfast's here!"

Briggs trotted to meet them. "Thanks. I'm starving! My stomach's started to make whale calls. You sure I can't pay you back?"

Foster handed Briggs half of the order and took a gulp from his soda. "I'm sure. It's the least I can do. Getting a new rollout would have cost me ten times more."

"Someone stole your rollout?" Claire asked, stunned. How could someone steal their portable boardwalk, knowing it was the only way wheelchair and stroller users could access the beach without getting stuck in the sand?

"Yeah, Ricky Bingle did. May Satan have his soul. He used to borrow it so his many girlfriends didn't get their high heels stuck in the sand." Foster made air quotes with his hands at the word 'borrow.' "The jerk thought it was funny to see me struggle to propel my chair through the sand to get back to the bathroom and the parking lot."

Claire gasped. "This is terrible."

"*Was* terrible and won't happen again. The guy's cockiness cost him his life. Goes to show that able-bodied people have limitations, too. Who's laughing now?" Foster said before rolling to the opposite side of the booth, where a few customers had gathered. "Best of luck out there, Briggs! Ride those waves with confidence. I'm betting on you!"

Briggs waved his sandwich and cup in the air. "Thanks, man!"

Claire followed Briggs out of the tent and into the dimmed sunlight. The morning mist was gone, but an overcast sky blanketed the beach in a palette of muted grey hues. June Gloom provided the perfect weather for photographers who didn't have to fight with the sunlight glare when capturing the competing surfers on their boards. But the overcast skies and low temperatures could be treacherous. The layers of clouds lulled tourists into assuming minimal UV exposure and forgoing sunscreen. It was a common misconception that one couldn't get sunburned on cloudy days.

"You're back on the Blue Crush team?" she asked.

"Yes, shouldn't I be?"

"I didn't say that. I think you should have never been kicked off the team in the first place."

"I didn't know I had a French fan club." Briggs settled on an orange beach chair and gestured Claire to the other empty one.

"I'm not really a fan. Just a curious mind searching for answers. Is it alright if I ask you a few questions?"

"Sure. But I'm eating." He ripped the wax paper wrapper with one hand and bit into the wrap like a hungry wolf.

Claire nodded and took a sip from her smoothie. Condensation drops lined the outside of her cup as the surrounding temperature rose. "Clearly, you love to surf. It must have been a disappointment to be kicked out of the team."

"It wasn't, and won't explain why, and I'm back."

Okay. "Did your personality clash with your teammates?"

"Only with Ricky."

"And now he's dead."

"I have nothing to do with his death if that's what you're implying," he said between bites. "I was in San Diego the night he died."

"What about Amy Walsh? Is there something between you two? She's really pretty."

Briggs spat out his mouth contents and laughed. "No way. The only thing between me and Em is friendship. Unlike you and that guy." He pointed at Torres, who was staring at them from the Osprey counter, his breakfast forgotten as if he was trying to decode whether Claire was actually flirting with Briggs, or worse, investigating. The way his jaw clenched suggested he was calculating something—probably how much trouble this could cause, and for whom."

"Who, Torres?" It was Claire's turn to laugh. She turned around and pointed at booth 27. "Now, to be serious. What can you tell me about him?"

"Lance? What about him?"

"Did he have a grudge against Ricky?"

"Everybody had a grudge against Ricky. The guy was a narcissistic prick. Always flaunting his wealth and trying to assert dominance with money. Was a sadist too. He loved to hit people where it hurt. He used to get drunk in front of Lance's booth and jingled his car keys pretending he was about to go for a ride when he perfectly knew that Lance lost his legs in a hit-and-run accident caused by a drunk driver."

"Would you say he had a motive to kill Ricky?"

Briggs choked on his sandwich and laughed another deep guttural laugh. "You think Lance killed Ricky? The guy's paralyzed from the waist down. Has been for many years."

"Who else had a motive to kill Ricky?"

"Beside Frank Fontaine? Thousands. At this point, it'd be easier to make a list of the people who didn't hate or resent Ricky."

Chapter Thirteen

When Claire returned to her apartment, Torres was getting out of the communal shower, his cropped hair glistening with water droplets like a freshly misted houseplant. Shirtless with only a towel draped around his waist, he trailed the scent of cocoa butter soap and men's deodorant—what Suggie referred to as a "pleasant assault to the senses," usually with an exaggerated fan of her hand.

With his two showers a day, one after his morning workout and one before heading out at night, Claire could literally say that she saw Torres half-naked more often than clothed. She wondered how he would react if she were doing the same, parading around the apartment with only a tiny towel wrapped around herself. But she wasn't going to try. She couldn't even get out of the house without a bra, feeling like she needed armor against the world. Men were too unpredictable, and she didn't want to send the wrong signal.

"Going anywhere special?" she asked, catching a whiff of his fancy aftershave—the one that probably cost more than her weekly coffee budget and only came out for dates.

Torres paused, his right bicep flexed as he dried his ear with a small towel, looking like he was posing for a bodybuilding calendar. "Why are you asking?"

"Just curious. From being your roommate, I can sense that you want to impress someone. Getting a fancy visit at the station?"

"No, and your senses are wrong. I'm headed to the Swim and Racquet Club for work. To question the staff about Ricky Bingle's death, an investigation you need to stay far away from, by the way." He said it with all the authority of a middle school hall monitor.

Claire grimaced. She didn't like being told what to do or not do, especially when her father was one potential suspect. "Do you have an appointment?"

Torres snorted. "Why would I need an appointment? I'm the police." He puffed up like a proud penguin.

I'm the police, ugh. As if his badge was a magical key to open every door in the world. "It's just, they don't like cops wandering around. Exclusive, membership-only places won't allow you to roam. You need an appointment or to be an invited guest."

"What, even for the police?" His expression crumpled like she'd just told him his protein powder was actually sawdust.

"Even for the police—unless, of course, you have a warrant. Your charm alone won't stop them from refusing you entry." The Fourth Amendment protected individuals from unreasonable searches and seizures, and this protection extended to people's private clubs and homes.

Torres inflated his chest like a territorial rooster. "You wanna bet?"

"I'd love to."

"If you lose, you're on cleaning duty for the month." With a confident smile that screamed 'I've never been told no in my life,' he offered his hand to seal the wager. They typically alternated kitchen and bathroom responsibilities on a weekly basis, though Torres never hid his disdain for the chore like a water-phobic cat avoiding bath time.

Claire hesitated for a moment, calculating the odds. The deal was appealing and didn't carry much risk, if any. She grasped his hand, agreeing to the bet. "If I win, you let me tag along in the investigation."

"I can't. You're too close to this. Your father's a suspect."

"What about letting me tag along and glance at the autopsy updates just today?"

Torres shook her hand, the warmth of his palm and fingers wrapped around hers like a promise. "Deal."

"I'll hold you to it." Torres might have a strong grip, but her legal and social acumen put her on top. Knowledge often beat brawn, especially when the brawn didn't know what it was getting into.

Chapter Fourteen

The Swim and Racquet Club was a sprawling, white stucco-walled structure with red-tiled roofs overlooking the ocean. Bougainvillea cascaded from wrought-iron balconies, and the scent of salt and citrus filled the air. Palm fronds rustled in the breeze, and the sound of waves provided a soothing backdrop. A uniformed valet stood at the ready to park or retrieve the club members' luxury cars, but Detective Torres waved him off, citing safety regulations and concerns over the handling of law enforcement vehicles. As per their bet, Claire followed him from a distance—far enough so people wouldn't assume they were together but close enough to listen to any conversation he might have with the staff.

Torres had barely stepped into the club's lobby with its gleaming marble floors and crystal chandeliers when the club's concierge stopped him from going further.

"Sorry, sir. The club is private. Unless you have a membership card, written permission from the board, or a warrant, I can't let you in." The concierge's smile was as stiff as his collar.

His jaw tight, Torres flashed his police badge a second time. "You're joking. I'm the police. I'm here to solve a murder."

As Claire had predicted, the concierge wouldn't budge. "As I said, sir, unless you're accompanied by one of our members, I can't let you in. It's the rules."

"Is there a problem?" A bald man in a blue Brooks Brothers sport coat and sockless leather loafers approached the red-faced detective.

"Yes. Your concierge refuses to let me in," Torres spoke between his teeth.

"May I ask who you are and what you need?"

"Detective Torres. Caper Cove PD. I'm here on police business. I need the wave pool and Blue Crush training schedule. I was told they trained here."

"Do you have a warrant?"

"I was thinking you would be willing to share such information without me having to get one."

"I'm sorry to say, but you thought wrong. Our clientele is very exclusive and we take our members' privacy very seriously." The managing director's tone suggested he would rather find a dead fly in his dish than cooperate with law enforcement.

"Can you at least let me in?"

"Are you interested in a membership? The initiation fee is ten thousand dollars with a recurring five-hundred-dollar monthly fee."

Torres gasped under Claire's knowing gaze. This type of fee wasn't unusual, and considered low by Washington D.C.'s most exclusive clubs. The price of privacy could buy a decent used car or feed a small army of hungry surfers for a year. In Caper Cove, the high initiation fee definitely kept the average resident from rubbing shoulders with the affluent residents, tourists, and celebrities.

Torres cleared his ear with his right pinky finger. "Ten thousand American dollars?"

A frown creased the manager's forehead. "I take this as a no, so I'll ask you to leave the premises and only return with a warrant. Your vibe is affecting the club's chi."

Torres grimaced, looking confused. "The what?"

"The chi. The life force or energy that flows through all living things, the mood," Claire explained as she reached Torres's side. She turned toward the manager and smiled. "Good morning, Judson."

The manager's face brightened like a sunrise. "Oh, hello Claire. How are you?"

"Great. How's Evelyn?"

"Wonderful. She can't stop smiling since the feast you catered. Can't stop talking about your strawberry shortcake. You really made her thirty-fifth birthday special. My mother can't thank you enough for doing it at cost."

"It was my pleasure, but please, keep this favor between us." Claire's mind flashed to the three sleepless nights she'd spent perfecting that shortcake recipe and planning an entire menu around a scented doll, her kitchen looking like it had been hit by a strawberry tornado. She had labored days to create the perfect celebratory meal at the Sunshine House, the local residential care facility, but she couldn't accept every favor request from people. She couldn't afford pro bono work the way she did it as a criminal attorney fighting to free the wrongly convicted. The days of her premium corner office and cushy expense account were long gone. She didn't have the financial support of a top law firm anymore and needed to get paid to support herself. She refused to live rent-free at her father's condo and have Torres as a roommate forever.

"What can I do for you?" Judson asked, his mood jovial, transforming from guard Doberman to a puppy golden retriever—a complete one-eighty from his previous interaction with Torres.

Claire placed her hand on Torres's forearm as if vouching for him. "I'm with my friend, Detective Torres. We are investigating together."

"Ah, yes! To clear your dad," Judson said.

"No, my father doesn't need to be cleared. He's done nothing wrong. But yes, finding the truth is what we're after."

"How funny, I was just about to give the detective the wave pool and team schedule. Please follow me." Torres's eyebrows shot up, almost reaching his hairline. The manager led the way through a beautifully carved door into the stately office and invited them to take a seat on the two leather armchairs facing an imposing antique-looking desk.

While waiting for Judson to return, Claire admired the décor. Design choices and personal touches in someone's office space served as a window into their personality and aspirations. The nautical maps and ceremonial tridents adorning the office walls revealed someone wanting to project strength and his mastery of the elements. Maybe to overcompensate weakness, she thought. Unless it was simply the default décor of all the coastal offices. A framed photo displayed a selfie with a beautifully costumed woman with blue skin, cosplaying one of the Vandstam merpeople—a fictional water tribe from a hit comic series and even more successful TV adaptation.

"Is there anything else I can help you with?" Judson asked as he returned.

"Actually, yes," Torres said. "What can you tell us about the relationship between Coach Kovac and Ricky?"

"Besides what everybody knew?"

"Which is?" Claire asked. She played dumb, maintaining her best poker face the way she did at countless negotiation tables. The first rule of investigating is to never assume anything, and the less you say, the more people will talk. Most are uncomfortable with silence and will feel the need to fill the conversation.

"Coach Kovac took Ricky on board on Ricky's parents' insistence. Without Ricky's money to sponsor them, the Blue Crush wouldn't be able to compete. The Bingles paid for the uniforms and promised to pay the next year of international travel expenses in exchange for Ricky assuming the position of team captain, and Ricky himself funded the wave pool in which the team trained. But Ricky wasn't a great surfer. Hadn't seriously trained in weeks. He jeopardized the team's chance at winning this weekend's competition." Judson's expression suggested Ricky on a surfboard had all the grace of a giraffe on roller skates. "On the opposite side, Briggs owns all the team records, including the tandem event with Tony Ramos.

"So Ricky was better off dead for everyone," Torres said.

"You said it, not me." The manager said as he rifled through the drawer of a wooden file cabinet. "With him dead, Coach Kovac could keep the sponsorship and get Briggs back on the team. That way, he could be guaranteed a medal for the team-based event."

"About the wave pool funding, isn't it usually the responsibility of equity members?" Claire's legal mind was searching for cause and effect, patterns in behavior, and motives. Equity membership meant that members were part owners with a financial stake in the club and responsibility for its operation and maintenance. If Ricky financially covered the building of the pool, how much of the club did he own? Could his increased share in the club be a possible motive for murder?

"Yes, it usually is, but it was Ricky's dream to join a surfing team. He didn't want to train in the cold ocean water, so he proposed to build the wave pool."

Torres snorted. "A bit extra, don't you think? Getting a surf pool to learn how to surf without getting cold. That's like becoming a sushi chef but being afraid to touch raw fish."

"No, the wave pool is a great incentive for people to join the club, and he agreed to foot the bill. So, who was I to say no?" Judson spread his hands in a 'what could I do?' gesture that seemed practiced in front of his office mirror.

Claire nodded. It was a harsh reality that rich people always got their way. The real question was whether Ricky had paid for the pool with his own money or left behind a trail of unpaid contractors and creditors who might hold serious grudges against him.

Chapter Fifteen

Claire stepped out of the racquet club's artificially chilled air into the bright daylight. The sun had won today's fight over June gloom's dreary atmosphere, to the joy of beachgoers. Under its signature sunshine, Caper Cove was again the postcard of Southern California paradise.

"I don't understand how Ricky could think paying to be team captain, when he clearly lacked the skills, would grant him success." The need for the appearance of leadership or dominance was ridiculous.

Torres followed her through the empty parking lot, groaning at the heat. "That definitely gives Coach Kovac a motive. By killing Ricky, he gets to keep the sponsorship money and his best surfer back."

"I agree." With Briggs, the Blue Crush were guaranteed a few wins, which means a boost in recognition, reputation, and visibility for Coach Kovac. "Winning the team event would propel Coach into the limelight and increase his earnings, cementing his own status in the industry."

"Sport coaches seeking fame and money, getting paid more than soldiers risking their lives for the country. Greed makes me sick." Torres shook his head in disgust.

"What about Tony Ramos, the teammate who vehemently opposed Ricky joining the team? Who needed Briggs to win the tandem event and increase his ranking?"

"I'm adding him and Kovac to the suspect list. I'll also get the list of all share-equity club members and anyone related to the pool construction. I can help run background checks on them all."

"No thanks. It's police business, remember?"

"But I won the bet. The only reason you got the membership list and pool schedule is thanks to me."

Torres paused at the car, keys jingling between his fingers. "Yeah, about that. How did you get in and obtain all this information? Do you have something on them? Are you blackmailing Judson, the manager, or are you involved with him?"

Claire snorted. "I'm the daughter of a policeman and worked for a criminal defense firm that catered to the wealthy. I know how the system works. All you need to do is connect with the staff and not act like you. Wearing fancier clothes might also help." Claire glanced at Torres. Though alluring, his half-buttoned and slightly wrinkled shirt wasn't to the standard of an elitist club. "Don't worry, I can mentor you through it all," she teased, straightening an imaginary tie.

"What was that favor you did him with Evelyn? Any compromising situations I should be aware of? If the guy's a suspect, I better make sure you're clean."

"You're kidding, right?" Claire rolled her eyes. "His younger sister Evelyn was one of my closest elementary school friends. At thirteen, she contracted a severe case of meningitis, which caused brain damage, leaving her with permanent cognitive impairments that required lifelong care in a special facility for individuals with disabilities. Because of the cost of her care, I agreed to do it at cost."

Torres's face fell, the accusatory edge in his posture melting away. A flush of embarrassment crept up his neck. "I...I'm sorry," he said quietly, clearing his throat. "That was unfair of me to assume."

Claire held her gaze for a moment, then gave a small nod of acknowledgement. "So who are we questioning next?"

"No one. I'm going to run background checks. You can't shadow me. I'm handling everything myself. Need the case to be airtight with Frank being a suspect and all," he said, opening the passenger door with an exaggerated flourish.

Claire froze, her jaw clenching like a steel trap. "Don't say that! He isn't a suspect. Just a person of interest." A suspect was someone believed to have committed a crime, while a person of interest was someone who might have information relevant to the investigation but wasn't necessarily implicated in the crime. The proper term mattered as much as the difference between a paper cut and an amputation when it came to her father's reputation. It was bad enough that her last night's client had suggested her father's guilt; it was another for his protégé and her roommate to assume the same.

"Sorry, person of interest. Do you need a ride home?"

"No, I don't need a ride to the *apartment*." Claire emphasized the last word like a verbal highlighter. She avoided the term "home" whenever talking about the condo she shared with Torres. "Home" felt too intimate, too "white picket fence," and was already the source of enough gossip to fill Caper Cove's social media feeds for a year. She wasn't living with Torres; they simply shared the same space. "And don't forget to clean the bathroom. Also, we're out of toilet bowl cleaner. You're on cleaning duty for the month, remember?"

Claire sighed as Torres drove away. She would have to investigate on her own.

"I'm sorry, I couldn't help listening. Did that cop take credit for your work and ditch you?" A woman with teal hair asked as she approached. She was wearing blue body paint over her entire body and the Vandstam fish-like uniform. She had sleep-deprivation bags under her eyes from what was probably a busy performing schedule.

"Looks like it." Claire forced an embarrassed smile, unused to having witnesses to her disagreement with Torres.

"I heard everything. I can sign an affidavit if you need to prove you did it all. Unless, of course, it's a lovers' fight."

"Not a lovers' fight, but I'm good. Thank you. And go Vandstam!"

The woman laughed. "Anytime. Being a trailblazer is rough. You set everything in motion, and the followers reap the benefit. We girls need to stick together. So if you ever change your mind, you know where to find me."

Claire nodded with a smile. The aquatic blue-skinned people were among the most conspicuous visitors. "I will, thank you."

"And my name's Sierra." The woman added as she trotted back to the group of Vandstam performers. She'd never sought recognition for uncovering the truth, especially in this case where she simply wanted to clear her father of all suspicion. But it felt good to be acknowledged for her work and contribution. It breathed new life into her motivation. She would find Ricky's killer before Torres, with or without him.

Chapter Sixteen

Claire stood in the empty Osprey kitchen, under its bright fluorescent lights, her hands busy with the familiar rhythm of chopping vegetables, the scent of fresh cilantro mingling with roasted garlic. Advanced preparation was essential during the busy season, especially when the number of daily customers would double over the competition week. The lively chatter of patrons and clinking glasses echoed from the bar, on the other side of the kitchen's swinging doors. As with every afternoon, the taco bar closed at five p.m. sharp and turned into the haunt for the local cops.

Suggie was on the opposite side of the counter, her newly blonde hair catching the light as she adjusted large swimming goggles that made her look like a scientist. She was impatiently waiting to receive a video call from her deployed husband and didn't want to ruin her makeup from chopped-onion-induced crying. She had propped the murder board on a side table and was refining their findings. The board looked like a conspiracy theorist's dream, complete with red string and pushpins that would make any crime show producer proud.

The picture of the victim topped a pyramid of strings connecting to suspect photos and their motives below:

Amy Walsh: save her reputation without having to have a very public breakup with Ricky

Coach Kovac: keep the sponsorship money while keeping the best surfers

Axel Briggs: keep his place on the team/captain

Tony Ramos: keep Briggs as a tandem teammate

Club equity member: to keep majority shares in the country club

"You really think the fiancée could have done it?" Suggie asked, her goggles fogging up slightly as she spoke.

"If Ricky was the bully people said he was, I wouldn't be surprised if he used his wealth and influence to prevent her from leaving him," Claire replied, the sharp thunk of her knife against the cutting board punctuating her words. "He didn't look like the kind of guy who would accept being dumped easily. She wouldn't be the first woman to be ambushed by an abusive boyfriend and fight to find a way out without having to go through a huge public breakup." Dating celebrities was like playing Russian roulette: one day you're a nobody, the next, you're thrown into the limelight and the line of sight of every imaginable ugly gossip.

"I'm adding Judson to the board." Suggie lifted her goggles briefly to get a better look as she erased 'Club member' with a brush and wrote 'Judson West' in its place.

Claire paused mid-chop, swept the onions into the sizzling olive oil, and lifted her gaze.

"Why, what have you found?"

Suggie grimaced and looked over her shoulder. "Judson owned most of the club's shares before Ricky built the wave pool last year. What if the club created news shares to represent the pool value—"

"And Judson lost control."

"Exactly. Judson might have resented Ricky for taking the club ownership from him. Isn't that reason enough to kill?"

"It is. Through history, men have committed terrible acts when someone takes what they believe belongs to them."

A ping sounded from Suggie's phone.

"Daniel's calling in five minutes. Okay if I leave the board here?"

"Of course. I'll take it to my room once I'm done."

"You're not afraid Torres is going to see it?"

"Not really. I won a bet and I'm now investigating with him," Claire said.

"Maybe he lost the bet on purpose so he can hang out with you more," Suggie waggled her eyebrows suggestively, the effect somewhat dampened by the goggles.

"Don't be silly." Claire sliced her last onion and added it to the giant skillet on the stove. Making enough caramelized onions for an estimated three hundred sandwiches was the biggest challenge she had taken on. Her father's famous grilled cheese, steak, and grilled vegetable sandwiches always included the freshest ingredients, including this homemade golden goodness.

"What? That's possible. Torres is upstairs in his room right now instead of flirting at the bar like he used to. Looks like he gave up on dating cop bunnies because he only has eyes for you."

Claire laughed, the sound mixing with the sizzle of onions. "I knew your obsession with romance plots, but I didn't know you were also living in high fantasy. You should consider fiction writing."

"How would you explain his absence from the bar? He's usually the first one at the counter."

"He's usually the first one at the bar because he helps my dad in exchange for extremely low rent. Frank charges him crumbs because Torres reminds him of himself when he was starting out—former Marine dropped by a long-time girlfriend. And he's not here tonight because police rules prohibit him from socializing with suspects or persons of interest in a crime to avoid conflicts of interest, maintain investigation integrity, and ensure public trust in impartial law enforcement."

"That makes sense. What about the fact that Frank is his landlord?"

"That's okay. It's not like Torres can move out and find an apartment on the beach at a reasonable rent, especially during the summer months."

"How are you feeling about all this, Frank being under the microscope?" Suggie asked, finally removing her goggles and revealing raccoon-like circles of pristine makeup surrounded by slightly smudged foundation.

"I'm not sure." She was still distraught by her customer's comment about Frank being a murderer and his past suspension. Did his superior officer believe his emotional involvement in Aurora's disappearance would compromise the investigation, or had her father committed an offense? Did the turmoil surrounding her sister's vanishing affect his professional performance, and was the suspension a compassionate decision by his superiors to give him time to deal with the personal crisis and seek support, or was the suspension the result of a personal vendetta against him?

"Did you find out why my father was suspended? Your mother must know something." Mrs. Oh was the fastest and most reliable town historian when it came to traditions and gossip.

"Sort of. Umma was reticent to talk about it, that's why I went blond."

"Wait. Your mom wouldn't answer your questions unless you dyed your hair?"

"Sort of. I was on the fence about it, but she's been pressuring me to do it, saying it'd be a great advertisement for the salon. So I went for it."

Claire blinked in surprise. "I don't know what to say. Thank you for your service to the investigation," Claire said with mock solemnity, placing her hand over her heart.

"I actually love it. It's a nice distraction while Daniel is away, and blonds do have more fun. Reminds me of our college days." Suggie laughed, removing her hat and flipping her hair dramatically. "Anyway, Umma mentioned professional jealousy. Your father was up for the captain position at the time, and someone reported him for roughhousing a suspect. The suspension was a way to discredit him; remove him from the captain candidacy."

"Who reported him? Who did he supposedly roughhouse?" Claire asked, suddenly worried. If her father had a violent past, clearing his name would be more difficult than she initially thought.

"Nobody knows who blew the whistle, but the guy who got promoted left soon after. And the suspect was Jim Stone."

Claire grimaced in disbelief. "The creepy pawnshop owner?"

"The one."

"That's weird. Aurora used to talk to me about a Jim. Didn't realize until today that it could have been him."

"You think he was involved?"

"I don't know, but it's worth considering."

Claire sprinkled sugar over the onion pan and reduced the heat under the skillet to medium-low. The aroma of caramelizing onions filled the kitchen, almost but not quite sweetening the tang of anxiety in the air. She started to clean the kitchen worktop when a man burst through the open emergency exit side door.

"This isn't an entrance. You need to go around the building," Claire said to the stranger, redirecting him to the back alley.

The man ignored her and shouted, "Inspection!"

"It's a bit late to conduct a food inspection, don't you think?" Suggie asked.

Three men followed him in the kitchen. They all wore black cargo pants, boots, and tactical vests with the "ICE" markings—Immigration and Customs Enforcement.

"There are no undocumented workers here," she said. "You're not allowed to enter. This is a private area. Unless you have a warrant, you're trespassing."

Suggie's phone appeared in her hand as if by magic, aimed at the intruders like a weapon, and Claire was happy her friend did—either as a preemptive protection against whichever agency the man said he was working for, or as content for a news article.

"I need to see your identification and your Form I-9," the man said. Form I-9 was used to verify the identity and employment authorization of individuals hired for employment in the United States. All U.S. employers had to complete Form I-9 for every individual they hired—citizens or not. Both employees and employers had to complete the form.

"Unless you have a warrant, I'm asking you to leave," Claire insisted, struggling to remain calm. Claire knew that without a judicial warrant, ICE agents couldn't legally enter private areas of businesses. The "employees only" signs weren't just for show; they created legal boundaries that even federal agents needed to respect. She stepped backward as two of the men approached menacingly toward her while the others blocked the door. One of them was holding a pair of handcuffs.

Claire's chest tightened, her breath coming in short, painful gasps. The fluorescent lights suddenly seemed too bright, the kitchen too small. Her hands trembled as the US-Mexico kerfuffle from the previous month flashed in her mind—the humiliation, the cold concrete cell, the guard who refused to believe her or let her make a call. The same panic that had overwhelmed her then was consuming her now. Sweat beaded on her forehead as the handcuffs glinted under the harsh light. Not again. She couldn't go through that again. Her mouth went dry, tongue sticking to the roof of her mouth as she fought to maintain her composure. People's assumptions of her non-Americanness was a heavy burden to bear, all because of a speech impediment that sounded like a foreign accent.

"Show me your I-9."

"She doesn't have one. She doesn't work here," Frank Fontaine said as he stormed into the kitchen.

"That's what they all say." The man glanced at his tablet. "You must be Frank Fontaine, the owner. We've received a tip that you're employing illegals."

"She's my daughter."

"Your daughter? Right. She sounds very American to me," he mocked as he motioned one of his agents. "Cuff her."

"You aren't taking her anywhere."

The man snorted. "Fine. Cuff them both."

"You've no legal reason to arrest us. Suggie, you're getting that on tape, right?" Claire called out.

The man noticed Suggie's phone and turned his back to the camera. "You've failed your Form I-9 Audit by refusing to provide the documentation regarding this woman and resisted her arrest."

"This is ridiculous. I have rights. I'm a U.S. citizen," Claire shouted.

"Really? Who can swear on their life that you are, huh?" the agent asked, smirking.

Bar patrons, mostly off-duty officers, entered the kitchen, surrounding the ICE agents. "I can," one said. Others echoed the same. Someone flashed Claire's law firm biography on their phone. "She's an attorney too."

The agent studied it with a grimace and motioned his team to retreat. He glared at Claire. "Why would someone tip us about you if it wasn't true?"

Claire's chest tightened as she realized how differently this could have gone if she didn't have white skin and a retired police officer father to vouch for her. How many people faced these same accusations without backup, without connections, without the privilege of being immediately believed when family stepped forward?

Claire's jaw clenched as she met his stare, refusing to be intimidated despite the adrenaline still coursing through her system. "I don't know."

There were many reasons motivating fraudulent whistleblowers: to taint someone's reputation or get rid of the competition. But why her? She hadn't caused harm to anyone. Neither did her dad. She exchanged a quick glance with Suggie, who was watching with narrow, suspicious eyes. This wasn't random. Was this related to Ricky Bingle's murder? And if so, was someone trying to stop her from investigating, or were they blaming her dad for Ricky Bingle's death?

Chapter Seventeen

I t was the official first day of the Pacific Coast Surf Championship. Competitors lined up at the registration area to check in and receive their competition jerseys, the morning sun glinting off their already-bronzed shoulders. In the shallow waters, Lance and a team of volunteers were helping disabled veterans learn to surf.

A sea of Vandstam merchandise flooded the beach—t-shirts and caps bearing the hit TV show's logo bobbed through the crowd like buoys. The show's surfers were scheduled to open the competition with their signature acrobatics, drumming up buzz before next month's Comic-Con, fresh off the news of their renewal for another season.

A few yards away, seated at the Osprey patio, families and supporters enjoyed breakfast while socializing with blue-skinned Vandstam performers. The scent of coffee, waffles, and coconut lotion filled the salty air. Suggie moved through the crowd with her camera, snapping photos of the dedicated fans while chatting with Vikram. One performer in particular had taken her craft to impressive extremes. Her modified body was a living tribute to the show's merpeople—nine nose rings marking each of her character's lives gleamed in the morning light, while a subdermal implant created a shark fin effect along her spine. Intricate gills were tattooed along her neck, complementing the iridescent scales that wound their way up her arms and legs. When she smiled, sharp veneer teeth caught the sunlight, making her look every bit the dangerous sea creature she emulated.

"This is impersonation to the highest level," Claire sighed, watching the Vandstam performer pose for fans, wondering if her appearance ever fused with her identity, whether people saw the lawyer or the caterer in her bearing and sartorial choice. If both sides of her could exist, or if her legal part was bound to die, or her chef one could never exist.

"That's Renata Efterlig, but everybody calls her 'Renée.' Her job has literally phagocytized her, transforming her into the perfect real-life Vandstam warrior," Vikram explained as he met her by the bleacher.

Claire handed Vikram his daily protein smoothie, noticing the presence of many of his colleagues on the bleachers' rows. "Did the entire office follow you here?"

Vikram laughed, water trickling from his dark curly hair. The top half of his wetsuit hung lazily from his waist, proving he belonged to the beach and the surfing crowd rather than the sterile halls of the morgue. "It's tradition. The Medical Examiner's office implemented a late start on mornings of the competition to boost staff morale."

Claire nodded. "I bet catching a glimpse of athletes in their prime is a much-needed breath of fresh air and a welcome change from handling corpses all day long. Mood-altering even," she said as she noticed Debbie, the perpetually grouchy medical examiner's office clerk. The woman was wearing a red 1950s-inspired dress and—miracle of miracles—an actual smile.

She settled next to Vikram on the sand, the grains still cool from the night air. "So you said you have something for me?"

"Yes, autopsy updates." His voice dropped to a whisper that barely carried over the sound of breaking waves. "We found particles in Ricky Bingle's wound. Silver paint flakes were embedded in the fibers of his jersey where he was initially struck, on the spine. We're looking for a medium-sized bar coated with shiny silver paint."

"Silver painted rod. Got it! We're going to need to check the teams' storage trailers."

"We also found cells embedded in his wound—the length of time the body was in the water should have washed it off, which means the contact must have been so hard, it could be the actual cause of death. With the type of algae, microbiome remnants, and level of salination found in the wound, we'll get a better idea of the rock he hit. We'll narrow down the locations. So we'll know whether he was struck or thrown against the rock that split his back." Vikram shuffled in place and sucked his smoothie hard through the straw, making noise as if he had reached the bottom. "Why don't you drop by my house for dinner tonight? I can go over the full autopsy report with you. I'll make fajitas—it's my personal tandoori version of the recipe you taught me."

"Or you can drop the report off at the station, and I'll give her a copy," a voice interrupted as a large shadow loomed over them like an unwanted cloud on a perfect beach day. Torres sat next to Claire, managing to spray sand on both of them in the process. "I didn't know you were giving private cooking lessons to Vic."

"He was referring to the recipes I taught him when he was a kid. I used to babysit him," Claire explained, brushing sand off her legs.

Torres snorted. "How cute. Next, you'll tell me you taught him to ride a bike, too."

"I better go," Vikram said as he rose to his feet, his enthusiasm deflating faster than a punctured beach ball. "Just let me know what works for you, Claire."

Claire imitated him, leaving Torres alone on the sand like the seaweed no one wanted to touch. "With everything going on, I'll take a rain check for your tandoori fajitas if it's okay with you. But I would love the updated autopsy results via text if you can."

"No problem. Just call me or visit if you have questions."

"I will. Thank you."

Vikram joined his colleagues on the spectators' bleachers, and Claire headed back to the kitchen, the scent of grilling fish and tropical fruits growing stronger with each step. Her break was over, and she needed to return to her workstation to make wraps for the incoming wave of customers.

Torres trotted after her, his footsteps heavy in the sand like a determined bulldog. "Hey, you can't go around asking for updates on the autopsy or for evidence. You need to stay out of the investigation."

"Why? I won the bet," Claire shot back, the salty breeze whipping her hair around her face.

"The bet was a one-day deal. Like those buy-one-get-one-free fish tacos deals.

"You're kidding, right? My dad's a person of interest. I can't relax and act as if everything's normal. I have the right to investigate on my own. Deputy Chief Ernshaw made me an official police consultant," she reminded him. The Caper Cove deputy chief had given her that title after she solved the murder of a rising designer and wife of the local gubernatorial candidate, two months prior—a fact she wasn't above wielding like a surfboard in choppy waters.

"Maybe, but you can't butt in on this case. Your conflict of interest could contaminate our findings. You need to stay clear of any evidence gathering."

"You're telling me you don't want my help in proving a member of the Blue Crush killed Ricky Bingle?"

"What do you mean?" Torres's eyebrows knitted together.

"The murder weapon may be in the gear trailer, which can't be searched without a warrant. A warrant you won't be able to get because you have no time to get it, nor reasonable cause. Which means, the murder weapon could easily be cleaned while we stand here arguing like seagulls over a French fry."

Torres's posture straightened, and tension filled his face as he realized he needed her help. "And you think they're going to let you go through the trailer because you're adorable?"

Claire shrugged, a mischievous glint in her eye. "Because Coach Kovac has a thing for French surfers." She recalled how, earlier that morning, Coach Kovac had enumerated all the French surfing teams, the top twenty French female athletes, and his unsuccessful attempt at speaking French.

"But you aren't a French surfer."

"No, but I sound like one, and the man is hungry and hates to wait in line," she said as she motioned to the coach at the end of a very long customer queue.

Chapter Eighteen

Ten minutes later, Claire and Torres were chatting with Coach Kovac in the parking lot, where the large asphalt rectangle had been transformed into a makeshift trailer park. Each competitive team had stationed their gear trailers and RVs, creating a chrome-and-fiberglass village that gleamed under the morning sun.

"Who had access to the trailer before today?" Claire asked.

"Besides me, only the assistant has a key, so, before today, it would be Briggs." Coach Kovac said, unconsciously mimicking her accent while running a hand through his silver-streaked hair.

"You kicked him off the team but hired him as an assistant? Isn't that a bit cruel, having to work where he should have been competing?" Claire continued, ignoring Torres's eye-roll that was practically audible.

"He asked me for the job. I wasn't going to deny him. The Swim and Racquet Club paid him a misery." With a swift pull, the coach unlocked the trailer door, revealing neatly stowed surfboards waiting for the next wave. "I must return to my team. Please be gentle with the equipment and lock behind you," he added as he winked at Claire.

Their phone flashlights in hand and latex gloves on, Claire and Torres sifted through the trailer's cluttered interior with precision. Each shelf, each corner, held a potential clue in their search for silver-coated gear. The tang of salt hung in the air, mingling with the faint scent of sunscreen, wet towels, and what might have been yesterday's forgotten banana.

Torres, his broad shoulders hunched over, examined a row of neatly stacked windsurf booms—the horizontal bar—handle windsurfers use to control their sails—while Claire scoured the ones in the back.

"There's gotta be something here," Torres muttered, frustration tainting his voice as he shifted the pieces of equipment aside with the delicacy of a whale in a porcelain shop.

Claire's eyes narrowed as she spotted a glint of metal wedged between two surfboards. With a deft hand, she extracted a bent windsurf boom and brought it to the light. The deformation in the aluminum was concave, resembling the curvature of a human back or torso. Its surface was dented and chipped, by what could be a violent impact.

"Blood," Claire whispered as she pointed at the crimson stain marring the metal, her heart drumming against her ribs.

Coach Kovac poked his head in the trailer and stepped inside, bringing with him a waft of expensive cologne that clashed with the trailer's salty atmosphere. "Blood? You sure?"

"Stay out!" Torres shouted at the coach as he rushed to Claire's side, nearly taking out a rack of wetsuits in the process. "Do you know who could have used this?"

Coach Kovac shook his head, his tan face paling slightly. "Any guy could have used it. They're supposed to hose down the gear once they're done with it. The assistant is the one putting everything back."

"So Briggs it is." Torres pulled his phone out and dialed. "Detective Torres here. I need a CSI tech here ASAP."

Claire exited the trailer and joined the coach on the parapet separating the parking lot from the beach while Torres welcomed the CSI team.

"Is it true you replaced Briggs with Ricky on the team because of money?" she asked.

"Briggs'd already quit, and getting Ricky on the team secured us a huge sponsorship. Surfing is a business like any other, you know. We can't work for free. The athletes and I need to make a living."

"Did Briggs ever tell you why he quit?"

"No, but Ricky told me he paid Briggs to take his place. I assumed it had to be a handsome sum because that kid, skilled as he was on a board, was on his way up. But I don't have time to think or question my surfers' motivation.

They do the job or they don't."

It was strange for a rising star to drop out of the competition for money. Passionate athletes didn't usually give up their dream and life's work so easily. Briggs had to be seriously pressured or even blackmailed. That's what she needed to find out.

Chapter Nineteen

laire stepped away as Torres secured the scene, his face pinched with frustration at the conspicuous absence of security cameras overlooking the now yellow-taped parking lot. Suggie had joined her, capturing everything with her camera. Murder wasn't a normal occurrence in Caper Cove, where residents still left their front doors unlatched. Even the resort section, usually bustling with sunburned tourists and lanyard-wearing conference attendees, had maintained its reputation for safety. The San Diego County CSI unit processed the Blue Crush trailer with methodical precision, while Torres and his team canvassed nearby trailers and RVs, questioning the surfing competitors and merchants.

"It can't be Briggs who killed Ricky. The guy doesn't even kill the flies or ants that get in his food. He's like a Buddhist, thinking all life is sacred." Lance Foster said as he approached Claire and Suggie in his wheelchair. He locked gaze with Suggie. "You should write that in your paper.

"I certainly can. You're Lance Foster, surfing champion, right?"

He shot Suggie a flirty smile. "I am also the paragliding instructor for the Vandstam at your service. He pointed at the sky. Above their heads, the colorful sails of hang gliders drifted slowly with the wind like giant butterflies showcasing the competition sponsors' brands, including the bright blue, fish-scale patterned ones of the Vandstam.

"Impressive. I'd be love to schedule an interview if you're up for it." Suggie leaned backward, her head tilted upwards, her camera pointed at the bright grey sky, and her finger tapped the shutter. Her professional camera rattled off shots like a caffeinated woodpecker.

"I saw your pictures of the Vandstam surfers in the Caper Cove Whisper. Your article on cosplaying as a lifestyle was very insightful."

"Thank you." Suggie's eyes sparkled with professional pride. "I'm hoping the Associated Press will snatch them up. These cosplaying surfers are perfect merpeople. I can only imagine what they'll do with the Vandstam Air People spin-off."

"Do I see hang-gliding in your future?" Lance asked them.

"I prefer to be anchored to the ground." The last time Claire "flew," she had been ejected from the third floor of an exploding building and had spent months of recovery in the hospital.

"Me too." Suggie adjusted the focus of her long-range zoom lens. "Hanging in the air, suspended horizontally face-down underneath a hang glider isn't my idea of fun."

"You can still fly and be seated comfortably upright if you are interested. I can personally show you, or explain to you over dinner," Lance said as he rolled his wheelchair right next to Suggie.

Suggie swept her long blond hair to one side with a tilt of her head, revealing pink streaks underneath, and smiled. "I'm flattered, but my husband wouldn't approve," Suggie displayed her wedding ring, giggling. "US Marine on his way home."

"No problem. I'm booth 27 if you change your mind and want to schedule the interview."

"Blonds do have more fun," Claire teased as the man rolled away.

"Yep, you should think of bleaching your hair. You could get guys this cute knocking on your door every night."

"I like to sleep, so I'll pass."

"You may be right. I heard Torres prefers brunettes anyway."

"That's also what I heard," someone interjected behind them.

Claire jumped and spun toward the voice. "Miranda! I mean...Deputy Chief Ernshaw. Hi. What are you doing here?"

"Checking the advance on the case. I need you to stay clear of the investigation."

"What do you mean?"

"You're too close to the case, Claire. Your dad's a person of interest, and I can't afford to be accused of preferential treatment and risk my position. I'm the one who had snitched on Jim Stone to Frank when Aurora disappeared. It's my statement that made him rageful and grab the guy by the throat, slamming him against the interrogation room wall. That's what got him suspended. If he's innocent, I'll prove it using proper channels and without your biased investigation."

Claire's jaw dropped, her eyes widening in disbelief. This didn't sound like the father she knew at all. "*If* my dad's innocent?"

'That's not for me to decide. The evidence will tell us."

"Right." Claire snickered. She had defended enough innocent prisoners to know that evidence could be planted or falsified. "Don't tell me: the mayor's pressuring you to find the guilty party before the end of the festival, and that the Bingles would rather find a scapegoat to blame for their son's death than catch the real culprit. Do I have it right?" Blaming someone, even an innocent, provided the Bingles with a way to make sense of the situation and created the illusion of closure.

Deputy Chief Ernshaw failed to reply, yet her eyes flickered with a telltale gleam, betraying her silent agreement with Claire's statement. "You better leave, both of you. And Suggie, the mayor asked that you not report outside of police sources."

Suggie gasped, her camera dropping to her chest. "He can't tell me that!"

The deputy chief raised her hands in surrender. "I'm just the messenger."

"Well, I have a message for the mayor. Tell him that if he has a problem with me, he can talk to my attorney, Claire. And if he doesn't like it, we'll sue him."

Claire jerked back in surprise, her spine stiffening. Her legal license was still active in California, but she hadn't worked on a case involving First Amendment law in ages. "Um, yes, of course. Just tell the mayor that Suggie and I are committed to uncovering the truth and that we refuse to be silenced by his attempt at suppressing Suggie's reporting. The Bingles' pressure on local officials only strengthens our resolve to investigate. We have a strong lead and hope to give you the name of the killer in less than a week."

Deputy Chief Earnshaw shot them a crooked smile and returned to the trailer area of the parking lot.

Suggie jumped in place and squeezed Claire's arms. "Oh my god, you were awesome. I wish I had recorded you. Your speech would have been phenomenal as a reel. You really know who's behind Ricky's murder?"

Claire grinned as if in pain. "Not really. I was being overly optimistic." The blood could be anyone's. No one locked their trailers here. Caper Cove was so safe, people didn't watch their belongings and could go swimming without worrying about their purse. "The blood means nothing. Getting cut or pinched to the point of bleeding when handling surf and windsurf equipment is quite common. Remember the summer we worked as a cleaning crew for the sailing club ? You sliced your hand on a fin, and I cut my finger when tightening a boom clamp."

Suggie grimaced at the memory. "I had forgotten."

A few yards away, Ernshaw and Torres were talking, their words carried by the wind to Claire's ears.

"We need to find out what Briggs is hiding. If we rush, we can sneak into the police's observation room before Torres and Ernshaw see us."

"Before they see us?"

"Yes, Torres always interrogates people in interview room three. The observation room's so tiny, they used it as a janitor's closet. If we get there before he does, he won't know we're there, watching."

"But people will see us coming in the station."

"The staff is so used to seeing me, they won't bat an eye at our presence."

"What about me?"

"I'll tell them you have a period emergency need for the bathroom and that I'm accompanying you. No man will dare question that."

Chapter Twenty

"I can't believe we're hiding in a police station. What if they find us?" Suggie whispered as she recoiled in the corner of the tiny, unlit room, her breath quick and shallow.

"Nobody's going to find us. Nobody ever gets in here, except for the janitor at the end of the day," Claire said, leaning casually against the two-way mirror. The room, a claustrophobic's nightmare, was barely large enough to accommodate them, and the stale air was heavy with dust. She doubted anyone would come here of their own will.

"What if Umma finds out? Aren't you going to be late for your shift at your dad's?

"Your mom won't know unless you tell her. And my shift starts at ten…oh, someone's coming," she whispered back as footsteps approached and a broad-shouldered police man escorted Briggs into the interrogation room on the other side of the glass and motioned him to sit at the table.

"We can't hear them," Suggie groaned, her breath fogging the mirror.

"There should be an intercom on your right, flick the switch up," Claire directed.

Suggie padded the dark room. "Got it."

The sound of a ringing phone filled the small room. On the other side of the mirror, the surfer picked up his phone. "Can't talk now. I'm at the police station. No, I won't. Will call you when I'm done." Then, he hung up as Torres entered the room.

The detective carried the blood-stained windsurf boom Claire had found in the trailer, wrapped in a giant plastic bag, and slammed it on the table in front of the surfer. "Whose blood is this?"

Briggs jerked back. "I don't know. Could be mine."

"So, you're admitting to killing Ricky?"

"Of course not, I cut my finger on a fin. You can ask the lifeguards. I went there to get a bandage."

"Why did you leave the team?"

"Ricky asked me."

"Just like that, because he asked?"

"Ricky was connected. If I refused or mentioned any of this to anyone, he threatened to have me banned from every surfing club in SoCal. Surfing is all I have."

"Where were you between ten p.m. and midnight two days ago?"

"I was in San Diego with a friend."

"What's your friend's name?" Torres asked.

"I prefer not to say."

"I bet the friend's the fiancée," Suggie whispered in Claire's ear. "They must be having an affair."

"Maybe." Claire stared at Briggs's face, trying to search for the lie.

Torres grunted. "So no alibi. I could arrest you right now and detain you the entire weekend."

"But...you told me this was a casual inquiry. Nobody told me I could go to jail. I can't miss the competition."

"The competition you killed Ricky for?"

"I swear, I didn't harm Ricky, but I know who had a motive. You will let me go if I tell you, right?"

"I can't guarantee that. Speak first and we'll see."

"Shouldn't I talk to a lawyer first?" Briggs scanned the empty concrete room in search of support. "I think I want a lawyer."

There was something in Briggs's demeanor—a subtle tell she couldn't quite pinpoint—that resonated with Claire's instincts about innocent clients. Maybe it was a micro-expression she had learned to recognize during her years of defending the wrongly convicted. But she couldn't stake Briggs's freedom on instinct alone, not when her personal stakes in the case and related emotions could easily affect her objectivity.

"You sure you want a lawyer? They complicate everything and are really expensive," Torres said.

"Oh no, he didn't," Claire muttered between clenched teeth, her criminal defense attorney instincts kicking in. How could Torres have threatened that man-boy with detention without informing him of his rights? She burst out of the observation room into the hallway, leaving a stunned Suggie behind. "See you at the Osprey tonight."

Claire charged into the interrogation room, her heels clicking purposefully against the concrete floor as she strode straight to Briggs. She was supposed to be done with the law, but she couldn't watch Torres narrowing down on an innocent like a passive bystander. "Hello, my name is Claire Fontaine. I'm an attorney," she announced with the same commanding presence that had won her high-profile cases. "Do not say one more word."

Torres jumped off his chair. "Claire! What are you doing here?"

Claire ignored the detective and smiled at the surfer, positioning herself between him and Torres with the practiced ease of a seasoned defender. "I will be representing you pro bono, so you won't have to pay me a dime."

"You can't do that! Get out," Torres shouted at Claire. "You're not his attorney."

Claire crossed her arms, unmoved by his outburst. She had faced down far more intimidating opponents in federal court.

"If not him, we're going to focus on your dad," Torres mumbled.

She knew that, but she couldn't, in good conscience, let an innocent take the fall for a crime he hadn't committed. She would have to prove both of their innocence.

Chapter Twenty-One

The Osprey kitchen crackled with lunch-hour energy. Each staff member moved with a sense of urgency, their movements choreographed with the precision of a well-oiled machine. The musical chaos of sizzling grills and clanging pots, and the pressure-cooker environment, weren't that different from Claire's past trial. Except this time, her workplace smelled of rotisserie and spices, and at least here, there were no losing parties. The kitchen staff churned out a steady stream of wraps and sandwiches, smiling. Frank's promise of a cash bonus at the end of the festival was a powerful motivator.

The lunch crowd was twice as large as the day before. The hundreds of Pan Bagnats Claire had made earlier were already gone, and tourists were ordering the classic French tuna sandwich faster than she could assemble them.

"Claire, there's a woman asking for you. Take five and then take over the ice cream station. The new guy doesn't know the difference between frozen yogurt, ice cream, sorbet, and custard."

"For me?" Claire traded her knee-length grey apron for a short turquoise one, happy to leave the frenetic pace of the sandwich assembly line. Bathing in the sweet aroma of freshly churned ice cream beat working close to an oil-splattering griddle. Plus, the simplicity of scooping would certainly free her mind, allowing her to mull over the murder case's every detail.

Her visitor turned out to be Amy Walsh, Ricky's fiancée. "Are you Claire Fontaine?" She asked, her manicured fingers drumming impatiently on the counter as she approached the booth's order window.

"How may I help you?"

"Are you a real American attorney?" she demanded unceremoniously.

Despite her years of handling unpleasant interactions with opposing counsels, Claire found this confrontation unexpected.

"Why are you asking?" Claire gestured toward the more private back alley. She didn't need or want another client—not when she was supposed to take six months off from law to let her brain recover from her law firm explosion.

"Briggs told me you're representing him. But you have an accent and..." Walsh's eyes swept over Claire's ice cream-stained apron, "don't real attorneys make enough money to make a living without needing to scoop ice cream?"

"I can't comment on whom I may or may not represent, but yes, I am a real attorney. Licensed in New York, D.C., and California," she said with a professional tone. Catering or serving ice cream didn't take away from her skills or qualifications.

"C'mon! How good are you, really?" Walsh's voice echoed off the alley walls.

"She's the best criminal lawyer anyone can get, and she's scooping ice cream to help out with the competition crowd for *her dad*," Suggie fired back as she approached. "Because that's what she does, she helps people. She doesn't hide the truth from the police and let her boyfriend hang high and dry without an alibi."

Claire jerked back at Suggie's fierce defense, making a mental note to thank her later for that BFF response.

Walsh recoiled and looked over her shoulder, her arms crossed tight against her chest. "I don't know what you're talking about. All I know is that Briggs doesn't need you as a cook or an attorney. You're officially fired. As his agent, I've secured a real lawyer to represent him." She handed Claire a piece of paper. "This is a certified letter with Briggs's signature officially firing you!"

Relief flooded through Claire. Her volunteering to represent Briggs had been a spur-of-the-moment mistake which was suddenly corrected.

"Good." She turned toward the chorus of excited chatter announcing the approach of coin-clutching children—Frank's one-dollar-fifty ice cream cones made the Osprey the most popular spot on the boardwalk for young families. "I've got to go."

"Wait." Suggie held her back by the arm and glared at Walsh. "We know you spent the night with Briggs the night Ricky died. So you can keep your condescension and fake morality to yourself. Briggs didn't tell the police because he didn't want to smear her reputation. Isn't that romantic?" Suggie added, her voice dripping with sarcasm.

The woman froze, her eyes widening like a deer in the headlights. For a moment, she seemed unable to speak, her confident demeanor completely stripped away. She glanced between Claire and the growing line of customers, as if searching for an escape route that didn't exist.

"Not sure about romantic, but certainly suspicious." Claire gave her friend's shoulder a gentle squeeze, surprised by the unusual anger. "You okay?" she whispered

Suggie nodded. "I'm sorry. I hate cheaters, and with Daniel deployed. I miss him…" She glanced at the ice cream booth in front of which a line of customers formed. "Continue here, I'm handling the booth." Suggie was familiar with the ice cream booth—their teenaged summers working together scooping ice cream had been the glue that had turned their friendship into an unbreakable bond.

"Don't apologize, I appreciate your support." Claire understood perfectly— for Suggie, newly wedded to a deployed Marine, the mere mention of infidelity released a pent-up resentment about military separations.

Turning back to Walsh, Claire asked, "Were you and Briggs having an affair?"

Walsh gasped, her perfectly symmetrical face contorting in shock and disgust. She glanced at the families lined up at the ice cream booth just a few feet away, then lowered her voice. "Oh god, no! This is not what you think it is! We are just good friends, long-time friends."

"How long?" Claire leaned against the wooden counter of the Osprey's boardwalk stand, positioning herself to keep an eye on both Walsh and the growing line of customers. "I'm on your side. I won't tell anyone."

Walsh shifted uncomfortably, glancing toward Suggie at the ice cream booth, then back to Claire. "On my side?" she scoffed. "That's rich. I've seen how you've been investigating, poking around where you don't belong."

"How long?" Claire repeated. "The truth is bound to get out."

The woman frowned, her gaze lowered as if searching for her answer on the sun-bleached boardwalk. "I don't know, a very long time. We grew up in the same town. I hadn't seen him in forever. Seeing him was a surprise. We just reconnected."

The genuine connection in the woman's expression told Claire she was speaking the truth. After all, Claire knew firsthand how childhood friendships often carry an unbreakable bond that survives the passage of time, like her and Suggie's friendship. "Where were you the night of Ricky's death between ten p.m. and midnight?"

"Asleep. I'm still on East Coast time, and I can't function without sleep."

"Did you know Ricky was cheating on you?" The familiar voice of Torres cut through the alley.

"Torres! Were you spying on us?" Claire asked, whirling to face him. She should have expected it—they were talking in the alley, right under Torres's bedroom window, right during his lunch break, at home since he couldn't hang out at the Osprey during the investigation.

"I was just passing by, just like you were at the police station earlier. Had a sudden craving for frozen custard," the detective said, his grin not quite reaching his eyes. "Can I get a double scoop, please?" He turned his attention to Walsh, his casual tone sharpening. "So, Ms. Walsh, did you know Ricky was cheating on you?"

The question didn't faze the woman. "Of course, I knew. Everybody did. I broke up our engagement three months ago, but Ricky asked me to wait until after the tournament to tell the team and the media. He didn't want the news to affect morale and create drama. It's important to have your head in the game without having the press gossiping about your personal life," she said with a hint of bitterness.

"Do you know who could have wanted to harm Ricky?"

"Besides Coach Kovac, who was forced to take him on the team, and the owner of the Swim and Racquet Club, who had to foot Ricky's pool bills, there are too many to count. I used to love Ricky, but it would be lying to say he was a gentleman."

"You mind elaborating on that? The bit about the pool bill?"

"Yes. What exactly did Judson have against Ricky?" Claire chimed in, her investigative instincts piqued.

"The wave pool where the team trained was supposed to be a gift from Ricky to the team and the club. Judson advanced the money by putting his club as collateral, but Ricky never paid the contractors. Judson was stuck with the bill, a bill he couldn't afford. When confronted, Ricky refused to pay, saying his mere presence at the club was payment enough, that his name brought enough customers for the owner to recover the cost."

Torres grimaced. "Do people really flock to the place to see him?"

"No, it was actually the opposite. Patrons wouldn't renew their membership because of Ricky."

"Why didn't Judson sue?"

"No local attorney would dare sue the Bingles, and Judson had no money for the retainer," the woman explained.

"And the only way he could get his money was if Ricky died, because Ricky's estate would have no choice but to pay the existing debt through probate," Claire concluded. But did Judson know that?

Chapter Twenty-Two

The INS field office's air hung heavy with tension, punctuated by the soft shuffle of paperwork and muted conversations. Fluorescent lights flickered overhead, casting stark shadows against the sterile walls. Claire stood in front of one of the service windows, force-smiling.

As if her father being a murder suspect wasn't enough trouble, now she had to prove—yet again—that she was born in San Diego, not Paris, and simply helping out her dad, all because some agent couldn't wrap their head around her French accent. The citation had been clear: present documentation within twenty-four hours, or her father's business could face penalties. She grabbed her birth certificate and passport, fighting the urge to pull out her law degree too. The whole thing was ridiculous, but she couldn't risk giving the authorities another reason to scrutinize her father's life. Not at the time of a murder investigation.

"Everything seems to be in order. Your citizenship status is confirmed," the ICE officer said as she returned Claire's passport and birth certificate.

"Thank you. I hope this will be the last time I have to go through this. It's tiring to be reported as undocumented and a waste of my time to have to prove my Americanness whenever someone doubts it."

"Well, you sound foreign, so it's normal to suspect you. It would be different if you were blond with blue eyes. Scandinavian illegals are rare. Or maybe work on your accent," the officer said with a smile that didn't reach her eyes.

"Why didn't I think of that?" Claire snarked. She bit her tongue, stopping herself from joking about adding blue contacts and hair bleach to her grocery list.

"We'll make a note in our system to hopefully prevent any future misunderstanding," the officer continued, shuffling papers with unnecessary force. "Is there anything else I can assist you with today?"

"Yes. Do you know who reported me?"

"I'm sorry, but we can't reveal that. First, I don't know, but whistleblowers are protected."

"But it wasn't a real whistleblower. It was a liar intent on hurting me and my father," Claire insisted, her hands clenching into fists under the counter. While opinions were protected speech, deliberately false statements meant to harm a business weren't. Making up health code violations or lying about the employment of undocumented immigrants crossed the line from protected criticism into actionable defamation. "That person filed a false report, which is a crime and a misuse of federal resources, without talking about defamation."

"Someone obviously has a grudge against you. Maybe try to be kinder? The French tend to be mean and arrogant."

"Again, I am *not* French, I just sound like one. How many French people do you know?" Claire challenged, thinking of the ones under whom Claire had studied French cooking, who had been amiable, and the ones in her D.C. social circles were maybe opinionated, but perfectly professional and kind.

"None, but that's what I heard," the officer shrugged.

"Oh, so, Elvis is still alive," she jested.

The agent frowned. "Elvis's dead."

"That's not what I've heard," Claire retorted with mock solemnity.

Chapter Twenty-Three

Ten minutes later, Claire was heading North on Highway 5, beneath an orange sky painted by the setting sun. She rode shotgun aboard Vikram's Honda, cradled in the supple leather seat, wrapped in the brand-new smell of a just-bought car. Indo-Western music played softly through the speakers, reminding her of her summer babysitting—when she couldn't have fathomed that the shrimpy dinosaur-obsessed, ten-year-old boy she babysat would become a handsome forensic pathologist giving her a ride home. His once wild hair was now carefully styled, and his former braces were replaced by a confident smile.

"Thanks again for picking me up."

"Not a problem. I was in the neighborhood. Had dropped off the surfers' urine samples for anti-doping analysis at a San Diego lab. I'm on urine duty every day this week, so if you need a ride in either direction, I welcome the company," he said, navigating through traffic with the same precise attention he used to measure ingredients when she taught him to cook eons ago.

"I see. Less bias and influence. We used to do the same with DNA testing. Outside labs ensure impartiality in the testing process. And compliance with international standards, of course."

"Exactly." Vikram lowered his window and let the warm air fill the car. "Remember when you used to let me watch those crime shows while you babysat?" he asked, navigating through traffic. "You'd pause them to explain why the forensics were wrong. I think that's when I knew I wanted to understand how bodies tell their stories."

Claire smiled. "You were always asking the questions no one else thought to ask."

"Still am. Sometimes I wonder if that's why I chose this field—to find answers for people who can't speak for themselves anymore."

"About that...do you think my dad could have something to do with Ricky's murder?" she asked.

"I dunno. You told me yourself: anyone can commit a crime under the right circumstances. Though killing a man over a parking lot feud, that's not your dad's style." Vikram's voice carried the weight of someone who'd spent countless hours at Frank's bar, observing the man's patient handling of the most difficult customers. "I think people got confused because of Ricky's posts claiming that Frank threatened to 'destroy him' and run him off the boardwalk. Without talking about the video."

"What video?" Claire typed her father's and Ricky's names in the search browser of her phone. A video of Ricky and Frank fighting violently filled her screen. "But it never happened. That's a deepfake!"

"Locals know Frank's character, but those posts got enough traction with tourists and outsiders to stir up trouble. Someone really hates you both. I reported it."

"Thank you." Claire stretched her neck by the window and took a big breath. There was nothing we could do about it right now. The faster she found the killer, the faster things will return to normal. "Any updates on the autopsy report?"

"Yes, the foreign substance embedded in Ricky's wound is a brooding anemone that doesn't usually thrive in southern California. The only place we find them is at the base of Launch Point, in the state marine reserve," he replied, his tone shifting from friendly to professionally precise.

"That doesn't make sense. There's no beach access, and the current couldn't have taken him there. He must have fallen from Launch Point." Launch point was the name of the cliff above, where the local gliderport was located. It included a runway for takeoff, an area for safe landing, and a café for spectators.

Vikram took his eyes off the road and glanced at her with a smile. "The presence of soil and grass under his fingernails supports that theory."

"So someone hit him with a steel rod, sending him stumbling toward the cliff. He lost balance and held on to the cliff's edge before he fell, and then hit the rock below?" Claire said, mimicking the motion with her hands.

"Could be. But why would he be in his surfing shorts and jersey at Launch Point at night?"

"Maybe he didn't have time to change, or he was prideful and wanted to impress his sports fans? He was on a date. Swim trunks and jersey are also the fastest clothes to get out of, when you're on a date." Her voice lifted with hope. "If we can prove Ricky fell off the cliff, that would exonerate Dad." Frank was working at the bar at the time, like he did every night between ten p.m. and midnight, serving his signature cocktails with the same steady hands that had once braided her hair for school.

"The bar patrons would have definitely noticed his absence if he drove to the Launch Point and back," he said, his eyes on the road, hands steady on the wheel despite the excitement of their deductions.

Claire kissed Vikram, a quick peck on the cheek that made him blush. "I know it's not conclusive, but it's a start. I need to check the top of the hill to see if there's any nail or claw marks."

"What, now?" The sky had deepened to a rich purple, the last sun rays painting the clouds a deep crimson. It started to get dark.

"Yes. You mind dropping me off at Suggie's?" Claire asked, already mentally mapping her investigation route.

"There's one more thing. The lab found minute traces of Rohypnol in Ricky's bloodwork. Someone wanted Ricky completely out of it."

"What, just now? Why didn't it appear on the preliminary report?" Claire demanded, her lawyer's instinct triggered by the procedural inconsistencies.

"The lab tech ran the blood panel twice," Vikram said, his voice tight with frustration. "Apparently, men getting drugged didn't fit his worldview, so he initially assumed it was a false positive."

"That changes everything. Being drugged *and* pushed. Someone took all the necessary steps to guarantee Ricky's death by making sure he was too incapacitated to fight back. The murder was premeditated and deeply personal."

Chapter Twenty-Four

The sun was gone, but light still streaked the sky with orange and pink lines when Claire and Suggie drove up to Launch Point—Caper Cove's highest lookout. The salt-laden breeze carried the distant cry of seagulls settling in for the night.

"We're not supposed to be here. The sign says the area closes at dusk," Suggie said as she parked her car in front of the closed gate, the gravel crushing under the tires. "I still feel bad about sneaking into the police station earlier. I'm not sure I've got it in me to break any more laws today. I don't want bad karma."

"Don't worry about what the sign says. It's just a suggestion to keep people at bay and avoid liability."

"Why don't we come back tomorrow? It's too dark and dangerous to check the cliff."

"I need to do it now, before the weather washes away the evidence. Ricky had soil and grass under his fingernails. If I can find his claw marks on the ground, I can prove he was here and clear my dad for good." Three of her clients had cancelled their catering orders because of rumors regarding her father's alleged involvement in Ricky's death. She needed to prove her clients wrong before they all cancelled their orders. She would also insist on a deposit from now on, so people couldn't cancel at the last minute.—especially when she had purchased the food and had to turn down other jobs to accept their reservations.

Claire grabbed a floodlight and a long rope from the trunk and walked toward the cliff, stopping at the giant steel anchor—a weathered sculpture that both symbolized the naval history of Caper Cove and served as a safety marker, warning people to be cautious near the edge.

She tied one end of the rope around her waist and the other end to the yellow ground anchor.

"Please, tell me you're not rappelling alone."

"I'm not alone. I have you. Plus, I've done this many times before. It was part of my law firm's quarterly bonding exercises." Claire's voice caught at the memory. She had gone to enough extreme sports-themed bonding work retreats with her former law firm—before someone detonated a bomb that killed everyone—to know her way around risk assessment, dangerous situations, and a rope.

"What about your outfit? Isn't your pantsuit silk?"

"Mr. Laver is a miracle worker," she said of the dry cleaner. "I'm sure he'll vanquish a few dirt and grass stains without a problem."

Claire positioned the floodlight so its beam cut through the growing darkness like searchlights, illuminating the cliff edges. She was crawling along the edge when flashing red and blue lights, accompanied by a sharp siren, sliced through the night.

"Park's closed at dusk! Can't you read the sign? What, are you French or something?" Torres's sharp, sarcastic tone shattered the evening quiet. Then, he grabbed the rope that held her to the edge and pulled her up with a grunt. "Vikram called me worried, told me your little plan, so I came to check out what he was scared about."

"Vikram called you?"

"Yep, your babysittee turned babysitter." He pulled her up to her feet. "What are you doing? The place has been trampled by hundreds of people in the last few days. If you find anything, it won't be accepted as evidence. Everything's been compromised since it's not from an unsecured scene."

"You have to let me find the mark. I can prove Ricky was here right before his death."

Torres crossed his arms over his chest and raised his chin. "You don't need to find the mark to prove it. We've got the evidence. Ricky had a date with a woman he met on GetLucky, the app for one-night stands. Someone called

Kinlay." He turned to Suggie: "Does that ring a bell?"

Suggie jumped back, shaking her head energetically, her silver bangles jingling. "You're asking *me*?! I don't do dating apps, I'm married!"

"I meant do you know anyone by the name of Kinlay? With the work at the spa, I thought…"

"No, but I can ask around the salon."

"That'd be great. Let me know if you get a hit. For now, get back to your car and go home. Also, I know you're just helping Claire, but if I catch you interfering with this investigation again, I'll have to arrest you both for obstruction of justice."

Suggie nodded, worry creasing her face.

"Wait. What's Kinlay's last name?" Claire asked, something nagging at the back of her mind. That name sounded so familiar.

"Don't know it yet. We'll find that out once the warrant clears. The company won't release the account holder's name or the registration IP address without it. Because, you know, lawyers."

Suggie gasped. "What if it's revenge? Someone who wanted to make him pay for what he did to them? Maybe a girl he date-raped?"

Torres shook his head and gave them a condescending smile. "What makes you think of something like that?"

"Because of the Rohypnol in Ricky's blood."

Torres looked stunned. "Damn you, loose-tongue Vikram," he grumbled under his breath.

Chapter Twenty-Five

At five a.m. the next morning, Claire sat straight up in her bed, ending a restless night. Her dreams had always been sneaky little detectives, dropping hints to help her solve problems. The circumstances of Ricky's death and Kinlay, the mysterious woman who met him at the cliff, weren't the first pairing she had encountered.

She grabbed her phone from her nightstand, typed "Kinlay + dive team" in the browser search box.

Nothing.

She tried spelling variations of the name—kinley, kinlay, or even kinlé—but nothing related to a fake girl, and nothing either when she scrolled through her contact names.

Outside her window, the birds' songs mingled with the sound of the waves as the inky blue sky stretched above the beach. A faint streak of pale blue lined the horizon, hinting at dawn. The cool, briny air slithered through, leaving a trail of goosebumps on her arms.

"How is that possible? I could swear I heard that name before," she mumbled at the murder board taunting her. It must have been in one of those pulp fiction paperbacks she had read in secret as a tween or in the B movies she watched with Suggie. They used to buy VHS tapes at garage sales and binge-watch them together during the endless summers of their teenaged years.

Then it hit her, so she texted Suggie.

SUGGIE: <you want to meet at the skyhouse now?>

<Sure, so no real running?>

CLAIRE: <Real running afterward. I'll explain when I get there>

<You still have our treasure box?>

The treasure box was a small suitcase in which Claire and Suggie had kept their most memorable teenaged memories, including all the rated-R movies they had watched without their parents' knowledge.

SUGGIE: <Of course I still have it. >

<I'll bring it up to the skyhouse>

CLAIRE: <see you in 10>

Claire slipped into her running gear and tiptoed out of her bedroom toward the entrance.

She was reaching for her shoes when the bathroom door slammed open. A blast of hot air hit her as if she had opened an oven door, and Torres appeared in front of her. He stood naked, but for a wide smile and a small white towel precariously wrapped around his waist.

"You're up early," he said." Faint tendrils of steam rose from his bare shoulders into the crisp morning air.

"And I thought I was in the foyer, but I guess I'm in a sauna now."

"Just trying to give the spa experience, free of charge."

"Very generous, but next time, can you leave some hot water for the rest of us?"

"I didn't think you were planning to take a shower right now. In fact, you've got your sleuth look. About to investigate some more, are we?"

"I don't have a sleuth look!" Claire glanced at the entrance mirror and frowned. "But speaking about investigating, did you get the full identity of the Kinlay woman Ricky had a date with?"

"Why are you asking? Are you secretly Kinlay?"

"Me, on GetLucky?" Claire laughed out loud. One-night stand wasn't her thing. "If I wanted a stupid one-night stand, I would jump in bed with one of The Osprey regulars."

He smirked. "So you're into cops."

"I didn't say that. What I mean was that you'll find me dead first before seeing my profile on an app like GetLucky. I can find dates the organic way."

"Really? Except I've seen you on any dates recently."

"How would you know? Are you keeping tabs on me?"

Claire's watch buzzed before Torres could answer. It was a message from Suggie. She found Kinlay.

Chapter Twenty-Six

Claire ran past the natural hedge of flowers that marked the limit of Claire's old neighborhood, along the paved road, and up to the backyard where a majestic Coast Live Oak tree stood tall. Hidden in the large tree's foliage, where their old treehouse once stood, was an updated shelter that mirrored their NYU dorm room—from the fifteen-year-old posters to an old Panasonic TV/VCR combo on which they used to watch movies scrounged from yard sales for fifty cents. Real glass windows, electricity, and a running faucet made the place a luxurious tree house, which could have its own vacation rental listing if it hadn't lacked a functional bathroom.

Suggie waited for her with matcha lattes and waved an old VHS tape. "I think I found what you're looking for. It's a French thriller called *Le Souffle*—Last Breath with a fake date named Kinlay and a murder."

"That's it!" Claire shouted. The movie was one of their tween-summer purchases at the local university yard sale, where all outdated and obsolete items were sold to fund new technology. They settled on the faux-fur carpet, and Suggie opened a box of Bungeoppang, the staple fish-shaped pastries of their childhood sleepovers.

"Halmeoni always makes extra, so I freeze them. I just warmed up a few. Want one?"

"If I want one?" Claire laughed at the question and took a bite of one of the crispy treats, the sweet red bean paste still warm. She grabbed a pen and paper and started to take notes as they watched the small screen.

The movie's plot was exactly as Claire remembered: a diving team created a fictitious girl to ambush and kill their fellow teammate. A swimmer stole someone's place on the championship diving team; angry to see their star diver expelled for unfair reasons and having to deal with a mediocre diver, the angry teammates planned the swimmer's death, creating a woman they named Kinlay to lure him to his death.

The similarities between the circumstances of Ricky's death and the movie's narrative were too uncanny to be a coincidence.

"You think the whole team is in on it...that they all wanted Ricky dead?"

"It's possible. It could also be someone who wants to frame the entire Blush Crush team." They would need more evidence to narrow down exactly how the killer or killers executed the murder before sharing this information with Torres. "We need to find out who knew about this obscure movie and had a motive to kill Ricky."

Chapter Twenty-Seven

The sun had barely risen when The Osprey kicked into high gear. Surfers needed fuel to power through their morning routine, locals heading to work, and tourists hoping to secure the best spots on the beach created a perfect storm of hunger and urgency that turned the bistro's usually peaceful patio into a bustling war zone. Hunger and time constraints can turn even the most pleasant, sweet baby birds into hangry and shrieking vultures. Even in a paradisiac setting like Caper Cove.

"Tom, order number eighty-five," Claire called out, managing the "athletes only" line where competitors grabbed pre-ordered breakfast without delay.

"Karine, order eighty-six."

A surfer with a French flag swimsuit, her hair still damp from a morning practice session, flashed her phone screen with the order's confirmation number. "Merci. Sorry you lost your clients. Glad you found this job. Food's everything."

Claire frowned, wondering what the French woman meant, and called the next order.

"Phil, order eighty-seven, that's me." A tall surfer with a bright blue jersey approached the counter and smiled. "I just read about you losing clients and all. Breakfast's easier to do than full meals, at least for starters, I guess."

Claire shook her head. "I'm sorry. I don't get it."

"No? Hold on." The man scrolled through his phone, then flashed its screen. It was a picture of her clearing a patio table the night before. The caption read: *Her bad food lost her clients. Now working at the Osprey cleaning tables because they won't let her cook.*

Claire gasped. "That's a lie!" She hadn't lost clients because of bad cooking. People cancelled her catering order because of her father's status as a person of interest in Ricky's murder. But it was over now. The latest forensic findings proved that Frank Fontaine, her father, couldn't have done it. Did they not?

Claire's stomach tightened as she read the rest of the post.

Maybe stick to one job next time? Stay in your lane! #badcook #badcaterer #fakechef #badfrench #confusedidentity #pickalane

Stay in your lane. The words stung as they echoed her own doubts. Was she fooling herself, thinking she could be a legitimate chef?

She searched the name of the offender, but the account had no specific name, just a single handle. Who was @fireinyourmouth?

Chapter Twenty-Eight

It was high noon when Claire ditched her apron and joined Suggie and Vikram on the beachside bleachers with their sandwich orders. Suggie had scored them VIP seats in the shade of the canopy—away from Torres. The entire medical examiner's office and police station had placed wagers on the surfing competition, and both Vikram and Torres were riding the crest of their fantasy surfing competition, vying for the top spot on the leaderboard. The rivalry was so intense that they couldn't be in the same room without dangerous sparks flying.

The air carried the scent of coconut sunscreen and grilled onion from The Osprey.

Suggie was tracking surfers through her telescopic camera lens while fanboy Vikram chatted with Sierra Thorn—the woman with teal hair Claire had met days earlier. Today, Sierra wore no blue body paint or makeup, just a plain shirt and shorts, with a Vandstam cap over her ponytail.

"Coming up after this heat, Danish champion Jürgen Pichler and the Vandstam Queen will showcase their surfing excellence!" the announcer's voice boomed across the beach, drawing cheers from the crowd.

"Didn't they just mention the V Queen? Are you supposed to perform next?" Vikram asked Sierra.

The woman smiled as if grateful for the recognition. "It's not me anymore. My friend Renée took over my role."

Suggie gasped at the news. "Renée Efterlig, the extreme cosplaying surfer whose body makeup withstands the waves?"

"It's not makeup. It's a skin condition. She's blue twenty-four seven like a true Vandstam," Sierra said, shrugging it off.

Vikram frowned. "But you were fantastic. Aren't you going to fight to get your job back?"

"Nah. Apart from the nose piercing, I can't keep up with her body modifications. Waist training and tattooing half my body isn't for me. I'm getting too old, plus I can't surf." She laughed.

"Are you staying with the franchise? What character will you be?" Vikram asked. "They can't get rid of you. You're the original Vandstam Queen."

"Aw. I'm grateful for the fans who remember who was there first." Sierra leaned in conspiratorially. "It's hush-hush right now, but be ready to watch me in the spin-off."

Vikram's eyes widened. "I can't wait for the release! But I love the first series. I wish I could rewatch the first season, but I can't find it."

"It's becoming a collector's item now since it had limited distribution. But they have a VHS copy of the first episodes at the athlete village community center," she said, referring to the converted motel housing the competing surfers.

Claire perked up and exchanged a knowing glance with Suggie. "They still have VHS?"

"The new generation calls it 'vintage.' The building has no wifi after nine p.m., so the tapes get checked out constantly. Are you looking for a specific movie?"

Claire's pulse quickened. "Yes, a movie called Le Souffle, spelled like soufflé."

Sierra scrolled through her phone. Spectators cheered in the background. "Lavigne with an explosive bottom turn!" the announcer called out over the crash of waves. "And there's the aerial—perfectly executed!"

"Here it is, Le Souffle, not a cookbook but a French thriller." Sierra flashed her screen in Claire and Suggie's direction. Is that it?"

Claire jumped from her seat. "Yes! Is there a registry that shows who checked it out?"

"No. Anyone can take anything without signing in. It's like a little free VHS library."

Claire settled back on the bleacher, her shoulders low. Everybody could have watched it. They were back to zero.

"A movie about revenge," Sierra noted, finishing reading her phone. "Fitting, considering the economy we Millennials inherited." She studied Claire's face. "I heard about your troll. Are you trying to find inspiration to retaliate?"

"Not at all. I'm pretending they don't exist." She bit into her Pan Bagnat sandwich, focusing on the crunch of the bread crust before her teeth reached the savory tuna and olives. Angry-biting into *pain de campagne* always made her happy.

"That's wise. You just need a few people to positively vouch for you in the comments," Sierra agreed. "Don't let the detractors intimidate you, and dive into other projects. When things get tough, I focus on the skin care line I created." She pulled out an iridescent blue tube with the Vandstam logo. "Would you like to be the first to try it? It's grapefruit with super light glitter. Gives you that perfect, smooth, and sparkly complexion too."

"I'd love to! Suggie set her camera aside, squeezed a small amount into her palm, and rubbed it in. "This feels and smells amazing. My mom would love this. The Vandstam logo guarantees its appeal at the spa. Can I take it with me?"

"It's my only sample. I should receive a case this week. Can't officially sell it before the list of the Vandstam royals comes out, and I'm officially endorsed. Let's exchange numbers, and I'll let you know as soon as I get it."

Claire's phone pinged several times in a row, calling her attention.

"That's a lot of texts. A boyfriend or a culinary emergency?" Suggie teased.

Claire forced a smile at her roommate's attempt at a joke. "Sadly, neither. Just more cancellations, no biggie."

Though she tried to stay calm, Claire's legal mind was already cataloging the damage. While online reviews were protected speech, deliberately false statements meant to harm a business weren't. Making up stories about her food or qualifications crossed the line from criticism into something legally actionable. But pursuing defamation claims could bring more attention than the damage was worth.

"What do you mean, *no biggie*? That's how you make a living," Suggie protested.

"Have you asked the police to trace the IP? You could get the troll's identity fast before they do more damage. That's what Vandstam security does with weird or threatening fan mail."

"I'll think about it." Using police resources for her personal gain would be unethical. She'd file an official complaint if it gets out of hand. The police couldn't act until the behavior escalated to harassment, threats, cyberstalking, or defamation.

Suggie checked the disparaging posts' comments on her phone. "Yes, I see. Good thing you've got great supporters, like Dr.Pangolin, who dubbed you a *culinary star*. Wait!" She pivoted to Vikram and chuckled. "That's you. You're Dr. Pangolin, aren't you? You picked an animal as a username?"

Vikram stopped mid-bite through his Mortadella-artichoke panini. "So what if I created it in middle school and didn't want to change it?"

Claire pretended not to notice Vikram's blush. She was the one who had taught him about the mammal when she gifted him a Beanie Babies pangolin to complete his collection of scaly animals for his tenth birthday. She had been sixteen at the time. Like many of the internet generation, changing a username meant deleting your account and rebuilding your online presence from scratch—something only a few were willing to do. Claire herself had to delete hers. No respecting attorney could have kept an account named "Stormy Claire" in reference to "it was a dark, stormy night."

Suggie squinted at the screen. "Could fireinyourmouth be Kerant Weber, the sandwich guy who's called you a French imitation? They both use the same syntax and overuse the poop and vomit emojis."

"If it's him, you need to stop him," Vikram interjected. "Make sure he doesn't do it again."

Sierra cleared her throat, looking pensive. "About the movie. You think that's what happened to Ricky? That he was taken down by a competitor?"

"Anything's possible. Did you know him?"

"Not really. Renée and he hooked up a few times."

Chapter Twenty-Nine

Two more clients had cancelled Claire's catering services without explanation since the false, malevolent post. So here she was in Suggie's backyard, in full running gear, stretching in the crisp, briny ocean air and morning silence. Running was the best remedy whenever stress or anger weighed her down.

Early morning birds started to sing audibly in the stillness of dawn.

"What did they say?" Suggie asked, performing a deep hamstring stretch beside her.

"That they had decided to go more casual American cuisine and less fancy French."

"Did you tell them you make a killer mac and cheese and fried chicken?"

"I did. Don't worry about it. I'm sure I'll find other catering gigs." It was high tourist season in Caper Cove, and if she didn't get a catering gig, she could still teach a cooking class at the local hotels. "Right now, I need a rush of endorphins. Ready to go?"

"Ready!"

The women were at the garden gate when Mrs. Oh burst out the front door. "They found another body!" Mrs. Bedoin just called. She said Fisherman Cooper just found a body in his fishnet. She called me before notifying the police."

Suggie glanced at Claire, wide-eyed. "That wasn't in the movie."

"Maybe it was an accidental drowning," Claire suggested. Bad things tended to happen in pairs, or triplicate. The championship attracted a lot of tourists, weekenders, and students, which meant a lot of partying.

The danger of swimming while drunk (or high) was highly underestimated. People ignoring the many warning signs about riptide currents compounded the problem.

"It was no accident." Mrs. Oh said, her voice trembling. "The victim had a spear in their chest."

Chapter Thirty

The crime site was right on the shore, yards from where the surfing competition was held, within shouting distance of The Osprey. The thick marine layer hung like a ghostly curtain, hiding the scene from the early-rising tourists out on a morning walk.

When Claire and Suggie arrived at the scene, the morning surfers had congregated around the body, blocking the grisly sight with a wall of surfboards and their leashes. The multicolored boards created a makeshift fence, their wet surfaces gleaming dully in the gray light. It reminded Claire of the tactic her father had directed when a surfer had suffered a shark attack. Frank had been mindful of sparing the vacationing families with young children from the trauma. Though this time, Frank stood away from the dead body, probably aware that contaminating the scene with his DNA would put him right back on the suspect list.

Smart to command from afar, Dad, Claire thought as she made her way to the corpse.

The victim was naked, her skin an intricate canvas of scale tattoos from her toes to her hips, and gills on her neck, giving her the partial appearance of a sea creature, the ink almost iridescent against her pallid skin. A metal shaft protruded from her chest, its tapered and grooved base indicating it was a spear from a speargun. There were no blood stains around the body, but that told them little. If she had been killed on the beach, the morning tide would have washed away any traces of blood in the sand. Either she had bled out elsewhere and been dumped here, or she had been killed right here on the shore, and the ocean had already erased the evidence.

"That's Renée!" A tall man in a Vandstam Speedo and a Viking beard and braids called out, distraught as he paced behind the surfboard blockade. Renée was the extreme Vandstam acrobatic surfer who had wowed spectators the day before.

"For god's sake, someone cover her!" Henry, the grumpy old man with a vet cap from the fish market, barked, shuffling forward with a bundle of seaweed in hand that he was about to throw.

"Don't." Claire stepped between the body and the old man.

The old man tried to push her aside, but Claire wouldn't yield. His weathered face reddened with indignation. "Why not? You French women with your casual attitude about sex and nudity."

A light laughter rose from the crowd of surfers, most of whom knew Claire and her French Foreign accent syndrome story from their morning breakfast at The Osprey.

Claire took a deep breath, mentally rolling her eyes. "I'm not French, and I doubt the French are into necrophilia. Touching her will compromise the evidence. We need the forensic pathologist to inspect her first before touching or moving the body."

Grumpy Henry glared at her. "Oh yeah, how would you know?"

Claire chose to ignore the question but ensured two of the surfers kept the old man at bay until the coroner arrived.

"You think Ricky's and her deaths are related?" Suggie asked, taking multiple shots of the scene, her camera's shutter clicking rapidly in the morning stillness, like a forensic photographer would. "Maybe someone has something against the Blue Crush."

Claire grimaced. "Possibly." The deaths of two surfers could be coincidental, but might not be. When it comes to investigating crimes, the first rule of thumb is to never follow one single path but to contemplate all possible theories.

"What if Ricky's death wasn't personal? What if we are dealing with a serial killer who's targeting all the competing surfers?"

"I doubt it." Claire shook her head, watching as the first rays of sunlight began piercing through the marine layer. "Most criminals stick to their particular way of operating, whether it's burglary, auto theft, or embezzling. But here the M.O. is different. Drugging and pushing someone over a cliff versus shooting someone with a speargun are widely different methods to kill someone…if it's the same killer, they're certainly emboldened."

Ricky's death was premeditated and carefully planned. Which meant an organized offender, often familiar with police investigation methods. A death by spear suggested a disorganized, impulsive attack, typically by a young, impaired, or mentally ill offender with poor social skills and low intelligence, who may act impulsively and leave the victim's body where the assault occurred. Jack the Ripper was a classic example of the disorganized serial killer.

Suggie lowered her camera. "You think we could be dealing with two killers?"

"I'm not sure, but the pool of suspects has exponentially grown. We need to widen the search and start questioning people now." Multiple deaths didn't automatically mean a serial killer. The law had specific criteria: a "cooling off" period between killings, similar victim types, consistent methods. These deaths here were too different, suggesting separate motives and perpetrators.

"We? Hasn't Ernshaw forbidden us to work on the case? " Suggie reminded her as the wail of approaching police cars pierced the morning air.

"Not for long." The media had a constitutional right to cover crime scenes from public spaces as long as they didn't interfere with police work or contaminate evidence. And she had a plan.

Claire rushed away and returned with a whipped espresso, the warm cup creating a small pocket of comfort against the cool morning air.

"Does crime really open your appetite?"

Claire laughed. "It's not for me. I'll be right back."

She trotted toward the parking lot where Deputy Chief Ernshaw was pushing through the throng of reporters who were held back by a police line, their cameras flashing like strobe lights in the dim morning.

"Deputy Chief Ernshaw, may I have a word?"

"Is this an ambush or what? You're working with the press now?" The chief's voice was sharp enough to cut glass.

"Not at all. I just want to be put on the case—"

"We've already talked about this."

"Not since my father's been cleared. I may have a new lead and I would love to see where it goes. You don't have to pay me. And I got this for you." Claire handed over the drink and a still-warm, fresh-out-of-the-oven pastry.

"What's this, a bribe?"

"Of course, not. It's so early, I assumed you hadn't had breakfast yet, so I brought you your favorite: two shots of espresso topped with whipped cream and a French brioche. Just making sure our police force is taken care of."

The Deputy Chief drew a sip from the drink and smiled, a bit of whipped cream catching on her upper lip. "Fine, I'm willing to listen, but hold on." She waved at Torres, who quickly joined their side. "Go ahead."

Claire inhaled deeply and shared her theory about the French movie. "Kinlay, the woman Ricky was supposed to meet, I think she was fake. Ricky was catfished."

"You mean Ricky was catfished and killed following a movie's plot?" Deputy Chief Ernshaw asked, her interest visibly piqued.

"Yes. There are too many similarities to be coincidences. I have a copy of the movie if you want," she said, gesturing at Suggie, who had come close.

Deputy Chief Ernshaw straightened, her posture shifting from skeptical to engaged. "The copy would be nice. And yes, you're welcome to work on the case as a consultant."

"Great. Thanks! I'll question the Blue Crush and the Vandstam and let Torres know what I find."

Torres's face crumpled, a muscle working in his cheek. "I don't remember you being made primary cop on the case."

Deputy Chief Ernshaw patted Torres's back. "Sorry 'bout that, Torres, but she's right. People who have things to hide tend to prefer talking to a pretty French-sounding woman than to an authoritarian alpha. But I'm sorry, Suggie. I can't officially have a member of the press officially working on a case, though I know you probably will."

Suggie gave her a thumbs-up. "No offense taken."

Torres grimaced. "You can't seriously give Claire that much authority."

"Claire gets results, and the sooner we're done with these cases, the better our town will recover from this infamy—the mayor's words, not mine." She glanced toward the growing crowd of onlookers gathering at the police tape. A murderous reputation wouldn't play in favor of the expanding resort town and would make it difficult for Caper Cove to win the bid to re-host the surfing competition the following years.

"A cop-consultant team like in *Castle*, the TV show," Suggie said out loud before whispering, "watch out for the sexual tension."

Deputy Chief Ernshaw stifled a laugh as she waved at the local oceanographer whose expertise had helped with the forensic analysis of currents and drift patterns.

Doctor Chen acknowledged everyone with a smile and pointed at her tablet displaying current patterns and tide charts, the blue lines pulsing with the simulation of ocean movements. "Based on the southward drift and morning conditions, your victim must have entered the water within that two-mile stretch. The coastal cameras along the Caper Cove shores would have caught any activity closer to the pier."

"I checked the surf monitoring feeds too, the ones surfers use to check wave conditions. Nothing unusual on those either." Torres added. "But the killer could have known about the camera's thirty-second intervals between snapshots."

Claire's eyes brightened with a spark of revelation. "Or they could have used the Forbidden Path. It's an old trail beneath the cliffs that disappears at high tide. Most locals don't even know it exists anymore. Perfect place to avoid being seen, if you know exactly when the tide will turn." The memory of salt-sprayed rocks and hidden passages flooded back to her. The hidden trail had been famous among high schoolers in search of a covert place to drink or hook up.

"I thought it had been sealed when we were in sixth grade, when…you know." Suggie didn't finish her sentence, her voice trailing off into the sound of crashing waves. Her alluding to Aurora's disappearance was enough.

"Can one path really be sealed from teenagers seeking privacy?" Claire knew from personal experience that nothing could have stopped her teenaged self on a mission. Not even danger or the risk of repercussions. She herself had broken a few civic rules when she started investigating her sister's disappearance. At ages twelve and thirteen, she had ventured down no-access trails and trespassed on a few structures and properties in search of clues on where her sister could have been.

Torres agreed with a head nod. "Unless you've got barbed wires and motion detection alarms, not even a secured building can keep unwanted visitors out. Think you can show me where it is, if you have time?" he asked Claire, his earlier hostility softening slightly.

"I'd be happy to do it right now." Her catering cancellations had turned out to be a blessing. Claire couldn't help but smile at the irony—her clients' cold feet had given her the very thing she needed most: time. Time to dig deeper; to follow leads that had gone cold; to finally track down whoever was responsible. Sure, her bank account might be taking a hit, but solving this case? That was worth more than any paycheck. Finding the truth and seeking justice was what she had been missing a lot since returning to Caper Cove.

Chapter Thirty-One

The Forbidden Path had been blocked by a brand new subdivision. While homeowners could own beachfront property, they couldn't completely block public beach access. But finding the path to get there required zigzagging between private driveways and backyards. It was a treacherous labyrinth of narrow paths, steep cliffs, and dense vegetation—a mix of Torrey pines and shrubland. The salty breeze carried hints of sage and coastal rosemary, nature's defiant reminder that this land had once been wild.

Claire led the way, following the faint trail left by the repeated passage of adventurers' shoes. Though years had gone by since she walked down the steep path, her feet remembered every rock and crevice from when she had searched this path for Aurora. It was strange how emotions and grief could etch the map of a place in your mind forever.

"You sure you know where you're going?" Torres asked, struggling to keep up.

The morning mist rose from the beach, enveloping the small hill in a cottony blanket, which made seeing beyond eight feet difficult.

"Feel free to go back to the car if you're afraid," she said, pushing through thick Torrey foliage. She tested the ground with one foot, assuring herself of the rocks' stability. Her teenaged-self had been way more limber and assured going down the forbidden path than she presently was. Each cautious step reminded her of how time had changed her.

"I can handle a little hike. I've been in raging sandstorms with no visibility back before," he snapped. "Just want to make sure we're not taking unnecessary risks. As a civilian, you're my responsibility."

"*Your* responsibility?" Claire snickered. The sound echoed off the sandstone walls, sharp and brittle like broken glass. "Whatever you say, Detective. Any updates on the camera search?"

"We've only got a grainy and dark video showing two silhouettes heading to and from the beach. Our IT guy's working on cleaning it up, but I'm not hoping for much."

Torres paused and stared out west. The morning fog lifted gracefully along the coastline, unveiling a pink horizon. Streaks of gold pierced through the clouds, painting the ocean in shimmering pastels. "Wow, I get why people would take their crushes here. The view's something else. Makes you almost forget there's a killer on the loose."

Claire glanced back with a sly smile. "Don't get too distracted by the sunrise, Romeo. One wrong step and it's a long way down."

"How many boyfriends followed you here?" he asked.

"None. I was investigating my sister's disappearance."

"Frank mentioned something about that. That's why you left Caper Cove?"

Claire inhaled deeply, as if the fresh salty air could rid her body of the grief she still felt twenty years later. "Yes. My mother took me to her native New York after finding out I was spending my nights scouting the area for clues."

"You ever thought of reopening the case?"

"Of course. But you can't tell Frank. He can get really obsessive about unfinished business."

They descended through a narrow passage carved into the sandstone cliff, emerging onto the clothing-optional beach where a naked yoga practitioner stretched in the dawn sun.

"What the hell is he doing?" Torres stopped.

Claire laughed. "This beach is clothing-optional. I thought you knew."

"That's why Dereck and Jess wished me a *good sightseeing* and grinned when I told them where I was headed."

"Just turn around, it's the hill that interests us, not the shore, right?" Claire pivoted on her heels and stared at the small hill, her back to the ocean.

Modern mansions with panoramic ocean views were sandwiched between older homes, their glass windows flashing like warning signals.

"You said only locals would know this path, right?" the detective asked, retracing his steps back up to the shrubby hill.

"Locals and seasonal tourists who rent these houses. But with social media today, one Instagram post is all it takes." She brushed sand from her hands and searched the rocks. Many swimmers used the crevices as cubbies for their clothes."

"I found something." It was a Blue Crush surfing jersey with Efterlig's name on it.

Torres hurried to her side, reached for his radio, and spoke to dispatch. "Hey Carla, I need the CSI unit to comb the nudie beach and the Forbidden Path." His voice was steady, his eyes scanning the area. He listened for a moment as the dispatcher confirmed the request, then clipped the radio back onto his shoulder.

Claire's eyes widened at once. "Since when does Caper Cove have a CSI unit?"

"Since today. It's only two people, a forensic photographer and an evidence technician. The town council put them on the payroll yesterday at Deputy Chief Ernshaw's request. She doesn't want a repeat of the Brooks-Poderas fiasco."

They walked back up to the cliff, waiting for the CSI unit. The morning fog was lifting, revealing the treacherous beauty of the forbidden path.

"You mind me asking what made you want to be a cop, especially here in Caper Cove?"

"My father was a cop and my mother always dreamed of seeing the sea," he said, eyes fixed on the horizon. "She asked me to settle near the coast so we could visit, but she passed before I had the chance. So I came here to scatter hers and my dad's ashes like she asked. I stayed because they were both here, in a way." He paused, his face tensing. "You mind waiting for the team and briefing them about the terrain? I need to address this."

Two hikers had crossed the police tape, and a third person was moving furiously fast up the trail. Torres broke into a sprint.

"Detective Torres!" The woman shouted—it was Amy Walsh. "How could you do this! Briggs is innocent!"

"Evidence is more important than your and your boyfriend's words."

"He's not my boyfriend!" Walsh shifted, facing Claire. "And you, aren't you going to help!"

Torres had arrested Briggs, apparently using him as bait to provoke reactions. Claire felt a spark of anger. Why hadn't he told her?

Chapter Thirty-Two

"I can't. You fired me, remember?" Claire replied, her mind still processing this information about Briggs being arrested. Knowing that she wouldn't approve, Torres had kept her in the dark. She shot him a questioning look, but he deliberately avoided her eyes.

The woman grimaced. "I know, but I've changed my mind. You're the best criminal attorney there is!"

Claire jerked back, familiar tension creeping across her forehead. The same woman who had questioned her legal skills two days ago was now asking her to represent her protégé. "Who told you that?"

"Fireinyourmouth in their post about you being a great attorney but a terrible chef…Hashtag 'stay in your lane' and 'leave the cooking to the real chefs'?"

"What are you talking about?" Claire pulled her phone from her back pocket and typed the hashtags in her social media search box.

The troll had struck again, posting one of the most unflattering pictures of Claire—hair tousled, half asleep, dragging The Osprey's giant garbage bags to the dumpster. Under it, the caption read: *from great attorney to lousy cook. A fall from grace: what happens when you quit your day job to become a private chef.* Another picture showed Claire's professional accomplishments and entire resume, which the troll must have screenshot from her law firm website. A wave of grief slammed into her, reminding her that she was her firm's only bombing survivor.

"This is not gossip, this is defamation." A long list of potential charges reeled in Claire's mind: libel, slander, harassment, cyberbullying, invasion of privacy, and intentional infliction of emotional distress. While taking photos in public spaces was generally legal, using them for harassment crossed a line. "I am not practicing law anymore."

Torres grabbed her hand to better see the screen. "Did they dox you?"

"Sort of, but the address posted is my old one in D.C.," she replied, her voice a whisper. The warmth of Torres's palm radiated against her skin, comforting her.

Why was this anonymous troll so relentless in hurting her reputation? Who were they to think they could define who she was or limit her potential based on her past career? Her worth and skills went beyond any past title or role. Her identity was hers to shape, not theirs to decide.

"Do a lot of people know about this?" she asked Walsh, angry at the fact that a complete stranger had posted her face, an unflattering likeness, online without asking her permission. While legally obtained, it felt particularly cruel to use such pictures for mockery. She had been careful not to post her full face. The explosion she survived was still being investigated, and she often wondered if the real masterminds had ever been caught or would try to finish the job by finding her.

The woman shot her a wry smile. "I'm sorry to say this, but you're the most popular hashtag trending in Caper Cove, after the competition and the murders, of course. Everyone's talking about you."

Silence fell. A salty breeze picked up, shaking the thorny shrubs around them. A woman and a man in blue "Caper Cove CSI unit" caps approached from the parking lot, carrying duffel bags.

Torres cleared his throat. "Let me know if you want me to check on that troll. And you, Ms. Walsh, keep your outbursts for yourself if you don't want to get a cell of your own," he said before jogging to meet the forensic team.

Claire shook her head to clear her thoughts. Her phone chirped with two unread texts. Two more catering clients had cancelled their orders. Which made too many cancellations this week to count. Instead of being angry at the unfairness, Claire returned to Walsh and smiled. She would feel and express her anger later.

"You're the only one who can help," the woman begged. "What you did in the Fenway trial was amazing."

"Fenway? You must have the wrong case." In this case, a transwoman had been wrongly convicted of robbery due to mistaken identity. The confusion arose because witnesses and outdated records continued to refer to her by her previous male identity, despite her legal transition to Ashley.

"I don't. You proved Ashley's innocence without revealing her former identity as male. She wrote her memoir about the trial and thanked you in the acknowledgements. See?" Walsh flashed her phone screen, where Claire's former client's face was plastered on the entire book cover. "People think fireinyourmouth made a mistake because you look different now… minimal makeup, longer hair…but I recognized you and your law firm's name instantly."

Claire felt her carefully constructed boundaries dissolving. She had learned long ago that identities were like Russian nesting dolls, each one containing another within it. The Claire who baked perfect soufflés contained the Claire who once cross-examined hostile witnesses. The Claire with the French accent housed the Claire who had grown up speaking pure California English. Every new layer didn't replace the previous one; it simply added complexity to the whole. The question was whether she was ready for others to see all those layers at once. She had come to Caper Cove to heal and needed to ensure her privacy remained intact. Her recovery hinged on it, especially her cognitive healing and eliminating that persistent French accent syndrome. The last thing she needed was clients finding her, desperate for legal help.

"I can pay you private investigator wages plus expenses. I have money."

Claire squinted at the woman, her head slightly tilted to one side. The casual mention of PI rates suggested someone was used to hiring private investigators.

"I had Ricky followed earlier this year, that's how I know about his cheating and how much PIs cost."

Claire inhaled deeply, counting to four, and exhaled at the same pace. She always struggled to reject cries for help. "I'm not agreeing to anything yet, but I'm listening." Though she should consider adding PI to her list of qualifications and get paid for it if her catering clients continued to cancel. " But why does it matter to you?"

"Brigg's my brother."

"You don't have a brother, only a sister." Torres had run a background on her. Born and raised in Richmond, Va. Preacher father. Sunday school teacher, mother. The oldest of two daughters.

Walsh looked over her shoulder. "I *had* a sister and now I *have* a brother."

"Briggs is your sibling?" The pieces clicked into place. The protective gestures Walsh had displayed in the photo Suggie had snapped of her with the trans surfer made perfect sense now. The way she had angled her body between Briggs and the camera, how her smile hadn't quite reached her eyes. She had been protecting her younger sibling.

"Yes, but nobody knows, and nobody can know about it. That would ruin his surfing career. Do you have any idea how tough it is to start anew?"

"I do." Beginning a new life as a private chef after years as a defense lawyer had been challenging—from her rocky start to these recent attacks from an angry competitor stealing away her clients. She couldn't have made it without the support of her father, her best friend Suggie, and her childhood community. She could only imagine starting from scratch with a new identity in a new state where she didn't know anyone.

Identity wasn't just who you were, but also who you weren't anymore. Briggs had left behind not just a name but an entire framework of expectations, relationships, and history. Claire wondered what it must feel like to be reborn that way—carrying forward only what you chose to keep, leaving the rest behind like a crustacean shedding its skin. Her own transformation had been more subtle but no less profound. The Claire who had once dominated courtrooms now served bouillabaisse with the same intensity and focus. Different identities, same soul.

Walsh stepped closer and held her hand. "Can you talk to him? I think he knows who killed Ricky."

Chapter Thirty-Three

Claire rushed past the front desk with a quick hand wave. Growing up in a police station headed by her father and serving as an on-and-off official Caper Cove PD consultant made her coming and going routine.

"I need to see Axel Briggs," she told the detention officer between breaths.

"Sure. He's in interview room three. Torres asked us to hold off on booking him but to tell anyone who asks that he's being charged with the murders." He gestured down the grey-blue corridor where the fluorescent lights cast harsh shadows on the concrete walls.

Relief washed over Claire, followed by anger. Torres was playing games, making people believe Briggs had been officially charged to create confusion, hoping the killer would reveal themselves by making a mistake or loosening tongues. Like gold panning—he shook things up, waiting for the gold to appear.

When the detention officer opened the interview room door, Briggs was balancing on a chair, watching a video on his phone, while sipping a large drink through a thick straw.

"Why is he wearing an orange jumpsuit?"

Briggs stood up from his chair and walked toward her with a smile. "That's because I asked them for one. I was in a swimsuit when Detective Torres brought me here. And not to complain, but the station is kind of chilly."

"I'm here because your sister asked me to come." She flattened the handwritten note Walsh had written for him on the table.

"What are you talking about? I don't have any family." He pushed against the table with his feet, putting distance between himself and Claire, the chair legs scraping against the linoleum floor, and crossed his arms over his chest, his eyes fixed on the handwritten note.

Claire leaned forward, watching his reaction carefully.

"I can't officially represent you right now for personal reasons, but I can help you until you need legal representation. Did Detective Torres tell you why he brought you here?"

"Yes, he asked if I would help with the murder investigation and pretend he arrested me. I thought, why not? If that can help draw the killer out."

"You need to unvolunteer from this." Claire explained the risks of pretending to be arrested. If Briggs went further into the pretense, the police would likely fingerprint him and collect his DNA samples as part of standard procedure. Those fingerprints would match the ones taken during middle school when he was still presenting as female, creating an unwanted connection between his past and present identities. The DNA analysis would reveal his chromosomal sex assigned at birth, potentially exposing his transition history through official records he's worked hard to leave behind.

Briggs settled back on his chair as if the weight of the world crushed him.

"Your sister told me you quit the team because Ricky found out about your relationship and threatened to out you."

"But I didn't hurt Ricky!"

"That's what I'm trying to prove. Torres's request to pretend your arrest might have been a ploy to reassure the mayor they had someone in custody, unless they hope to find incriminating evidence linking you to Renée's death and make sure you're already in custody."

"Renée's dead?"

"Yes, we found her this morning, and the police have a witness who saw you two fighting."

Briggs's entire body stiffened, his face went pale, and his eyes widened in disbelief. He opened his mouth as if to say something, but nothing came out.

A heavy silence filled the room, broken only by the distant hum of the building's ventilation system.

"It wasn't a fight. She wanted me to be open with my transition, something I wasn't ready to do…. I don't understand. Why would someone kill her?" he said, his voice shaky and his words broken.

"That's what we're trying to figure out. Your entire team might be a target."

"Our team isn't a target. I know who wanted Ricky dead," he whispered, his voice barely audible. "I overheard the team planning to pay a girl to ask Ricky out, get him naked, and steal his clothes to humiliate him. They thought the embarrassment would violate the club's morality clause, so they could put me back on the team. They talked about getting Ricky drunk to meet the girl at Launch Point. It had to be an accident."

"Anyone else know about it?"

"Judson West, my boss. He heard them, too, but didn't intervene. Said Ricky deserved whatever happens to him. Told me to shut up or I'd lose my job. I work there full-time during the year but get time off during competition. It's hard to get a job like that."

"Do you know the name of the girl?"

"Lucy or Julie…I'm not sure. But she's new. She might have been one of the redheads working at the club the night before Ricky's death. She's one of the temps Judson hired to handle the competition crowd."

"How much do you know about Judson's love life?"

"Not much. He used to brag about dating one of the Vandstam girls, but he got dumped hard a few months back. Why, you think he's the one who killed both Ricky and Renée?"

Chapter Thirty-Four

"Ladies and gentlemen, welcome to an electrifying evening here at Brave the Wave! The moon is shining bright, the waves are perfect, and we're about to kick off an unforgettable night surfing session," the surf commentator's voice boomed over the beach. "After a touching minute of silence to honor our late predecessors, our surfers are now ready to take on the waves under the stars. First up, we have Alison Miller, known for her incredible agility and unique style."

Despite two tragic deaths, the surfing competition pressed on. The death of the Vandstam Queen made the headlines, calling it an accident. The autopsy results haven't yet been released, and Suggie had promised Torres to keep details of the death quiet for the next twenty-four hours. The organizers, under pressure from corporate sponsors, had refused to cancel, and the athletes had refused to give up on their Olympic dreams. But Claire couldn't shake the feeling that someone here tonight knew more than they were letting on.

The weather conditions for night surfing were optimal with moderate offshore winds and a clear sky. Floodlights illuminated the beach but didn't reach as far as the surfing waves, forcing the surfers to rely on the brightness of the moon, creating a show with their LED-lit boards that traced glowing arcs through the darkness. Perfect conditions for surfing—and for killers to hide in the shadows.

Claire was manning The Osprey's "hot drinks booth," serving chocolate oat milk, herbal teas, and lattes for the crowd of spectators. Steam rose from the cups, carrying the scent of cinnamon, ginger, and nutmeg into the cool night air. Suggie was by her side, taking a break from shooting pictures for her news articles.

"Pumpkin spice herbal tea…isn't that a fall drink?" Torres asked as he approached the counter, still moody from his afternoon fail. His interrogation of the Blue Crush team had led nowhere. Their plan to humiliate Ricky had fallen apart when their bait—the young woman they had recruited—hadn't followed through. Instead of meeting Ricky as planned, she had spent the evening partying, claiming someone had cancelled the plan.

"It's a June Gloom drink in Caper Cove," Claire said cheerily. June nights had been unusually cold, and nothing felt cozier than a fall drink. The aroma reminded her of the first day of fall when she would spend the last Saturday of September at the local coffee shop, enjoying pumpkin spice lattes and scones with her mother and sister. "Plus, it's comforting to the grieving community."

Claire glanced in the direction of the private booth where the Vandstam performers had gathered away from the assaulting crowds of fans. Their hushed conversation stopped abruptly when they noticed her looking. Their presence at the party, hosted at the Osprey and sponsored by the studio, was a 'contractual duty' according to their supervisor. And when your job consisted of seasonal, temporary gigs, missing one meant the risk of being quickly replaced and therefore unemployed. "Most of them don't drink."

"Me neither, so a pumpkin spice latte with extra whipped for me, please." Lance Foster wheeled up to the counter. "So what's new, Detective? Is it true what they say, that Renée's death's a murder?"

"Can't comment. The medical examiner hasn't released the autopsy report yet."

Suggie scooted closer to Lance, her phone open on her digital notebook. "You think it's a serial killer?"

"It would make no sense. Ricky was a pest, a parasite, driving drunk, risking people's lives. He won't be missed. Why start with someone everyone hated and then kill Renée, who everybody loved?"

Torres stared at Lance and leaned forward. "You're not mincing your words. Do you know something we don't?"

Lance's eyes narrowed slightly. "More than you might think." He paused, as if weighing his words carefully. "The other night, late, Ramos was pacing like a caged animal. I've never seen him so worked up. He was ranting about Renée. Said she had agreed to meet him at Lover's Beach but stood him up. Man was obsessed with figuring out who she was with instead."

Torres's pen scratched against his police issued notepad. "Did he mention anyone specific?"

"Nah, but he thought it might be someone she'd chosen over him. Kept bringing up how Renée had been on and off with a guy before, but wouldn't give him a chance." Lance shook his head. "The way he was talking…might be worth asking him who he thought that someone else was. Maybe she was with the killer."

Claire and Torres exchanged a meaningful look. Renée had to have been with Ricky.

"So you think Ramos could have hurt Renée?" Claire asked. It wouldn't be the first time someone tried to take out the competition at work or in love.

Lance left a bank note on the counter as a tip and grabbed his drink. "An alpha male with wounded pride, you tell me."

Torres groaned as Lance Foster rolled away to meet a woman. "Everybody is a detective this week."

"Any updates on who Kinlay is?"

"We've traced some digital evidence that's given us a strong lead," Torres replied, his expression grim. "The investigation's pointing toward someone associated with either the Blue Crush or Vandstam teams."

"Do you know who?"

"Closing in on them. About to make an arrest soon."

"Who?"

"I'm not telling. You've already ruined my strategy by getting Briggs released."

Claire frowned. "But I was right. His and Walsh's alibis were rock solid. There's no way he could have done it. Without new evidence to shed light on the case, I don't see how anyone could be arrested based on the little evidence there is."

"So let's gather some more," Torres said, heading to the Vandstam table.

"What, right now?"

"Go!" Suggie slid behind the counter and tied an apron around her waist. "I've got this."

"You sure?"

"Of course. Go! I need that scoop!"

Chapter Thirty-Five

The Vandstam performers clustered against the back wall, some curled in the giant booth, others standing. Their iridescent fish scale pants and skirts shimmered and caught the light, their blue face makeup beginning to fade into patchy patterns. With the lost look on their faces and their intricate braids and elaborate Viking-inspired tattoos, they looked like ancient warriors who had been pulled through time into an era they didn't recognize. Through the open emergency exit door, the breeze carried in the scent of melted chocolate from s'mores and dying firewood, mingling with the salt-heavy coastal air.

"Hello everyone. I'm Detective Torres with the Caper Cove Police Department, with our consultant, here to ask questions about Renée."

"Was it an accident?" A young character performer with intricate knotwork tattoos snaking down his arms stepped forward. His voice trembled despite his fierce Viking-like appearance. "Could she have... speared herself while diving?"

Claire bit her tongue, resisting the urge to reply. The preliminary autopsy report stated that the spear went straight to the lung at a perfect ninety-degree angle. Something that only happened if someone shot straight at her. Her left lung collapsed and filled up with blood. She tried to get help, but she died within ten minutes.

The Vandstam crew gathered around the table, forming a semi-circle around them. A towering man with a salt-and-pepper beard and elaborate braids stepped closer, concern marking his weathered face. "Could it be murder?" he asked.

Several of them visibly flinched at the word, their collective gasps filling the silent pause. The word hung in the air like a curse.

Torres shifted his weight as he chose his words carefully. "That's what we're trying to determine. At this stage, we're exploring all possibilities. Are you the team leader?"

"Ja, Jürgen Pichler," the man confirmed, his voice thick with emotion. "I cannot believe this happened to Renée. Why her?"

"We don't know, but we're going to find out. Did Renée have any enemies within the surfing community?" Claire directed her questions to the women—they were often more attuned to social dynamics and discord than their male counterparts.

Jürgen shook his head, his braids swaying with the movement. "None. She got along with everyone, mostly." His eyes darted to Sierra Thorn, who stood at the opposite end of the table.

"Renée went out with Ricky a couple of times, but she saw through his act quickly enough after what he did to us. If you want suspects, you should talk to Ricky's conquests or fiancée. Maybe one of them got jealous or someone he wronged had had enough."

Torres's pen paused over his notepad. "Had enough? What did Ricky do?"

The question sparked a collective murmur of discontent. The performers exchanged dark looks, their earlier nervousness transforming into something more heated.

Jürgen's face darkened. "That jerk bought the exclusive rights to film the surfing exhibition. Then he started restricting locals from posting their own surf videos on social media. Said it violated his contract. Then he set up VIP areas that blocked the best viewing spots, spots local families have used for generations."

"Yeah, and his drones were everywhere, buzzing over surfers' heads during practice, all for what he called his premium content," a woman with shimmering scaly leather pants said, making air quotes with her fingers. Her voice dripped with venom. "If he did this to us, imagine what else he did to others. How many people he stepped on."

"Did Renée have financial problems?" Torres asked.

"Hardly. She was living a pretty lavish lifestyle. Since becoming the Vandstam Queen, she was earning high six figures, easy. Her casting agent had her doing appearances weekly, not to mention the sponsored social media payments and the huge seven-digit endorsement deal with the Vandstam franchise she was about to sign."

Torres scribbled in his notepad. "What about her health? Was her blue skin affecting her?"

"No, Renée was healthy." Sierra stepped forward. "She turned blue from taking colloidal silver supplements she found online. Trusted some scammy health blogs instead of doctors."

"Sierra discovered Renée at ComicCon," Jürgen chimed in. "Took her under her wing, taught her everything about being a Vandstam Queen."

Sierra flinched at the word 'queen.'

"She was self-conscious about her skin at first, but our community helped her see it as beautiful, perfect for a Vandstam sea warrior," Sierra added. "Then she learned how to surf and even learned to speak Danish. She was the personification of the Vandstam Queen."

"But she had her own troubles," a snow white-haired woman interjected from the crowd. Her timing felt deliberate, as if she'd been waiting for the right moment to drop this bombshell. "Renée had a huge falling out with Doctor Harrison, her plastic surgeon. You tell them, Sierra. You knew her better than anyone."

Sierra's face went pale beneath her fading blue makeup. Torres shifted to fully face Sierra. "Yes, tell us."

"There isn't much to say. Renée started with the usual: breast augmentation, lip fillers, you know, what most Hollywood actresses go through. But then she went into body modifications, which became an obsession. Her surgeon told her to stop. Said she was taking it too far, that he wouldn't do any more procedures. He even served her with a cease and desist order, claiming her cosplay modifications were damaging his reputation for beautification, and demanded she stop using his name.

Claire exchanged a glance with Torres. The pieces started to form a disturbing picture. A surgeon with a conscience—or one worried about liability? But more importantly, what wasn't Sierra telling them?

* * *

Claire and Suggie walked away from the noise of the gathering, moving toward the quieter edge of the beach where the floodlights didn't reach, when a twenty-something Vandstam fan jumped into their path. His vest jangled with Vandstam pins—everything from limited editions to ComicCon exclusives—the metal clinking over the crash of the waves and the announcer's voice calling out surfer names. "You're Suggie Oh, the reporter, right? I've got a scoop to give you."

"What is it?"

The fan's eyes gleamed with an unsettling intensity. "I want a VIP pass or a ComicCon badge in return."

"I have neither, and I don't pay for information." Suggie's voice was firm. Checkbook journalism could easily compromise the integrity and accuracy of her reporting.

"Fine!" The fan was about to walk away when Claire asked him to stay put.

"If the scoop was related to Renée, it could help us with the case," she whispered to Suggie. "At this stage of the investigation, any lead is a good lead." She turned back to the fan.

"How about all the soda you can drink at the Osprey for the remainder of the festival?" Claire knew justice shouldn't be transactional, but reality often proved otherwise.

"Deal!" The fan pulled out his phone, swiping through images as he spoke. The blue glow of his screen competed with the distant LED surfboards tracing paths through the dark water. "I saw Renée with a surfer last night. Got proof right here." He held up his device, the night vision quality of his picture startlingly clear. "I was planning to sell it online to pay off my student loan or take my girlfriend to Europe, not sure yet," the student added with a mercenary grin. His casual tone made Claire's stomach turn. The photos showed Ramos and Renée, nude on the beach, engaged in more than a simple kiss. "I left before things got too heated," he said, "and before Grumpy Henry started shouting at them."

Behind them, the surf announcer's voice echoed across the water: "Beautiful form on that cutback! The LED lighting really showcases the power of that wave!"

Claire half-blushed. Before it got too heated? Unless they were going to engage in Cirque-du-Soleil moves, the scene couldn't get any more heated than it already was.

"Okay, we've seen enough!" Claire snatched the phone from the man, her movement swift and decisive, the device disappearing into her dress pocket.

"Hey, that's my phone!"

"Not anymore. It's evidence. Isn't it?" Suggie asked, glancing at Claire.

"That's right. Recording people engaging in intimate activities without their consent is a crime."

The man protested, his voice cracking. "But it's a public beach. It's not like they were in some private room or anything."

Claire shook her head and raised her voice as cheers erupted from the crowd watching the surfing demonstration. "It doesn't matter. They have a reasonable expectation of privacy when they're engaging in intimate activities. Filming them without their knowledge or consent is a crime, plain and simple. Plus, you were trespassing when you filmed this." She recited the charges like a well-worn prayer: invasion of privacy, eavesdropping, and wiretapping if he recorded their conversations, before or after the act, with possible additional charges of harassment, blackmail, not to mention possession and distribution of obscene material. All of this meant a felony punishable by a fine and/or up to three years in state prison.

"Look, I wasn't trying to hurt anyone. I…I didn't mean for things to get this far…" he stammered before running away. His pins jangled frantically as he fled toward the crowd gathered around the surfing area.

"Do we run after him or call Torres?" Suggie asked." I can't run in those heels, especially not on sand."

Chapter Thirty-Six

Still half-asleep, Claire shuffled into the kitchen in her fuzzy flip flops, making a beeline for the coffeepot only to find Suggie and Torres chatting at the counter. The rich aroma of freshly brewed coffee and fresh pastries filled the air. Torres was lounging in casual clothes, a crisp polo, and khakis that somehow looked wrong on him after weeks of seeing him either shirtless in boxer shorts or in his tight summer bicyclist police uniform.

"Did I miss the memo for the early morning meeting?"

"Torres caught the killer! Caper Cove can return to being the peaceful paradise it has always been," Suggie sang in a happy tone that sounded a little forced. "He called me over to give me the scoop and celebrate with you."

Claire rubbed her eyes, wondering if she was still dreaming. "What are you talking about?"

"You can stop investigating now and leave the matter to the police," Torres said between gulps of coffee.

Claire yawned, happily surprised to see raisin brioches from Le CoffeeShop, her favorite bakery, their golden crusts still warm and glistening with a light egg wash. But her stomach churned at the sudden, too-easy victory. "Who's the killer?"

"Tony Ramos. The warrant for his place went through. We found Rohypnol in his belongings. His teammates folded fast after that, confessing that Ramos was the one who drove Ricky to Launch Point. Plus, we found his rant-text about Renée snubbing him, and then she died just after they hooked up. We've got our killer and solved the two murders!"

Claire's blood ran cold. "But that doesn't make any sense. Why kill her after spending the night with her?" Claire asked. She didn't mean to be a party pooper, but something felt very wrong.

Suggie shrugged. "Don't ask me. I'm no psycho. Must be something like revenge porn but with murder."

"And where did Ramos get the spear? Have you found the spear gun it came from?" Claire's voice sharpened with suspicion. The weapon was too sleek, with no handle. Renée would have seen it coming. It's not like Ramos could have hidden it in his Speedo.

Torres shrugged. Too casually. "These are all details that I'll iron out later. Right now, I'm meeting the mayor at the station. Hasta la vista, baby."

"What about Grumpy Henry's threats? The peeper said the old vet threatened both Ramos and Renée that night," Claire interjected.

"Henry? Come on, Claire. He's all bark, no bite. Guy served his country… he's just having trouble adjusting to civilian life. No way he'd do this." Torres waved dismissively before leaving the room, his footsteps heavy on the parquet.

Claire frowned. The strong evidence he had for Ricky's murder was useless to charge Ramos for Renée's murder. The real killer was still out there, and Torres was about to close the case on the wrong man. She grabbed a brioche, her appetite gone but needing something to do with her hands, rushed to her room, and settled on her bed, facing the murder board.

Suggie followed on her heels, her steaming cup of tea perfuming the air with notes of chamomile and lavender. "You don't think Ramos did it, do you?"

"Something's off."

They both stayed silent for a few minutes, sitting cross-legged on Claire's bed, sipping chamomile lavender tea, their eyes fixed on the collage of photos, writing, pins, and strings. The morning light streaming through the window turned the red string connections into a messy spider web or a trap.

Claire's gaze traced the connections on the murder board. Ramos seemed the most likely suspect, but what if that was exactly what the real killer wanted? Judson, with the unpaid pool bill and the ex-girlfriend (maybe it was Renée) also had a strong motive.

Claire paused and took a giant bite of the brioche, letting the crème patissière melt on her tongue while she thought. Ramos wanted to get rid of Ricky to get Briggs back on the team to qualify, and he was the one who drove Ricky to the cliff and roofied him. He was also the last person to see Renée alive. That made him the perfect patsy.

"Did the police recover Ricky's murder weapon?" Suggie asked.

"No, that's what bothers me. The MOs are so different, and a calculated killer would know better than to spend the night with his second victim hours before killing her...and we have two other suspects."

"Who?"

Claire stood up and added the names to the board, her marker squeaking against the glossy surface like fingernails on a blackboard. "Doctor Harrison, Renée's former plastic surgeon, who had a conflicted relationship with the victim, and Grumpy Henry, who threatened to kill both Ricky and Renée for noise disturbance. Have you heard anything about him?"

Suggie shrugged. "Nothing special. Everybody knows Grumpy Henry. He used to be a Navy diver before he retired here after his wife passed away. He barks loudly and complains a lot. He's like one of those chihuahuas that thinks they're Rottweilers. He hasn't hurt a fly so far, but he has a mean streak to him."

"A military background as a diver makes him more than capable of handling specialized equipment like a spear gun. What about Doctor Harrison? As a plastic surgeon, someone at the spa must have heard of him."

"Is he the one who gave Renée a new face?" Suggie swiped through pictures on her phone and showed the screen to Claire—Beautifica LLC's social media account that showed a parade of before-and-after pictures of plastic surgery patients, including Renée. The phone's screen glowed brightly in the dim room. "This is how she looked before."

Claire frowned, studying the before-and-after surgery photos. The transformation was so dramatic it was unsettling. "Are you sure it's the same person?"

"One-hundred percent. And look at this. These were taken at the spa by our beautician. They knew Renée before she went blue and became the Vandstam Queen."

Claire kept staring at the picture, a chill running down her spine. Why would someone erase themselves so completely? Unless they were running from something—or someone.

"I can see why a plastic surgeon would want to quiet a former client who turned herself into an otherworldly character. Renée was the opposite of the Barbie-perfect-beauty publicity he was looking for."

"His before-and-after portfolio probably didn't include 'From High School Musical Extra to Smurf Shark Princess' as a selling point," Suggie agreed. Her attempt at humor fell flat in the silence.

Claire closed her eyes and exhaled slowly. She wondered what drove someone to remake themselves so completely. Maybe Renée had looked in the mirror every morning and seen a stranger until the day she fully resembled the Vandstam Queen. In a world where so little was within our control, perhaps there was a power in transforming yourself, even if it meant becoming something that only existed in comics or fantasy series.

"I have a free consultation with him at ten this morning," she said.

Suggie gasped. "Wait…you're considering plastic surgery?"

"Not for me, for the investigation! Unless, of course, he can excise my French accent."

* * *

Dawn bathed the fish market in gold. Inside its weathered blue halls, the usual morning crowd of local chefs and restaurateurs jostled between stalls—a detour on the way to the plastic surgeon's office to find an answer to her questions. Claire lingered near the entrance, pretending to examine a crate of fresh oysters while her eyes darted across the market floor, searching for Grumpy Henry.

"G'morning, sweetie. Your dad already picked up his order. Something he forgot?" Alma asked. Her weathered hands gestured toward an empty ice-filled bin.

"I'm just looking for Grumpy Henry. I was hoping to ask him a few questions," Claire explained.

"Oh, honey, you won't see him today. Hasn't come for a couple of days now. He isn't well. Been under the weather, saying someone broke into his house and went through his things. Harvey and I have been delivering him his fish and bread on the way back home after work."

Claire tensed up. A man skipping his years-old routine right after the murder of a woman he had threatened reeked of guilt, especially when that man was a former Navy diver who knew his way around spears.

Chapter Thirty-Seven

Doctor Harrison's office exuded luxury with its dramatic waterfall wall, Italian leather seating, and museum-quality artwork. Before-and-after photos lined the cream-colored walls, showcasing the surgeon's self-proclaimed artistry—refinements that transformed ordinary faces and bodies into magazine-worthy perfection.

Claire waited by the reception desk when Torres entered the room. "What are you doing here?"

"I could ask you the same question. I told you to stop investigating."

"You told me?" Claire laughed. Who did he think she was, his subordinate? "A plastic surgery consultation is kind of an intimate matter, don't you think?"

"Yes, it is, but this isn't the case here, am I right?" Torres's cocky smile appeared before he gave a quick wave to the receptionist, who must have given him the heads up. "You can't get around HIPAA privacy laws without this," he said, waving a warrant at her.

"Fine. I thought you caught the killer."

"I want to cover all the bases. Don't want the mayor's pressure to affect my objectivity."

"About that. How can you be sure Ramos did it and not another member of the team or someone else entirely?"

"Because Ramos roofied Ricky and drove him to the cliff himself."

Though damaging, it was circumstantial at best. "What did he say in his defense?"

"That he didn't mean to hurt Ricky, just wanted to incapacitate him, and didn't expect he would fall down the cliff." Torres's jaw tightened. "After that, his attorney told him to shut up and had the balls to suggest I had no evidence. Said Ricky was hit with a pipe, and that I had no case without the murder weapon. But I have Ramos's phone messages ranting about Ricky, plus one from the day we found Ricky's body saying he 'didn't do it on purpose.'"

"Doctor Harrison is ready to see you," a medical assistant said, guiding them into the surgeon's office.

The doctor remained seated behind his desk, pointing at two metal chairs. His calculating gaze made Claire's skin crawl. "You're here about Renée Efterlig."

"What can you tell us about her?"

"She started as a regular patient, asking me to make her pretty." He pushed a folder of medical files and pictures across the desk.

Claire studied the file's content—Renée's progressive transformations documented in before, during, and after pictures. Torres's face tightened at the images of jaw reconstruction and cheek implants that transformed one woman into someone unrecognizable.

"This is barbaric," Torres spat. "Why would anyone go through this?"

"The patriarchy, media pressure, societal expectations," Claire replied, matter-of-factly. The list was a mile long.

"Men go through this as well," the doctor added. "Beauty requires sacrifice."

Harrison leaned back in his ergonomic chair, his silver-streaked hair catching the morning light. "My work is about empowerment," he said, though his tone suggested he was trying to convince himself as much as them. "But Renée...she was never satisfied despite multiple procedures. She took my art and twisted it into something unrecognizable. The pointed chin was just the beginning. She wanted subdermal implants, iris alterations. She was obsessed with becoming this mythical water creature. I had to refuse further treatment."

"Maybe Renée's deviation from traditional beauty standards was the point," Claire interjected. "True artistry isn't about transformation into someone else, it's about feeling at home in your own skin. The problem isn't people modifying their bodies. It's a society that makes them feel they have to conform to someone else's idea of beauty. Renée wanted uniqueness, to be the Vandstam queen she was inside."

Harrison's expression soured. "There are standards. Proportions. Aesthetics. What Renée wanted wasn't beauty, it was self-mutilation. I filed a cease-and-desist order when she started getting dangerous procedures elsewhere. She was affecting my professional reputation."

"Who was funding her surgeries?" Claire asked. Before becoming the Vandstam queen, Renée was barely scraping by.

Harrison pulled up Renée's file on his tablet. "Judson West, owner of the Swim and Racquet Club. He guaranteed payment for her procedures. Put his club up as collateral."

Claire studied Judson's signature. She had seen this story play out before: the older man bankrolling a young woman's transformation, expecting devotion in return. And when Renée got famous and cut ties with her benefactor? Nothing wounded male pride quite like being discarded after outliving your usefulness.

"When did you last see her?"

"Two years ago. She wanted gill-like implants in her neck. Said she was becoming her true self, the Water Tribe Queen." He shook his head. "I refused."

Claire stood, gathering her notes. She could feel Harrison's clinical gaze analyzing her features, mentally cataloging potential 'improvements.' She met his stare directly. "Don't bother, Doctor. I'm quite at home in my skin." She got up, ready to leave, but paused before pushing the door. "Is there anything else related to Renée you can think of?" Torres asked.

Harrison hesitated, as if weighing whether to reveal something. "Another woman wanted me to transform her exactly like Renée, asking for the same body modifications. I don't remember her name, but she showed me the page from a comic book for reference. She seemed desperate, like she wanted to beat Renée at her own game."

"What did you do?"

"I refused. That's when I realized that Renée must have been giving out my name. I don't need that kind of referral. My reputation's at stake." Harrison's voice hardened. "I'm not in the business of making monsters."

Claire and Torres exchanged a worried gaze. Half the Vandstam crew is supposed to fly to Comic-Con Texas tomorrow. If one of them was the killer, they would need proof tonight.

* * *

Outside Harrison's office, Claire and Torres stood in the parking lot. The heated air shimmered above the asphalt, making Claire miss the usual coastal gloom.

"I have to head back to The Osprey to pick up the lunch orders for the medical examiner's office," Claire said, shielding her eyes. "I'll meet you there?"

Torres shifted his weight, keys jangling in his hand. "No. I'll read the autopsy report later. I'm meeting with the prosecutor first." He paused. "Something about Ramos's arrest…it all wrapped up too neat, too fast. The mayor's been pushing for quick results, but…"

"Having second thoughts?"

"I hate to admit this, but you might be right. I know Ramos killed Ricky—the roofie, the texts. That case is solid. But Renée?" He shook his head. "Judson had more reason to want her dead than Ramos ever did. I feel like I'm missing something. Want to meet me at the Swim and Racquet Club later?"

"You're focusing on Judson now?"

"He bankrolled all of Renée's surgeries." The detective ran a hand through his hair. "First Ricky's debt, now this. The guy seems to be everyone's favorite ATM."

"Could be a pattern," Claire mused. "People taking advantage of him…"

"Or a motive. Getting rid of the people bleeding him dry." Torres checked his phone as she strode toward his car, his shoulders rigid despite his casual tone.

"Good luck with the prosecutor."

"Have fun on your date with Vikram," he called back.

Chapter Thirty-Eight

The transition from Harrison's office to the medical examiner's morgue was like going from a glossy fashion magazine spread to a black and white flyer. Sterile eggshell walls and practical laminate flooring replaced the dramatic waterfall and travertine tile floors. But, here, truth replaced illusion. There were no curated artwork or transformation photos lining these walls, just anatomical charts and safety protocols. The autopsy room might have been cold, with its stainless steel tables and surgical instruments, but it dealt in certainties rather than promises. There was something honest about the sharp scent of disinfectant after Harrison's office's flowery fragrance. In death, people were all equal—no artifice, no seduction, no pretense. Just the truth laid bare under unforgiving fluorescent lights.

Claire followed Vikram to the small viewing room adjacent to the autopsy suite, away from the bodies and the smell of antiseptics. He handed her the report and motioned at the X-rays illuminated on the wall, the harsh backlight casting shadows across his face. "The report is self-explanatory, but let me know if you have any questions," he said, unwrapping the chicken marsala sandwich Claire had brought him. The warm aroma filled the small room, temporarily masking the institutional smell.

Even in black and white, Renée's modifications were striking—her reshaped skull, shaved mandible, and a series of subdermal implants that created an otherworldly topography beneath her skin. Silicone forms carefully placed to raise her skin to transform her human canvas into the fictional shark-human hybrid Renée wanted to emulate.

"She had over twenty procedures done?" Claire asked, scanning the autopsy report.

"Yes, but from different sources," Vikram explained. "Her plastic surgeon was quite forthcoming about the conventional work—facial reconstruction, chin reshaping. He handed over her entire case file, insisting he was only responsible for her 'beautification' and not her 'bestialization.' His words, not mine." Vikram touched the X-ray where Renée's chin came to an unnatural point. "Though the line between the two seems rather thin."

"What about the artists who did the rest?"

Vikram's expression darkened. "Unknown. These modifications fall into a gray zone. Subdermal implants like these are usually done by traveling body modification artists. They work outside the conventional medical establishment." He paused, running his hand through his hair. "You know, I've been losing sleep over this case. In med school, they teach you that bodies tell stories, but Renée…it's like she rewrote her entire narrative in flesh and bone."

"But don't licensed surgeons perform similar procedures all the time, like skin pockets for pacemakers or chemotherapy ports?"

"Technically, yes. But there's a world of difference between medical necessity and…this." He gestured at another X-ray showing the intricate network of implants. "The American Medical Association doesn't recognize these procedures. Most doctors won't touch it. Primum non nocere—first do no harm."

Claire leaned closer to examine the images. "So, bone shaving and rib removal toward beauty standards is fine, but anything else is unethical?"

There was irony in how society sanctioned some body modifications while condemning others. Celebrities flaunted nose jobs and Brazilian butt lifts despite their risks. Doctors approved jaw sculpting that permanently altered faces. Yet step beyond those accepted beauty norms, and suddenly it's about mental health and ethics.

"According to the medical establishment, yes. Doctor Harrison was adamant that anyone who had taken the Hippocratic Oath shouldn't be involved." Vikram shuffled through more X-rays. "A lot of extreme body modifications are done by artists who don't have medical training, but in her case, you can see the expertise. The way everything was done showed a deep understanding of anatomy and surgical precision. Since most body mod artists work in an unregulated space, it's hard to trace procedures."

He switched to a different set of images. "The tattoos make it challenging to identify certain injuries, particularly bruising or subtle surface trauma. But we work around it—UV lights, CT scans, MRI. Technology reveals what the eye can't see."

Claire's attention shifted to the trident sealed in an evidence bag. A chill ran down her spine. "Is that the murder weapon?"

"Yes, a three-prong spear, manufactured in the mid-1900s. The lab's analyzing a blue fiber embedded in the wound and a shiny substance found on the spear. Could be anything," Vikram said, crumbs from his sandwich falling onto the small table. "You recognize it?"

"I think so." She had seen a pair of similar tridents gleaming on the wall of Judson's office at the Swim and Racquet Club, and, now that she thought about it, at The Osprey too. The realization hit her like a punch to the gut. Dad!

"You alright?" Vikram asked.

"I've got to go," she said, nearly knocking over her chair as she bolted out of the room. She needed to get to the Racquet Club to check Judson's tridents, to confirm her suspicions. To see if they were still proudly displayed on his wall. If one of them was missing, Renée's murder would be quickly solved.

Before her father made the suspect list again.

* * *

Torres stood outside the entrance of the Swim and Racquet Club, his polished shoes impatiently scuffing against the sidewalk as he checked his phone, looking annoyed.

"What's going on?" Claire asked, gasping for air from running.

"The attendant isn't allowing me entry because of their stupid members-only rule."

Claire pulled her phone from her crossbody purse, fingers flying across the screen as she sent a text.

Seconds later, the entrance attendant met them outside and invited them inside. "Mister West will be here in ten minutes. He told me to let you in and to be free to wait in his office, but to make sure Ms. Fontaine remains with you at all times."

"Of course." Claire thanked him and headed straight to the manager's office.

"Where are you going?" Torres grabbed her arm and glanced through the French doors behind which surfing celebrities sunbathed on lounge chairs, their skin glistening in the afternoon sun. "I'd prefer to wait by the pool."

"We need to check the office first." She twisted away, freeing herself from his grip, and speed-walked to the office's door.

"What aren't you telling me?" Torres trotted after her, his leather shoes clicking against the marble floor as he struggled to keep up with her wide, powerful stride.

"Look at this," she said, pausing once she reached the room. She showed him her phone screen, which displayed a picture of the murder weapon. "And this," she added, pointing at a glass frame on the wall. Inside the case where two tridents used to be, only one remained—which looked identical to the murder weapon.

Torres's gaze darted between Claire's phone and the framed trident. "We need to take this into evidence." He was heading toward the frame, his hand already reaching out to grab it, when Claire stopped him.

"You can't do this!"

"Of course I can, the spear's in plain view!"

"The Plain View Doctrine doesn't apply here. Seeing one decorative trident and speculating that its missing pair is the murder weapon doesn't make its evidentiary value *immediately apparent*. It's circumstantial at best. You need a warrant." Merely matching the murder weapon wasn't inherently incriminating.

Torres yanked his phone from his pocket and called the station for reinforcements.

A few minutes later, Judson froze at the door, keys still dangling in his hands, the mid-afternoon sun shining on his bald spot. "Can I help you?"

"Yeah. You mind telling me about this trident?" Torres asked, his voice artificially casual, as he gestured toward the ornate frame where a single trident hung beside an empty bracket.

"It's a first-generation Vandstam exclusive." Judson's manicured hand swept through the air with practiced showmanship. "Produced before the TV show took off. Been on the wall for six years. Why, are you a collector?"

"Not quite, but I'm particularly interested in this one." Torres's shoes creaked against the floor as he stepped closer. "Isn't it supposed to be a pair?"

"Yes." Judson's Adam's apple bobbed. "I sold one of them two days ago."

"To whom?"

"I don't know. They paid me cash at the Vandstam fan tradeshow."

"How convenient!" Torres's voice sharpened.

Judson's fingers drummed against his thigh. "Convenient for what?"

"How well did you know Renée Efterlig?"

"Renée?" The name seemed to knock the air from his lungs. "What does she have to do with this…wait…" The smooth confidence drained from his face. "Was she killed with a trident?"

"I don't know, you tell me. "How do you know she was murdered?" Torres's shadow fell across Judson's face.

"So, it's true…." Judson stumbled back, confusion then panic marking his face. "You don't think I have anything to do with this?"

"Did you?"

"Of course not!" His voice cracked. "I loved her!"

"You loved her?" Torres asked with a cold, mocking tone. "She could be your granddaughter!"

"Age is just a number." Judson lifted his chin, but his hands trembled.

"That's what creeps always say."

"I didn't kill her. Tell him," he pleaded with Claire.

Claire glanced at the photo on Judson's desk—Renée in her early Vandstam costume, standing next to him with the practiced smile of a character performer with a paying customer. If Judson had been treating their relationship like an extended meet-and-greet, that would explain both his delusion of love and her distance once real fame arrived.

But the case wasn't over.

Chapter Thirty-Nine

The evening sun cast long shadows across The Osprey's patio as Claire tended to the grill, the aroma of merguez sausages and spices drifting through the air. Behind her, on the gravel path, her father and his former colleagues were playing Trident Toss —players aimed their tridents at scored target zones, competing for the highest points through turns and special throws.

An invisible noose tightened around her neck. She had stolen and Ziploced one of the tridents earlier to keep as evidence, praying it wouldn't be the same set as the trident that killed Renée.

The bar's evening menu usually consisted of five items—chicken wings, French fries, quesadillas, fried calamari, and sliders—but her father had made an exception that night. Since her client's cancellation had left Claire with premium ingredients and a need for company, she was serving couscous to the bar's regulars.

Off-duty cops and first responders filtered out from the bar, drawn by the smell of North African spices. They had shed their uniforms but not their bearing, gathering around the wooden tables. Torres sat apart, phone in hand, his shoulders tense as he scrolled through what Claire guessed was the day's headlines. His strange mood suddenly made sense.

"First page!" Suggie's voice carried across the patio as she rushed toward Claire, tablet in hand, Vikram following with his characteristic quiet smile. "And a reporter from The Washington Post called my research 'impressively thorough.' Can you believe it?"

Claire flipped a sausage, hiding her conflicted smile. "That's amazing,

Suggie. Though maybe don't wave it in front of you-know-who."

"Torres?" Suggie dropped into a chair, undaunted. "He should be thanking me. The whole town's talking about how both suspects were released." Both Ramos and Judson had walked free on bail and insufficient evidence. "How many more clues do they need?"

"Don't tell me." Torres didn't look up from his phone. "Judson running his mouth about the murder weapon is bad enough. The mayor's breathing down my neck. If we don't solve this by next Sunday, he's bringing in the FBI and making us all look incompetent."

Claire quickly began plating the couscous, layering it with grilled vegetables, and addressed the line of waiting patrons. "Hey, who wants the first batch? Frank said you all had a rough shift."

"I do," a burly man sporting a thick mustache and a Hawaiian shirt shoved a five-dollar bill into the empty coffee can Claire had placed on the nearest table—she couldn't charge for the dish but welcomed donations, which would hopefully be enough to cover the ingredient costs. She couldn't do anything about clients canceling, but did her best to prevent the financial loss.

"Speaking of work," Suggie interjected, accepting the second steaming plate, "Your dad told me you got a last-minute booking for tomorrow?"

"Yeah, at 179 Golden View." Claire handed a local firewoman a loaded plate, pretending not to notice how Torres's head snapped up at the address—the rental villa and first murder scene where Torres and Claire had first met. "They need brunch for about a hundred people."

Suggie nearly dropped her fork. "Wait…is your client Shonda Greenfield by chance?"

Claire nodded, arranging more sausages on the sizzling grill. "That's the one. You know her?"

"That's Renée's agent. She's probably here for the funeral arrangements. Renée didn't have any family." Suggie leaned forward, food momentarily forgotten. "I heard that she's holding auditions. Can I come?" she asked, eyes bright.

Claire hesitated, then shrugged. "Sure, why not? I could use the help." She didn't mention how the booking had come through her website, wondering if Shonda knew about the house's deadly history. The local social media storm hadn't reached everyone, apparently. "I don't know who referred me to her, but I'm eternally grateful."

"That was me." Vikram claimed a plate of fragrant couscous. "She came to the morgue to ID the body and asked the front desk if they knew a good caterer. I passed along your name. You're the best one around."

"What can I do to repay you?"

"Have dinner at my place when all this craziness is over."

"Deal!"

The conversation drifted as more patrons claimed their plates. Talks of sports and politics filled the air, and Claire's tip jar overflowed when Claire caught Torres watching her with an unreadable expression. Unlike before, when Frank was merely a person of interest, discovering the same trident—potential evidence—at a police gathering would make him an official suspect. And a guilty cop would destroy the department's reputation. Torres had to be conflicted about making a move that could discredit her father, and cast a shadow on the entire police force and first responders of Caper Cove. He looked unsure about how to proceed.

The couscous disappeared quickly, and the warm evening air carried away the scent of grilled vegetables and merguez into the twilight. Claire cleaned up the grill and brought all the utensils back to The Osprey kitchen, followed by Vikram, whose arms were laden with the remaining dirty pans, and Suggie, carrying two small gift bags.

"Umma got samples of Sierra Thorn's new skincare line! When they announce Sierra as one of the new royals, these are going to fly off the shelves.

Claire frowned. "Wait...the Vandstam logo? I thought Sierra lost her endorsement as queen." Logos required proper authorization or licensing from the Vandstam franchise, as they were protected intellectual property.

"The chosen royal court still gets that privilege. They're announcing the new Vandstam aristocracy—princes and princesses—at the end of the festival competition." Suggie's enthusiasm bubbled over. "Sierra may have lost the crown, but she's still one of the favorites. After everything she did for Renée, of course, she'll make the list. Which means she can use the logo for marketing. Try it," she encouraged as Vikram opened the tube. "Gives you that perfect, smooth, and sparkly complexion too."

"Sparkly like the vampires in *Twilight*?" Vikram asked dryly.

Claire half-giggled as she dried her hands, but quickly lost her smile. "Who had access to the cream before today?"

"Just Sierra and us. We were the first ones to try it when we chatted with her on the bleachers. Why?"

Vikram tensed up and exchanged a knowing glance with Claire. "I'm going to compare these to the mysterious substance I found on the trident." He was about to leave when Claire stopped him. "Wait. I need your help with something."

Vikram perked up. "Anything."

She pulled the bagged trident from a cupboard and handed it to him. "Would you mind checking one of these?" she asked.

"Wow. It looks exactly like the murder weapon," Vikram whispered, his gaze darting between the bag and the Trident Toss players outside. "You sure about this?"

"Yes, I'm sure." Her mind was already mapping out defensive strategies. Her father had already weathered suspicion about Ricky's murder—she couldn't let another shadow fall over him. If one of these tridents matched the murder weapon, if someone from the local police or first responders was involved, she needed to get ahead of it fast. She would need a PR strategy, character witnesses, documentation of The Osprey's security measures, and most importantly, solid proof of her father's innocence. In her years of criminal defense work, she had learned that the most devastating evidence was often the kind you discovered too late to counter. Better to find the truth now, even if it hurt, than be blindsided in front of a grand jury or the media.

Chapter Forty

At eight a.m. the next morning, Claire was settling into the Golden View villa's gourmet kitchen. The cool morning air carried the salty ocean spray through the open window, mingling with the fragrance of freshly baked pastries. The space was a chef's paradise with its shiny commercial-grade stainless steel appliances, a six-burner range with double ovens, and a giant refrigerator with transparent doors that she had just stacked with a rainbow of fruits and vegetables. Two islands topped with white Italian marble provided ample workspace. The kitchen flowed seamlessly into an airy great room where floor-to-ceiling windows framed ocean views.

She texted Suggie, reminding her to pass by the florist on her way up, and checked the clock—she had two hours before serving brunch at ten o'clock for "about fifty to one hundred people." The approximation was rather large, but Claire didn't mind. She was grateful to get a job after so many client cancellations and aimed to provide the best and most delicious experience, even with minimal preparations. Thanks to her father, who had remodeled her apartment, she benefited from a double oven and had already baked over two hundred muffins—blueberry, lemon poppy seed, and apple cinnamon—and scones—crispy-edged and tender-centered savory ham and cheese, buttermilk lavender, and cranberry orange by seven o'clock. Her pre-cooked quiches and pastries went straight into the oven, and her overnight oats and fruit salad into the refrigerator. She just needed to assemble the parfaits and plate the charcuterie and smoked salmon onto platters. Then it was on to cooking the Canadian bacon that would soon fill the kitchen with its smoky-sweet aroma and lobster for the eggs Benedict, plus grilling the spiced tofu and vegetables.

"So weird to be here," Suggie said as she dropped the jars of local honey that caught the morning light like amber and bags of edible flowers on the counter. The first time they had entered this beautiful kitchen, a teapot, three mugs, and a plate of Linzer cookies had been set on a tray, waiting for them. Their host was gone—the first murder in Caper Cove and the first one Claire and Suggie had solved together. But the place also held the memory of her friend's wedding.

Suggie eyed the spread of international cheese and ingredients. "This is way fancier than I thought. Hope you still serve normal coffee."

"Of course." Claire handed her friend a cup of steaming coffee. "Shonda asked for an *original, semi-extravagant brunch*, so I brought baby lobster for the eggs Benedict and brioche sausage. I even made boeuf bourguignon last night—the slow cooker saved my life."

"Is that enough for one hundred?"

"It should be just right." As long as the guests were wannabe actors, people usually careful about their weight and calorie intake, she would be fine. Better too much than not enough. When clients didn't want the abundant leftovers, Claire knew of local soup kitchens that would love them.

"Here." Claire handed Suggie an apron. "Catering first and investigative journalist note-taking second, please. I really need to make a good impression."

"You can count on me! So, how is Shonda? Did you get to meet her?"

"I only talked to her via the intercom when she opened the gate. She told me to set up brunch in the kitchen. People will enter the property through the garden's side door, along the tile patio, and through the kitchen's sliding door. She asked me to direct them to the conference room."

* * *

The kitchen's quiet rhythm was interrupted when Shonda's assistant, Marcus, burst in, his designer shoes clicking against the marble floor.

"Claire? I'm here to help direct traffic. Shonda wants the actors to grab their food and head straight to the conference room." He adjusted his tortoiseshell glasses, taking in the elaborate spread. "This looks incredible. The aroma alone is making my stomach growl."

The first wave of hopefuls began trickling in around 9:45 a.m. They moved through the kitchen in small clusters, their voices echoing off the high ceilings as they loaded their plates with quiche and pastries. Claire noticed they all seemed to be wearing variations of the same "casual-but-camera-ready" outfit—fitted jeans, flowing tops, and impeccable hair and makeup despite the early hour.

Every half-hour, a new group would arrive. Twelve stood out from the crowd—some were covered head-to-toe in shimmering blue body paint with Ragnar braids, while others wore elaborate winged costumes that barely cleared the doorframe. They were clearly hoping to be cast in the new Vandstam spin-off show—Vandstam: The Air People.

Claire had to suppress a gasp when Lance Foster rolled in. The adaptive gear vendor from booth 27 had transformed his wheelchair into what looked more like an experimental aircraft than medical equipment, complete with retractable wings and a cockpit-style canopy. It was true what they said about Southern California—absolutely everyone wanted to be an actor.

"Did you hear about Ramos and Sierra?" A young woman in a cream silk blouse whispered to her friend while waiting for Claire to finish plating a chive and cheese omelet. She carefully angled herself away from one of the blue-painted cosplayers who was enthusiastically explaining his method-acting approach to someone. The scent of melted Gruyère cheese wafted between them as she continued, "Apparently, they were pretty serious until she lost the Vandstam Queen role."

Her friend, carefully selecting a cranberry-orange scone, rolled her eyes. "Classic Ramos. He only dates queens—literal TV queens. Remember how Renée totally shut him down at first? She wanted nothing to do with him right after he and Sierra split."

"Right?" The first woman leaned in closer, her voice dropping even lower as she studied the edible flower of her yogurt parfait. "But the minute she got cast as the new queen, suddenly she was interested. They thought they were being so discreet, too. Nobody would have known they were hooking up if she hadn't been killed."

Claire kept her face neutral as she garnished another plate, but her ears perked up at this revelation. The women moved on, their voices fading as they headed toward the conference room.

"I mean, everyone knows Ramos would never hurt his 'queen,'" the second woman's voice drifted back. "But Ricky? That's a whole different story…"

Claire glanced at Suggie, who had been refilling the pot with fresh brew. Her friend's eyes were wide, and she had frozen mid-pour, the dark stream of coffee overshooting its mark and splashing against the metal rim. She shot Claire a complicit look—the same one they had shared since childhood.

"Need any help refreshing the platters?" Marcus appeared at Claire's elbow, making her jump, seemingly oblivious to the gossip swirling around them. Through the kitchen windows, Claire could see more actors arriving, their shadows moving across the dewy grass as they made their way to the side entrance.

"Thanks." Her mind raced as she handed him a fresh tray of muffins.

"The Lobster Benedict is a hit," Suggie said casually, mopping up her spill. She lined up clean mugs, the porcelain clicking softly as she arranged them in neat rows. "We've gone through two pounds already. These actors may watch their calories, but they sure don't skimp on caffeine."

Brunch was almost over, and the number of wannabe actors was dwindling. Claire was cleaning the buffet, removing the empty trays, when she nearly collided with a twenty-something redhead who was reaching for a blueberry muffin.

"Oh, sorry!" the woman said, steadying herself, flattening her sticker name tag that read 'Lucy.' "The food smells amazing."

Claire's heart skipped a beat at the name. Lucy—the same Lucy who was supposed to meet Ricky at Launch Point? There couldn't be that many red-haired aspiring actresses named Lucy in Caper Cove. She glanced at Suggie, who had suddenly become very interested in wiping down an already spotless counter.

"Lucy? I heard you're quite the actress," Claire said carefully, adjusting a platter of smoked salmon. "Are you a waitress at The Swim and Racquet Club? The Blue Crush team told me you gave them the best tables during the evening rush."

Lucy's expression brightened momentarily at being recognized as a good server, then quickly dimmed as if she recognized Claire. "You're the lawyer chef who's helping the police." She glanced around the busy kitchen, then lowered her voice. "Look, I know I should have come forward after what happened to Ricky, but I never actually met him that night."

"What happened?" Claire pretended to arrange a garnish while moving closer. "I won't say anything to Shonda or anyone else. I just want to hear the truth."

"The team hired me to help them prank Ricky. You know…meet him at the cliffs, get him drunk, steal his clothes. Just stupid hazing stuff." Lucy's bangles clinked nervously against her cup. "But then I got this call at work, on the club's landline. Someone said the whole thing was off, to forget about it."

"Did you recognize the voice?"

"No, but they still paid me. Left me a hundred-dollar bill so crisp it crackled. I thought it was a fake at first." A small, embarrassed laugh escaped her. "I actually framed it. My first almost-acting gig, you know?"

"Why didn't you tell the police after…?" Claire let the question hang in the air.

Lucy's gaze darted toward the conference room, where voices could be heard rehearsing lines. "Look, I'm trying to get noticed by the right people. Being mixed up in a murder investigation isn't exactly the kind of publicity I need. Besides, I figured since I never actually met him…." She shrugged.

"Who else knew about the prank?"

"Just the Blue Crush team, as far as I know. I assumed they were the ones who called it off." Lucy dabbed at her lips with a paper napkin, leaving a faint coral lipstick stain. "I should go. My audition's starting soon, and I need to prep."

As Lucy walked away, Suggie abandoned all pretense of cleaning and hurried over to Claire. The smell of coffee and fresh pastries suddenly seemed too sweet, cloying in the air between them.

"Claire," Suggie whispered, "if the Blue Crush team didn't make that call—"

"Then someone else knew about the prank," Claire finished. "Someone who didn't want Lucy at Launch Point that night so they could be there instead."

Chapter Forty-One

As the last of the hopefuls filed out, Suggie glanced at her phone and grimaced, hastily untying her apron. "I have to go. Umma just texted about the spa's quarterly reports, which I completely forgot to make, and she mentioned that Judson wants to meet me to tell his side of the story about being arrested for Renée's murder and making bail," she added, her eyes still on her phone.

"Probably an exclusive for an article," Claire cheered. Though, as a former defense attorney, she would advise against Judson giving any press interview until the investigation was complete. Literally every word could be used against him in a court of law. Until the murder investigation was concluded, it was too risky, even if he was innocent. Facts and words could easily be twisted when analyzed through a biased lens.

"Exclusives are journalists' gold."

Claire nodded sympathetically, wiping down the last of the marble countertops. "Go. You've been an amazing help. Text me about the interview?"

After Suggie left, Claire was just unplugging the coffeemaker when Shonda Greenfield appeared in the doorway. "Wait—is there any of that amazing coffee left?" The woman was a striking, commanding presence—a statuesque woman with blond cornrow braids that contrasted beautifully with her complexion. "This roast is divine. And that kale smoothie earlier? Perfect balance of sweet and green."

"I'm glad you liked it. I'm just finishing up here. I'll be out of your hair in a minute."

"Oh no, please, stay. I want to talk with you, if you have time, of course," she said, her statement bracelet catching the late morning light.

"I do," Claire replied, pouring the coffee and settling onto one of the barstools at the kitchen island across from Shonda. Sunlight streamed through the windows, warming the marble surface between them.

"First, I wanted to say the food was incredible. Especially impressive with less than twenty-four hours' notice." Your drive is impressive. Which brings me to an interesting proposition. How would you feel about playing a villain in Vandstam?"

Claire blinked. "A villain? I didn't realize I was giving off evil vibes."

Shonda laughed and slid her phone toward Claire. "You're famous, Claire. Your social media following has exploded, and drama seems to follow you everywhere."

The screen showed a new post from @fireinyourmouth—a photo of ICE agents entering the Osprey's kitchen from a few nights ago. The caption beneath heavily implied she was undocumented. Claire's stomach dropped as the number of comments and shares grew.

"That thread is getting longer by the second," Shonda said, shaking her head.

Claire's fingers itched to grab her own phone and see the extent of the damage, but she resisted. She needed to finish her work here, and the last thing she wanted was to let a client see how much this lie was affecting her. "This troll is lying."

"Of course he is. He claimed you were a terrible cook, and obviously, he's wrong," Shonda gestured at the spotless kitchen that had recently held a feast. "Probably a jealous competitor who can't match your skills. But you need to use all that noise somehow. No publicity is bad publicity."

Claire suppressed a grimace, thinking about recent events. Being taken for target by a troll, being doxed, and losing all her catering gigs were definitely bad things.

"So, how about joining the Vandstam crew. With your French accent, you'll fit perfectly as we're seeking accents from around the world."

"I'm flattered, but as exciting as it sounds, acting isn't for me."

"You might be the only one around here who doesn't want to be on TV," Shonda smiled. "Oh! And one more thing. Would you be interested in judging the Gidget competition? We're doing a segment on the best Vandstam cosplayer."

"Me?"

"Yes. Renée was supposed to be one of the judges, and since she can't…" Shonda's voice trailed off before brightening again. "Your online infamy, if I call it that, would bring excellent publicity to the contest."

"Can I think about it?"

"How about five minutes? I'll use that time to send your payment." Shonda pulled out her phone and made a few taps.

Claire's phone pinged in her pocket. She retrieved it and checked the message flashing on her screen. "I think you made a mistake. This is too much."

"I added a thirty percent tip for the extra delicious factor. And I'll definitely be recommending you." Shonda took a long sip of coffee and closed her eyes, enjoying the midday sun and sudden silence. The birdsongs that had been drowned out by the crowd of auditioners now sounded pleasantly loud. "If you change your mind about acting, or have any questions, let me know."

Claire straightened. "Actually, I do have questions," she said, her voice taking the careful tone of an attorney about to take a deposition. "About Renée."

Something shifted in Shonda's expression, a mix of pride and sadness. Marcus, who had been quietly organizing the auditioners' portfolios at the far end of the kitchen island, moved closer.

"Renée was a dream client," Shonda said softly. "I first met her at a fan convention…" Shonda's smile turned wistful. "Renée just felt right at home. Nobody questioned her blue skin there."

"She didn't need makeup," Marcus added, adjusting his bow tie. "Made her perfect for last-minute appearances. The fans loved that authenticity."

"Did you see anything unusual about her behavior recently?"

Shonda shook her head. "Renée was driven. She was constantly pushing herself, both physically with her body modifications and emotionally. Trust me, working in an industry where people judge your acting and appearance all the time is soul-crushing." She took another sip of coffee. "But Renée was dedicated to embodying the Vandstam Queen. Her fan base speaks for itself."

"Did she have any enemies?" Claire asked.

"Everyone rising to fame has some," Marcus said. "Whether she meant it or not, Renée challenged everyone who stood in her way. Sierra wasn't too happy about that, being forced to watch Renée supplant her at casting calls."

"When Renée took up surfing, that was it for Sierra." Shonda sighed. "Can you imagine having a real-life Vandstam queen who could actually spend the entire day with fans? No makeup to worry about, no constant reapplication needed. She could stay in the water, hang out in the sun, and it was all genuine." Her voice softened. "Renée physically erased and rebuilt herself. Even her name. I'm sure you know that Renée means 'reborn' in French. She always felt like a stranger in her own body and wanted to show the world who she truly was inside."

"The transformation was remarkable. Her skin color became her signature instead of her burden."

Claire nodded. "The world can be harshly judgmental."

"You've got that right!" Shonda set down her empty coffee cup with a gentle clink. "Embracing who you are is an act of courage." She met Claire's eyes. "And sometimes, modifying your body to reflect your reality is an emotional necessity."

Claire considered this silently. How many people were trapped between who they appeared to be and who they felt they were? For Renée, the skin had been both curse and liberation—a bridge between her inner and outer worlds. Claire's own accent had become part of her identity, too, whether she had wanted it or not.

The kitchen fell silent but for the soft hum of the refrigerator and the distant sound of waves through the open window.

"Thank you," Claire said finally. "For telling me about her."

Shonda stood, her bracelet catching the light again. "Just...find out what happened to her, Claire. She deserved better than this ending."

As Claire gathered her things to leave, she couldn't shake the feeling that understanding Renée's transformation was key to understanding her death. She just had to figure out how all the pieces fit together.

169

Chapter Forty-Two

Claire's knuckles whitened against the handlebars of her Vespa as she navigated through the midday traffic, her mind methodically sorting through her options like files in a well-ordered cabinet. The photo of ICE agents attempting to detain her—a moment of terrifying confusion that had lasted mere minutes—was now spreading across social media like wildfire, accompanied by false accusations about her immigration status.

A John Doe lawsuit would be the proper first step, she mused, signaling for a turn onto Main Street. The court would likely grant her request for pre-lawsuit discovery, and from there, a subpoena to the social media platform would follow naturally. This was a clear case of defamation.

Her phone chimed softly from her purse for the twentieth time since she left the Golden View villa, but she ignored it—she never checked messages while driving, and she needed to be home fast. Reading whatever text or notification she was receiving was sure to incense her further. She could ask Torres or Deputy Chief Ernshaw to use their cybercrime tech to find the troll's IP address. When she finally parked in her assigned spot behind The Osprey, she retrieved her phone and scrolled through message after message: the first were from clients requesting she reduce her contracted catering prices by half or more—figures that would leave her breaking even or operating at a loss. The rest were cancellations, each client more apologetic than the last. All her catering gigs for the next two months, gone.

Pick a lane, the troll's words flashed in her head. Maybe they were right. Maybe trying to be everything meant being nothing. Her law license was still active. She could go back to D.C., back to being just Claire Fontaine, attorney. No more confusion, no more questions about who she was or where she belonged. Her phone buzzed with another notification from @fireinyourmouth: When you can't hack it as a lawyer, why not pretend to be French? #FailedAttorney #FakeChef #StickToOneThing

The words hit like a physical blow because they articulated her deepest fear: that she was running from her real identity instead of toward a new one.

Chapter Forty-Three

The afternoon sun had finally broken through the thick June gloom when the paddle-out for Renée started. Over fifty surfers, some in their competition jerseys and others in Vandstam attire, formed a circle about one hundred yards offshore, their boards pointed inward as they joined hands to honor Renée "The Vandstam Queen"—the one who had united the world of surfing and 'living cosplay.' Fans and spectators stood on the shore as the Vandstam theme song played from the speakers. Someone had accidentally queued up the wrong track first, blasting "Baby Shark" before correcting the mistake. Then, the circle erupted in a splash of joy and color. The surfers splashed water toward the sky while cheering, calling out her name, and pounding loudly on their boards. The rhythmic thunder of their tribute echoed across the water. A couple threw flowers into the center of the circle, white and blue flowers that floated on the swells.

"What are they doing?" a spectator asked Claire. "I thought this was supposed to be a memorial."

"The cheering may seem strange, but this moment represents Renée's life and spirit rather than mourning her loss. It's like sending her spirit off with energy and love, like a standing ovation at a final performance."

"Oh, I see. Like a celebration of life."

"Exactly," Frank Fontaine said as he reached his daughter's side. His tall shadow moved across the sand as he wrapped one strong arm around Claire's shoulders and squeezed her tightly, the way he used to do when she was a little girl, afraid of the night. "You okay, kiddo?"

"I think so." The ICE post implying she was undocumented had gone viral with thousands of commenters either sharing their immigrant stories or debating the country's immigration policies. "At least some of the commenters are creative—one suggested I must be from Mars because 'no Earth woman could make smoothies that good.'"

It was strange how people latched onto the most visible parts of her identity—her accent, her cooking—while completely missing the deeper currents. The explosion, the coma, the loss of her colleagues…these invisible traumas had reshaped her far more profoundly than any surface change ever could. Identity wasn't just what others saw. It was the accumulated weight of experiences, both visible and hidden, that people carried within themselves. Claire wondered how many people walking along the beach below wore similar invisible marks of transformation.

She had untagged herself, but her face in the picture remained there.

"I reported the post and filed a complaint with the police and sent a message to the troll, asking him to stop spreading lies and remove the post, that if he continues, I would have to take action."

"What did he say?"

"He replied, 'You're the liar.'" Claire shook her head in frustration. "I'm angry. His lies made me lose catering jobs."

"You know you can always work here and live for free," Frank said. "Though fair warning—Torres might really grow on you."

"I know, Dad, and I'm really grateful for that, but you know. I need to be financially independent for my own mental health and pride."

"I understand. Want a smoothie or feel like a game of toss?" He asked, pointing at the trident toss pit. "I've finally fixed that wonky trident that kept landing pointy-end first in people's sandcastles."

"About that, Dad. We need to talk." She pulled her father aside. "Your tridents look exactly like the murder weapon. Do you think one of the guys could have done it?"

"What? No way!"

"Do you ever run a trident inventory to see if they are all accounted for?"

"C'mon, Claire. They're not even sharp, just part of a game. The most damage they've done is to people's pride when they miss the target completely—which reminds me, we should probably take down that 'World's Worst Throw' photo wall." He gestured at the worn brass police badges that decorated the walls. "Didn't Torres arrest Judson for the crime?"

"What if he made a mistake and it's one of the Blues?"

"Claire, it's Caper Cove for Pete's sake! The most controversial thing our police force has done is that time Officer Johnson tried to arrest a shirtless man for public indecency, thinking he was a topless woman. Plus, I know everyone."

"Maybe that's the problem. You can't stay objective when it comes to suspects. For you, it has to be an outsider."

"Speaking of the devil," Frank mumbled as Torres approached them. He had his police-issued bike helmet in one hand and a small black Vandstam-branded briefcase in the other. The helmet sported several small dents and a sticker that read "My other vehicle is also a bicycle—budget cuts, you know." Torres dropped the case and the helmet on the counter and asked for a cold lemonade. He was wearing the bike patrol's navy blue bike shorts and a tight top with the large golden star with CCPD embroidered on his chest. "Those bike shorts are getting more attention than actual crime prevention," Frank whispered to Claire.

"Bad day?" Frank asked as he served Torres a cold lemonade. "Problem with your case?"

Torres gulped down the lemonade in one go and set the glass back down with a clink. "The only thing worse than finding a clue is finding the wrong clue," he sighed. "Judson was telling the truth. He really did sell one of his tridents for cash. Found the buyer who asked for his money back. Turns out, the trident's a fake. Was supposed to be a special 1960s US Divers Sea Hunter Pistol Speargun, the one the US military divers and SEALs used back in the day that the Vandstam team had rebranded. But this one, the one Judson bought for an insane amount of money, is lead-filled plastic. So cheap, its shine is water-soluble."

"So Judson's innocent," Claire muttered.

"I'm not sure about innocent. But his trident isn't the murder weapon." Torres glanced at Claire and the trident toss. "Though he did try to convince me he was being framed by a gang of vengeful merpeople."

"Don't be coy with me, Torres. Claire already told me about my tridents," Frank said. "What are you waiting for? Aren't you going to interrogate the entire police force?"

"I wouldn't…"

Claire frowned. Her father's pressure on Torres wasn't fair. As both Torres's mentor and landlord, Frank held too much leverage over the detective, especially now that the murder weapon might match The Osprey's tridents.

"There's no need to do that. At least not yet," she said.

"What do you mean?"

"I sent one of the tridents for analysis. The results will tell us whether to follow this path."

Her father frowned. "You did what?"

"I'm sorry, Dad, but I had to know. Are you upset?"

Frank burst into laughter. "Of course not. Look at you, not afraid to find out the truth despite your possible conflict! That takes guts. That being said, I don't think you'll find your killer here."

Claire wanted to believe him. After all, most cops and first responders working in Caper Cove moved here because of the quiet nature of the town: to be able to surf, and fish, and enjoy a work-life balance that no other cities could offer. Except for the double murder last spring, the most exciting thing in the police blotter usually involved rescuing cats from trees or breaking up heated arguments about proper surfboard waxing techniques.

Claire leaned against the boardwalk railing, watching the festival crowds seated on the bleachers. The wooden planks vibrated beneath her feet with the constant shuffle of patrons.

"So many people," she murmured, more to herself than to Torres, who had joined her at the railing. "Any one of them could be—"

"That's what everyone's thinking," Torres interrupted, his eyes scanning the crowd. "You should hear the talk at the station. All about watching the outsiders, the tourists, anyone who 'doesn't belong.'" He made air quotes with his fingers.

Claire turned to face him. "But that's exactly our problem, isn't it? We're all so busy watching the strangers that we're missing what's right in front of us."

"What do you mean?"

"Think about it. We see these people every day—at church, at the grocery store, at town council meetings. We wave, we smile, we think we know them." She gestured toward the crowd. "But do we really?"

Torres's face hardened. "You're not suggesting—"

"I'm suggesting that while we're all watching these thousands of visitors, searching for monsters in unfamiliar faces…we might be keeping our backs turned to the real threat. Someone could be counting on exactly that."

A cool breeze swept across the boardwalk, carrying the scents of cotton candy and sea salt. Behind them, the festival lights began to flicker on one by one, casting long shadows across the weathered wood.

Torres was quiet for a long moment. "You know how that sounds, right? These are our neighbors you're talking about. People you and your dad have known for years."

"Sometimes," Claire replied, her eyes fixed on the darkening horizon, "the killer is someone you'd never suspect."

***

The setting sun streaked the sky in pink and orange, silhouetting the festival vendor booths below. Claire and Suggie had retreated to the sanctuary of Claire's bedroom, where the sounds of the bustling boardwalk drifted up to her second-floor apartment like a college dorm party they hadn't been invited to.

Their murder board dominated one wall—a maze of red string, photographs, and Post-it notes illuminated by Claire's desk lamp. Three new faces had joined the web of suspects: Dr. Harrison's professional headshot from his plastic surgery practice website, a grainy security camera still of Grumpy Henry scowling at someone off-frame, and a glossy promotional shot of Sierra Thorn in full Vandstam regalia, taken before Renée had claimed her crown.

"Pass the kimchi?" Claire asked, not taking her eyes off the board. Suggie had brought the spicy fermented cabbage, along with steamed rice and huraideu-chicken, turning Claire's desk into a makeshift Korean feast. Their dinner sat neglected as they processed the day's revelations, though the kimchi's tangy aroma was making it harder to focus on murder by the minute.

Suggie handed over the jar, then dabbed at a spot of gochujang sauce on her shirt. "You're not going to believe what Judson told me," she said, her voice carrying that particular tone that meant she had uncovered something big.

"I'm listening." Claire spooned kimchi over her rice, the tangy aroma mixing with the salt air drifting through the open window.

"So you know how everyone thought he was just some creepy stalker?" Suggie leaned forward, her eyes bright with discovery. "Turns out the reason he was Renée's financial guarantor for her surgery was because she needed someone to sign off for her because she couldn't use her hands for weeks after her hand webbing procedure."

Claire set down her chopsticks. "Wait, what?"

"Yeah, and here's the kicker. He really loved her. He was her first real fan. Before anyone even knew who she was. He's got these pictures of her from her early days, before the whole Vandstam phenomenon took off. He believed in her when she was just a kid with a dream and some sketches."

Claire turned to study Judson's photo on the board. "That changes things, but doesn't exonerate him. Why didn't he mention this during interrogation?"

"Maybe he was embarrassed about being a superfan to someone way younger than him and realizing he's been used." Suggie trailed off, then suddenly sat up straighter. "What about Dr. Harrison?"

"His alibi is airtight." Claire sighed, her shoulders low. "That leaves Grumpy Henry and Sierra Thorn."

A loud burst of laughter from the festival below interrupted her brooding. Both women moved to the window, watching the growing crowd of revelers below. The festival lights brightened the twilight, transforming the beach and boardwalk into a carnival of color and shadow. Couples strolled hand-in-hand, pausing occasionally to admire the local artisans' displays; teenagers linked arms, swaying to music together; children darted between stalls, their laughter carried by the breeze.

"You thinking what I'm thinking?" Suggie asked, already reaching for her jacket.

Claire grinned, gathering up their empty containers. "That we should take a break from this investigation?"

"Exactly. No talk about work or the investigation. Just fun times like when we were teenagers and all we cared about was getting a nice tan and kissing boys."

"Great idea, minus the boy-kissing part," Claire said, moving Thorn's photo to the prime suspect location and crossing Dr. Harrison's artificially whitened smile. The remaining suspects stared back at them, each hiding their own secrets. Somewhere in this web of relationships and rivalries lay the truth. They just had to find it. Preferably after funnel cake.

"Ready?" Suggie asked, already heading for the door.

"Behind you," Claire replied, giving one last look at the murder board before following her friend into the night.

Chapter Forty-Four

The boardwalk pulsed with energy as the seventh day of the festival drew to a close. Tomorrow would mark the start of the international competition, but Claire couldn't shake the case from her mind, even amid the ceremony's spectacle. Sierra Thorn might not have been Renée's friend as she suggested to be, especially after her protégée took not only the Vandstam crown from her but also her boyfriend. And there was Grumpy Henry, whose threat to Ramos and Renée was left uninvestigated on the pretext that an old vet couldn't kill a fly. Their possible culpabilities kept circling in Claire's mind like hungry seagulls over a discarded bag of chips.

"Let's check out the art walk." Suggie pulled Claire away from the main stage, where the show continued. The local artists' booths lined a quieter section of the boardwalk, their handmade purses, jewelry, sculptures, and paintings illuminated by warm spotlights.

"You're the guide," Claire humored. Having not attended the festival in years, everything looked and felt new: the balloon artist sculpted sloths and tapirs, as well as the classic dog and giraffe; the face painters drew flowers and dragons, but mostly Vandstam symbols on children, as well as adults' faces.

"This is so pretty," Suggie said as she stopped at one display where a myriad of small oil paintings represented Caper Cove's landmarks—the lighthouse, the centuries-old library and post-office, the main shores with its lifeguard tower. "Look, there's even the Osprey!"

Seeing her father's taco shop immortalized among the town's beloved landmarks filled Claire with pride until another canvas called her attention. Her hand gripped Suggie's arm. "Look at this one."

She pointed to a watercolor that captured the craggy coastline where Renée's body had been found. The perspective was from the Forbidden Path looking down—the treacherous rocks overlooking the secret beach rendered in stark detail, including a piece of clothing which looked like a Blue Crush jersey.

"Oh, that's one of Henry Morgan's pieces," said the vendor, a cheerful woman wearing a name tag identifying her as part of the Local Artists' Cooperative. "He rarely shows his work, but he's quite talented."

"Henry Morgan...as in 'Grumpy Henry'?" Claire asked, studying the painting more closely. "The one who lives alone in that old house on the cliff?"

"That's him. Took me weeks just to convince him to let me display anything. He just drops off his work and disappears back to his hermit cave, as we call it."

"When did he bring this one?" Claire pressed.

"Just this week. Gorgeous morning light, isn't it?"

Claire studied the painting more closely—the yellow and red festival tents dotted the beach in the background, several distinctive buoys floating in the painted waters. This was recent work, and that perspective from the Forbidden Path meant Henry had been there recently, despite his supposed frailty.

"We should get back to the ceremony," Suggie said, but Claire could tell by her friend's expression that she was thinking the same thing: Grumpy Henry's solitary house on the cliff would have given him both the perfect vantage point to observe Renée's movements and the skills to reach that treacherous outcropping where Renée was attacked.

The drums from the opening ceremony reached a crescendo in the distance as Claire stared at the painting, her mind racing. The reclusive veteran in his cliff-top house suddenly seemed a lot more dangerous than just a grumpy neighbor.

Chapter Forty-Five

"This is insane," Suggie said, gripping the steering wheel as she pulled up to the dirt turnoff near Grumpy Henry's property. The headlights caught the 'No Trespassing' sign before she killed the engine. "Let me come with you."

"If I'm right about this, I need you at the beach entrance," Claire said, checking her flashlight batteries. "If anything happens, that's where backup should come." She didn't mention that she was counting on Grumpy Henry being less likely to act if he spotted a lone trespasser rather than two.

"Need I remind you what happened during your last solo investigative trip to Mexico?" Suggie's voice was tight with concern. "You might not be with me right now if I hadn't followed my instincts and checked on you that day."

Claire touched her friend's arm. "I'll be fine. I just need to confirm the connection between the path to his house and the murder scene. Twenty minutes, tops. If I'm not back at the beach access point by then, call it in."

"Promise me you won't do anything stupid."

"Define stupid," Claire grinned, then softened at Suggie's expression. "I promise. Twenty minutes. I'll buy you a funnel cake afterward."

She slipped out of the car, the festival's distant lights creating a colorful haze over the coastline. The moon hung high over Caper Cove, lighting the Forbidden Path as Claire navigated around rocks and shrubs. Her flashlight beam caught glimpses of loose gravel and twisted roots as she traced what she now realized was a well-worn trail from Grumpy Henry's backyard. Rock formations and dense coastal shrubs screened the path from neighboring houses and the main road—a perfect cover for someone who knew these cliffs intimately.

She clicked off her light, letting her eyes adjust. The path was easier to access than she'd expected. So much for the story of the grumpy old veteran with the bad knee.

A twig snapped behind her.

Claire spun around, but before she could react, a familiar gruff voice cut through the night air. "Curious about my painting, Detective?" Grumpy Henry emerged from behind a rock formation, something long and metallic gleaming in his hands. "A guy from the co-op told me people were asking questions."

Claire's breath caught in her throat. The moonlight glinted off the weapon Grumpy Henry pointed at her—a speargun, loaded with a spear identical to the one that had killed Renée. The same distinctive notching near the tip that the forensics team had documented.

"That night," Henry continued, stepping forward, "Renée and that boy were making so much noise. No respect. None of them have any respect for this place." He gestured with the speargun toward the secret beach below. "I served my country to protect places like this."

Claire took a step back, the loose gravel shifting under her feet. "Henry, you don't—"

The spear whistled past, grazing her upper arm. A sharp sting, then a warm wetness trickled down her sleeve. Henry was already reloading, his movements practiced and efficient despite his supposed frailty.

"You shouldn't have come here," he growled, advancing steadily. "Why didn't you go back to your country instead of sticking your nose where it doesn't belong?" he snarled.

"I'm not a tourist, I grew up here," Claire replied, stalling for time as her eyes darted around for escape routes.

"Yeah, right, with that accent!" He snorted.

"I'm Frank Fontaine's daughter," she said firmly.

"You don't fool me. You all want to make me believe my fall made me crazy, but it won't work. Only thing that makes me mad is all the noisy tourists and kids!" Henry's voice rose with indignation. "They have no respect for people's sleep schedules with their drones, and now, they're even paragliding at night, kicking rocks down as they fly off the cliff!"

Claire paused. "Have you filed a noise complaint with the police?"

"Why do you care? Move!" Henry barked, gesturing with the speargun toward the beach. "That way!"

She retreated step by step until she felt empty air behind her heels. The cliff edge. Claire paused, understanding his tactic. At high tide, a fall might look like she'd jumped into the water, but now, at low tide, a fall would look like an accident. The perfect cover for murder. Waves crashed against the rocks below, the sound nearly drowning out her pounding heart. Moonlight glinted off the newly loaded spear as Henry raised the gun again. She was trapped between a killer and a forty-foot drop into darkness.

Chapter Forty-Six

A car door slammed in the distance. A flashlight beam cut through the darkness.

"Claire?" Suggie's voice carried across the cliff top.

Henry's head snapped toward the sound. In that split second, Claire lunged forward, grabbing the barrel of the speargun and yanking it sideways. Henry's trigger finger tightened reflexively—the spear discharged harmlessly into the dense shrubs. Years of swimming had given Claire upper-body strength that surprised Henry.

"I had to protect this place!" Henry shouted as they struggled. "These kids with their parties, their noise, their disrespect—"

"Like you protected Renée?" Claire twisted the speargun from his grip and tossed it out of reach. The speargun clattered to the rocky ground.

Henry threw a wild punch, but his footing was unsteady on the uneven ground. She blocked it easily, then swept his legs out from under him—a move she had learned in self-defense class after too many late nights walking alone to the subway station in Washington, D.C.

"You nosy bit—" he went down hard, his bad knee apparently not bad enough to stop him from killing Renée, but real enough to betray him now.

Before he could recover, Claire had him face down, one knee in his back as she secured his hands behind him. Her arm stung where the spear had grazed her, but adrenaline kept the pain at bay.

"You okay?" Suggie called out as she appeared from behind the rocks, her phone pressed to her ear. "Torres is three minutes out," she announced.

"I'm good," Claire replied, maintaining a secure but gentle hold as Henry stopped struggling beneath her. "Your twenty minutes weren't up."

"Yeah, well, after what happened last time, I started the timer at fifteen instead of twenty." Suggie kept her flashlight trained on Henry. "You're not the only one who learned from the last investigation."

Sirens grew closer, red and blue lights pulsating through the night. "I didn't mean to do it," he mumbled. "This was my post. My watch. For years I've kept this coast safe—"

"Safe?" Claire said softly. "You killed an innocent girl."

"I never meant anyone to get hurt," he whispered. "I just wanted them to stop. Every night, more kids, more noise. They steal things from my patio—chairs, planters, anything not bolted down. Every night with their laughing, their music. This isn't some party beach, this is—"

"This is a crime scene," Detective Torres's voice preceded him as he emerged from the path, weapon drawn. "You okay?" he asked Claire.

Claire stepped back, letting Torres take over. She pressed her hand to her arm where the spear had grazed her.

"You're really okay?" Torres asked again, handcuffing the old man and handing him off to another officer.

"I'm fine. He missed, remember?"

"He could have killed you!" Torres faced her, his hands clenched at his sides. "Do you understand that? You could have died tonight!"

"But I didn't—"

"Because you got lucky!" His voice cracked. "Jesus, Claire, when I saw you on that cliff edge…"

She turned to face him fully. In the moonlight, she could see something raw and vulnerable in his expression.

"I can't do this again," he whispered.

"Do what again?"

"Watch someone I…." He stopped, running both hands through his hair. "I can't afford to lose you." The words hit her like a physical force. "When Suggie called tonight, when she said you were at the cliff, all I could think about was finding your body on the rocks." His voice was barely audible. "Frank would never forgive me…."

"Well, we won't have to worry about that, won't we?" Claire said, following Suggie to the flashing red lights of the ambulance.

"I told you not to do anything stupid," Suggie said later, as an EMT cleaned the wound on Claire's arm.

"Technically, I didn't. He's the one who came at me," Claire replied. "So, how about getting that funnel cake…."

Chapter Forty-Seven

The grazing injury was so light that Claire was able to resume her cooking and delivery duties the next morning, despite her father's concerns. She was now in Oh La La Spa, the luxurious resort spa, arranging two hundred blue macarons—blueberry and chocolate sea salt—on an ocean-themed display that matched the Vandstam logo. Mrs. Oh had placed the catering order to celebrate the release of Sierra Thorne's collection of Vandstam-branded skin care.

"Henry spent the night in custody. He claimed he didn't mean to kill anyone, but confessed to firing a warning shot, nothing more."

"He used to be a good man, always trading fishing stories at the farmers' market on Sundays. He's a different man since his accident last winter," Mrs. Oh added as she scurried across the spa floor to make sure that every cream tube was the first thing clients saw through the store window. These products would bring in new clients—Vandstam fans who might have never been in a spa before and wanted to try it out. "Shooting a warning shot… that's not the Henry I knew."

"It's crazy how an injury could change someone's personality or brain processes like that," Suggie agreed, absently adjusting the crystal display stands.

"Not being able to control the way your brain works is terrible. I understand the frustration." Claire knew all too well how an accident could rewire your brain without your consent. Her French accent had become both a defining characteristic and a source of scrutiny—something she neither wanted nor could escape. The frustration of being constantly misunderstood, of having others make assumptions based on how she sounded rather than who she was…it was exhausting. Identity should be something you craft, not something that happens to you against your will.

"I'm happy your neurological speech disorder didn't turn you into a murderer," Suggie said.

"Alright, girl, no more talk of murderers. We've got Sierra Thorne's products to launch," Mrs. Oh said as she pointed at the reception counter. A live feed of the surfing festival stage streamed to the reception counter computer. "In a few seconds, the names of the lucky Vandstam Court will be announced," the announcer declared, followed by the shouts of spectators.

Claire stood by Suggie and Mrs. Oh, the three of them watching the live stream. Shonda Greenfield approached the stage, microphone in hand, explaining the honor it was to be counted among the court, that the benefit of being among them was to appear regularly in the TV series, but also to attach the logo to their products like a franchise agreement. Then, the casting agent started to read the names out loud: " Julie Lee, Sarah Faxon, Connie Smith, DJ Jackson…." Claire and Suggie waited to hear Sierra Thorne's name so they could leave the spa and return to their occupations—helping out at the Osprey for Claire and photographing the athletes for Suggie. "…and last but not least, Kristina Grifant ."

"Did they say Sierra Thorne?" Mrs. Oh asked.

"Let's check." Suggie's fingers flew over the keyboard. The official Vandstam website jumped to the screen, displaying the list of the new court. There was no "Sierra Thorne." Suggie did a site search for "Sierra," which led to the alumni page, stating that Sierra was no longer with the Vandstam and that a third new Vandstam queen would soon be announced.

Panic crossed Mrs. Oh's face. "I can't sell these products if she isn't on the list."

"It's okay, Mrs. Oh. Nobody's seen them yet. We're taking care of it," Claire said, understanding how combustible the situation had gotten. Without being part of the Vandstam court, Sierra didn't have the authorization to sell products with the Vandstam logo. The hundreds of little tubes they had arranged as waves on the transparent display shelves were now considered counterfeited products; selling them was considered trademark infringement and could cost Mrs. Oh her license. With the competition and camera crews around, she had to remove the infringing products from the shelves stat.

Claire handed Suggie a box and, without telling her what to do, the pair worked in unison. As Suggie held the box below each shelf of products, Claire swiped the shelf with her arms, sending dozens of tubes falling into the box, removing in two minutes what had taken them an hour to create.

"What are you doing with my products?" Sierra Thorne screamed as she pushed the spa employee who had just opened the door. She grabbed tubes from their hands with increasing panic. "You need to put them back on the shelf!"

Mrs. Oh frowned. "I can't. Your products aren't officially licensed."

"They don't need to be. I am the Vandstam Queen. It comes with the title." Sierra contradicted, her voice more despair than anger.

"You *were* the Vandstam Queen, but not anymore."

Sierra's face crumpled at those words. For just a moment, the composed performer mask slipped, revealing the devastation underneath. This wasn't just about losing a title; this was about losing everything.

"Renée is dead, isn't she? I'm the only Vandstam Queen standing, aren't I?" she screamed, grabbing tubes from the box Suggie was holding and trying to place them back on the shelf, her blue nails scratching against the glass.

Claire called Torres before it got out of hand. When the detective appeared in the doorway, Sierra's demeanor shifted instantly—her rage melting into calculated charm.

"I'll find another seller," she said, running a finger along one of the cream tubes. "But you should know, Mrs. Oh…when the Vandstam Court scandal breaks tomorrow, you'll wish you'd kept these on your shelves. And you, Officer," she said as she turned to Torres, "don't you have better things to do than harass legitimate businesswomen? Like catching actual killers? Aren't Ricky's and Renée's murders still unsolved?"

"About that, anything new?" Suggie asked as Torres watched Sierra leave.

"There's movement on the case, but I can't discuss it yet," Torres replied.

"Come on. I held back the Grumpy Henry story because you asked me to, and now it's too old for breaking news," Suggie protested. "You owe me."

"Suggie!" Mrs. Oh interjected. "Help me clean this up before the clients arrive."

"Claire, do you mind going to the station with me? I need your expertise, and something about Grumpy Henry is off."

Chapter Forty-Eight

laire met Torres at the station and followed the detective to his desk—a cubicle made of a denim blue soundproof partition that faced the window, where the afternoon light shone on the cluttered surface. There, they watched the video of Henry's interview. The veteran looked as tired as he sounded confused, his weathered hands trembling slightly as they rested on the metal table.

"You might want to put him through a psych eval," she suggested, the scent of Torres's coffee lingering in the air between them. "You can't accept a confession if he's incompetent."

"He's not. You saw when he said he had proof he didn't do it."

"On his surveillance video?"

"Yes, he gave us consent to retrieve the video from that night from his surveillance app. Gave us his security account number and password. "Here it is," Torres opened another video, the click of his keyboard punctuating the unusual hushed atmosphere of the office.

The footage streamed clearly from the security app, the screen's blue-white glow illuminating their faces. The veteran might be an old hermit, but his surveillance setup was military-grade.

They had already reviewed the first part of that night's footage: Renée and Ramos's laughter echoing up from the beach and the comings and goings of the skinny silhouette of the voyeur who had filmed the lovers' encounter before Henry threatened them, his jacket pins glinting in the moonlight, catching the camera like tiny stars against the darkness. But it was the second half of the recording that demanded their attention.

"Here," Claire pointed as Torres scrolled through the timestamps, her finger leaving a smudge on the glossy screen. "That night."

The black and white footage showed Henry on his back patio, shouting toward the beach. The audio crackled with his threats, "Clear out! This is private property!"

Then he was moving, speargun in hand, following the Forbidden Path toward the nude beach, his footsteps crushing the dry vegetation.

"Play it again, with the sound on max," Claire requested, leaning forward, her chair creaking as she shifted her weight. Sure enough, the distinctive *clink* of the trident hitting rock came through clearly on the audio, a metallic ping that echoed in the small office, followed by Henry's frustrated curse. "He didn't shoot Renée."

"He claimed he went back the next morning to retrieve the trident, but it was gone," Torres said, making notes.

"Wait," she squinted at the screen, her reflection ghostly in the monitor's glare. "Can you rewind? There."

After Henry retreated to his house and Ramos left the scene, Renée was still laughing, calling him a chicken in the background. Then, a few minutes later, another figure appeared on the path. Unlike Henry's bent, shuffling gait, this silhouette moved quickly, purposefully, with the agility of a predator. The figure had come from the opposite side of Henry's house, from where Ramos and Renée were—as if it had been there all along, unseen by the young voyeur— and it paused at the exact place they had heard the spear fall, then disappeared from the frame.

Torres tapped the screen. "That's definitely not Henry."

He played the sequence again. The mystery figure's movements were fluid, athletic—someone much younger than Henry. Someone who would have found the murder weapon, still warm from its discharge, lying there in the darkness, and took it to use against Renée?

"So Henry's telling the truth," Claire said, watching the footage loop again, a chill running down her spine. "His 'warning shot' was turned into a murder weapon, but he wasn't the one who used it to kill Renée."

Torres submitted his findings to Deputy Chief Ernshaw, who agreed. The video partially exonerated Henry.

"He could have gotten around behind the camera to make us believe there was someone else that night and finished the job by hand," Ernshaw said. "Can we clean this up? Get any identifying features?"

Torres shook his head. "Not from this angle. But now we know that we're looking for someone young, lean, and athletic, who knew about the path and was already there that night before Henry."

Claire studied the silhouette move across the screen again, her eyes burning from fatigue and concentration. They had ruled out Henry as the killer, but the real murderer had been clever enough to use the vet's angry outbursts as cover. Someone who knew the area well enough to navigate that treacherous path in the dark. Someone who had a reason to want Renée dead.

"I want every frame analyzed," Ernshaw said, standing. "Height, build, gait analysis. Anything that might help us ID our shadow friend." She paused at the door. "Good work bringing Henry in, Detective. He could still be our killer, but even if he's not, this footage just broke this case wide open."

Claire nodded sadly, wondering if Henry truly understood the gravity of his actions. The fishmonger's words echoed in her mind about how Henry hadn't been the same since his fall on the icy dock last winter—a memory that still made the locals wince when mentioned. Still, his actions would likely result in multiple criminal charges, as this would be considered a dangerous and threatening action. She wrestled with whether to press charges against him for shooting his speargun at her. The only charge she was certain about, though, was against fireinyourmouth, the internet troll who had been spreading lies about her.

"Back to the murder board with this new piece of the puzzle," Claire shouted. Somewhere between Henry's warning shot and Renée's death, someone had walked that path. Someone who saw an opportunity to kill and took it.

"I don't think you should continue here, Claire. And try not to hang out with Torres in public too much, would you?" Ernshaw added.

Claire frowned. She wasn't purposefully following Torres around. The detective was not only her roommate, but they both hung out at The Osprey, just below their apartment. She would bump into Torres whether she wanted to or not.

"Can I ask why?"

"It's just your troll created another controversial post and used today's newspaper picture to create friction."

Claire checked her phone and saw it. A picture of Frank standing next to Renée, with the trident toss in the background, both with tridents in their hands. She prayed that the tridents were not of the same set as the murder weapon. The optics were bad.

"What have I done for them to spew so many horrible things about me and my dad?" she shouted, exasperated.

"No idea, but one thing is certain. You can't go behind our back and ask forensics to test things for you, understood?"

"I don't know what…"

"I'll stop you right here," the deputy chief scolded in a harsh tone. "We know Vikram was testing your dad's tridents for you. The alloy isn't the same, in case you're wondering. Frank and The Osprey's patrons are officially cleared, at least from using these as weapons. But next time I catch you, you'll have to answer to me and the Fraud, Waste, and Abuse board. Forensics has to go through proper channels, understood?"

"Yes, ma'am. Did the lab find something else?"

"This is a police matter, and you're not consulting on this case anymore. Goodbye, Claire."

Chapter Forty-Nine

"This was supposed to be a photo marketing op," Frank Fontaine groaned, staring at the Instagram post captioned: *Frank Fontaine showcasing his trident throwing skills to the Vandstam Queen.* "This fireinyourmouth troll is out from under his bridge!"

Claire leaned against The Osprey's counter, trying not to wince. "Dad, maybe we should pause the trident-throwing game for a while, given everything that's happening..."

"Because of a bully who hides behind a social media handle? Sweetie, this is Caper Cove. Half the town has known me since before you were born, and the other half are tourists who'll be gone next week. That's the beauty of living next to a fancy resort." Frank laughed.

"That's not the point. I care about you and your business's reputation." She had already lost all her catering clients, but she knew from her criminal defense days that lies traveled faster than truth and repairing damaged public images could take time, if it was even possible.

Frank set down the paper and studied his daughter, his eyes crinkling at the corners. "Why don't you enjoy the day for once. No work, just watch the competition and relax. When's the last time you took a day off? Really took one? And no, stress-eating an entire chocolate cake while reviewing case files doesn't count."

Claire opened her mouth to argue, then stopped. "Fine. I'll be upstairs if you need me."

"Want something from the kitchen? I can have one of the servers bring it up."

"Thanks. I still have those truffle shavings Shonda Greenfield insisted I keep from brunch. Might make an omelet or a chocolate mug cake."

Claire climbed the exterior stairs to her second-floor apartment, breathing in the salt air. Below, the beach was transforming into a stadium. The bleachers overflowed with spectators, their excited chatter mixing with the crash of waves. Sponsors' tents dotted the sand like exotic flowers, and news crews positioned their equipment near the judges' platform.

She settled under her balcony awning and unpacked Suggie's camera with its specialized lens. Her best friend was stuck at the spa—her mother, also her boss, wouldn't let her leave until the month-end reports were filed. Suggie had texted a picture of herself drowning in receipts with the caption 'send help', asking Claire to take pictures for her. Suggie needed these shots— one perfect photo of each competitor for her Associated Press portfolio submission—and Claire's balcony offered the perfect vantage point above the competition zone.

Through the viewfinder, Claire focused on her targets: Briggs adjusting his wetsuit, Ramos conferring with his coach while simultaneously trying to fix his hair for the cameras. It felt surreal, photographing murder suspects preparing to compete in the Olympics qualifiers as if they hadn't ended someone's life or been suspected of it because everyone was innocent until proven guilty, or until they tried to flee the country in a paddleboat, which hadn't happened...yet.

"Get ready to witness the incredible Lance Foster, American adaptive surfing champion who's been dominating the waves!" The announcer's voice boomed through the speakers, echoing off the cliffs that cradled Caper Cove's beach. "This athlete redefines what's possible on a surfboard. His upper body strength and control are mind-blowing! Foster has proven time and time again that nothing can stop him from conquering these waves!"

Claire steadied the camera against the railing, capturing Lance as he maneuvered his board through a perfect aerial rotation, his adaptive surfboard working as a seamless extension of his body. The crowd erupted in cheers, and Claire found herself joining them, nearly missing the shot but managing to capture his triumphant finish. Suggie needed to write an article on this guy.

"Siri," she said, lowering the camera, "tell me about Lance Foster, the national surfer."

The AI responded with his story: an Olympic hopeful whose dreams were shattered by a drunk driver during the Hamptons competition, who went on to found the VersaFit Surf Academy, now one of the country's leading programs for athletes with disabilities. He continues to compete in—"

Her phone buzzed with an incoming call, cutting the AI's monologue short. "Hello?"

"Ms. Fontaine." The familiar voice sliced through the festive atmosphere like a knife. "This is Special Agent Devreaux with the FBI."

Claire straightened, her hand trembling as she lowered the camera. "Yes," she answered, wondering if the doxing by the online troll had consequences that required the FBI to call her.

"Ms. Fontaine." Special Agent Devreaux's voice was clear despite the announcer's enthusiastic commentary in the background. "I apologize for interrupting your afternoon, but we've had some significant developments on the explosion investigation. Do you have somewhere private we can talk?"

Claire glanced at the camera, then at the two surfers she was supposed to be photographing. From her elevated position, she could easily spot Axel Briggs warming up near the judges' stand, while Tony Ramos spoke with his coach just beyond the safety barrier. They would have to wait.

"Give me a second." She stepped inside, closing the sliding glass door to her apartment behind her with a soft click, muffling the roar of the crowd and the constant crash of waves.

"Yes?" Claire said, settling on a chair that faced the ocean. Through the glass, she could see Lance being helped onto the beach, his bright smile visible even at this distance.

"We identified the bomber," Devreaux said without preamble. "His name was Kevin Reeds. He had a twin brother, Jacob. Ring a bell?"

Claire's blood went cold. "Jacob Reeds, a wrongfully convicted man whose evidence I tried to exonerate?"

"His sister Hannah found a post about you online, saw you were still alive, and didn't know whether to contact you online, so she contacted us," the agent continued.

Claire's fingers tightened around her phone. On the beach, the next surfer was taking position. The announcer's voice was a distant hum now, like the ringing in her ears after the explosion. "Go on."

"The evidence you found three years ago? You were right. And there's something you need to know about why you survived that day, and about your firm. Hannah Reeds would like to meet with you. She has her brother's journal. She thinks you should read it."

"And then what?" Claire asked.

"Then you can come home, Ms. Fontaine. Back to D.C., back to the law. There's no one left to hurt you. The threat is over."

Claire pressed her forehead against the cool glass of her sliding door. Below, life went on—the competition, the cheering crowds, the endless waves. Her new life, the one she'd been trying to build in Caper Cove, suddenly felt as fragile as a soap bubble. She thought about her briefcase, still packed away in her closet, about the case files she sometimes dreamed about. About how she missed Washington, D.C.'s urbanism and diversity. But also about her new apartment and the way her balcony offered clear sight lines in all directions. In D.C., she had been Claire Fontaine, rising star attorney. In Caper Cove, she was Claire, the chef with the French accent. Neither version was more or less authentic—just different facets of the same person. Perhaps that was the truth about identity: not something fixed and unchangeable, but fluid and evolving, like the tides reshaping the shoreline outside her window.

"I'll need to think about it," she said finally.

"Of course. Hannah's contact information will be in the email."

The call ended. Claire set the phone down with deliberate care, as if sudden movements might shatter something fragile inside her. She pressed her palms against her eyes, but couldn't block out the flood of images rushing back—Olivia's laugh echoing through the conference room, Jess arguing passionately about a pro bono case, Marco's desk cluttered with family photos he'd never see again. Survivor's guilt pressed against her ribs like a weight she couldn't shift. Why had Kevin Reeds deemed her worth saving while condemning everyone else? The randomness of it felt like a cosmic joke.

Outside, the competition continued, waves rolling in as they had for millions of years. Claire picked up Suggie's camera again, but her hands were shaking too much to hold it steady. Below, the beach had become a tableau of suspects: Briggs riding his final wave while Ramos stretched for his heat. Judson stood with his arms crossed near the judges' tent, deep in conversation with Sierra Thorne. Coach Kovac paced the shoreline, occasionally glancing at his phone, while Walsh sat primly in the VIP section, her Blue Crush cap casting shadows across her face. They all looked so ordinary, so at home in this world of sand and surf—just as her law partners had looked perfectly at home behind their mahogany desks.

Claire's phone pinged. An email notification had just appeared with "Hannah Reeds' email + contact information as the subject line. Pages of the bomber's journal waited inside, along with whatever closure it might bring.

Claire stepped back onto her private balcony, returning to the familiar view of the beach she had grown to appreciate. From here, she had a perfect vantage point of all six suspects. She steadied the camera against the railing, thinking how strange it was to be hunting killers again, even if only through a lens. The past, she decided, could wait a few more hours.

Chapter Fifty

The email from Hannah Reeds contained pages from Kevin's journal: *She was the only one who tried to help Jacob. The only lawyer who saw the truth. When they ignored her evidence, when they let him rot in prison for money...I knew the whole firm was corrupt except her. Wednesday is her courthouse day. I'll make sure she's safe.* Claire's hands shook as she read further: *Sasha Petrov owns them all. The law firm launders his money through 'legal fees.' Thirty million last year alone. Claire Fontaine is the only clean one. She has to survive to expose his entire operation, and all the others must perish with me.*

The knock came just as the last competitors cleared the beach. Claire hadn't moved from her spot by the window, watching the sky turn pink. The crowd had dispersed, leaving the cleanup crew to check the bleachers for forgotten items and rake the sand.

"Are you alright?" Torres asked from the sliding door.

"Why wouldn't I be?"

The detective stepped outside, trailing the fresh fragrance of soap, his hair wet from his post-work shower. "You haven't moved since I came home an hour ago. Is it about the FBI call?"

Claire silently gasped, tense. "How would you know about that?"

"Special Agent Devreaux called the station asking about you. He didn't have your new phone number."

"I see." Her voice sounded distant. She'd changed her number after last spring's kerfuffle when she became semi-famous for catching a killer, and people were calling her non-stop for interview requests. She'd forgotten to update the FBI, a Freudian forgetfulness meant to put as much distance between her past and her present. "There was an update in the investigation."

She told him about Kevin Reeds' diary, about being the only one spared, about Jacob Reeds' upcoming release, like she was reciting someone else's story.

Torres studied her. "Usually, when people get news like this, they react. They shake, cry, sigh, or just…something. But you? You're standing here like nothing's changed."

"Nothing has changed, really." She paused. "Or maybe it's too big to feel all at once." She thought about Ricky and Renée's murder investigations, the online troll with a PhD in harassment from Twitter University, the weight of clients' cancellations. "Maybe I'm not ready to break."

"You don't have to. Everyone processes trauma differently." Torres stepped closer, his voice soft. "Though I should warn you, if you're planning on bottling it up, it's technically against California's environmental protection laws."

Claire half-giggled at his legal joke. "Are you psycho-analyzing me?" she asked, her voice breaking.

"I'm not certified. My only qualification is binge-watching three seasons of 'My Psychiatrist and Me' last weekend. But as your roommate and colleague, you can count on me if you need to talk or cry. I know you have Frank—"

"No, please, don't tell my dad. He'd go into overprotective mode. " Frank had enough on his plate with the onslaught of consumers and his sixteen-hour shifts between the taco shop and night bar.

"My lips are sealed."

The gentleness in Torres's voice undid something in her, and tears began to fall. Torres reached for her hand. His touch was grounding, which surprised her. Their physical contact was usually limited to passing at the door. The warmth and strength of his hand steadied her, tearing down the wall she had built around her. The scent of sea salt and coffee that always seemed to cling to him made her want to lean closer.

But she couldn't. She wouldn't. Vulnerability romance, a.k.a. crisis-born hookup, had never solved anything and would only complicate her living arrangement. She pulled away, wiping her eyes with the back of her hand.

"I need some air," she managed, moving toward the door. She could feel his eyes on her as she left.

She descended the stairs, leaving Torres and the comfort of his arms behind in the growing twilight. She ran to the only safe place she could retreat—back to her last era of innocence, when the hardest decision was choosing between chocolate and vanilla ice cream, and 'adulting' was just a made-up word that made her parents laugh.

Chapter Fifty-One

The skyhouse creaked gently in the evening breeze like a ship in harbor. For Claire, stepping into this perfect recreation of their '90s NYU dorm was like slipping through a time portal, away from her present worries and past trauma. She traced her fingers along the corkboard, pinned with concert tickets and Polaroids from her college days. The scent of fresh wood and Gap fragrances lingered in the air.

What she wouldn't give to return to that time of fearless possibilities, when their biggest concern was making it to morning classes after late-night study sessions at that Washington Square café where the barista always drew inappropriate doodles in their latte foam.

"Incoming." Suggie's head popped through the trap door like a whack-a-mole, her arms thrust upward with a massive tote smelling of Korean cuisine.

"Is that bibimbap?" Claire unpacked the bag onto the kitchenette counter, each container releasing a steamy cloud of spices into the air.

"Umma made it for us," Suggie said, hauling herself up. "I didn't say a word, but she's already heard about the FBI calling the station asking for you. She doesn't know what it's about, but she wanted to make sure you had comfort food to help you with whatever you're going through. You know how she is."

Claire laughed, settling on one of the two wooden stools. The Caper Cove gossip chain moved faster than light—Einstein would have been impressed. Despite the breach of privacy, Claire couldn't help feeling a twinge of envy. If only the murder investigations could gather information with that type of efficiency, Ricky's and Renée's cases would be closed.

"Actually, I'm fine." Claire shared the conversation she had with Special Agent Devreaux between bites of steamed rice, detailing the explosion and subsequent investigation.

Suggie's eyebrows shot up. "So fireinyourmouth's malicious doxing actually helped the bomber's sister find out you were alive?"

Claire snorted. "In a weird way, yes. The internet's chaotic god strikes again."

"Are you going to talk with her?"

"I don't know yet." Claire poked at the sautéed mushrooms with her chopsticks. "That's something I really need to sleep on longer than one night. Chatting via phone or video call is not my favorite method of connection. Half of the time, I end up staring at my own face anyway, wondering if that's really what my left eyebrow looks like.

"I can relate to that. Daniel barely calls, and when he does, the screen freezes so much that I'm starting to think he's in a club under a strobe light." Suggie's shoulders slumped. "I miss seeing his actual non-pixelated face so much."

"Any word when he might be back?"

"The unit's spouses mentioned the possibility of an earlier return if the mission wraps up ahead of schedule, but I'm trying not to get my hopes up. Plus, I don't know where we'll be living yet."

"Why don't you both stay in the apartment? There's an extra bedroom, and the second bathroom should be installed by next week."

"An extra bathroom, huh?" Suggie wiggled her eyebrows suggestively. "So no more bumping into naked Torres then?"

"Half-naked Torres," Claire corrected, fighting a blush.

"Well, if Daniel and I decide to move in, I'd make sure to keep the bathroom busy so you get to enjoy the sexy soap thief a little longer." Suggie gave a wicked grin.

The two women dissolved into laughter that echoed through the treehouse. Childhood friends are amazing that way—they could lift mountains of hardship off your shoulders with nothing more than inside jokes and shared giggles.

"I really hope you're not returning to D.C. I've missed you all these years. Same with your dad and Vikram." Suggie gestured toward the window with her chopsticks.

Through the glass, across the neat lawn and carefully trimmed hedges, stood Claire's childhood home with its grey shingles and warm red brick walls. On the second floor, straight across from the skyhouse, Claire's old bedroom glowed softly. Its new owner, Vikram, was pushing a vacuum cleaner back and forth like a man on a mission.

"Must be cleaning for you." Suggie's voice dripped with suggestion. "When's your date already?"

"It's not a date. Just dinner." Claire stabbed at her bibimbap. "He's about to renovate the rest of the house and invited me to check my and my sister's old bedrooms for keepsakes. My dad seemed to have left everything in it when he sold it." Her father had put the house on the market right after her mother passed away, finally accepting that his dream of seeing his family under the same roof would never come true.

"Your dad didn't leave everything. He gave Umma all your clothes. They are in a trunk in the basement." Suggie's voice shot up several octaves in an eerily accurate impression of her mother: "I wouldn't let a weirdo get hold of her pantyhose!"

"Vikram is a bit awkward, but he's very smart and sweet and—"

"Hot, you can say it."

"I was going to say kind." Claire focused intently on her dish. "He got in trouble because I asked him to compare The Osprey's tridents to the murder weapon. Ernshaw kicked me out of the investigation and won't let me check the lab report. I don't even know what the lab found out about the gooey substance on the murder weapon." She scooped a ball of sauce-soaked rice and placed it on her tongue, savoring the moment instead of dwelling on her frustrations. "Today's been kind of a blur."

"Why don't you text Vikram. I bet he can tell you."

"What, now?"

"Sure. It's not like he's got something better to do besides making your old bedroom sparkle like a Disney princess suite," she said, glancing through the window as Vikram fastidiously fluffed Claire's childhood pillow.

Claire pulled her phone from her purse and, before she could overthink, texted Vikram.

CLAIRE: < hi, Vic, did the lab find out what the gooey substance on Renée's murder weapon was?>

The message whooshed away in the digital void. On the other side of the property, in the house across the yard, Vikram snatched up his phone, his fingers flying across the screen.

VIKRAM: <No but I can find out. When do you need it?>

Claire checked the time. Eight p.m. was pushing it for lab results, but…

CLAIRE: <As early as you can?>

VIKRAM: <I can drop it by your place within an hour>

CLAIRE: <that would be amazing, but I'm not home right now. You mind texting it to me?>

VIKRAM: <No problem. Will text you when I get them>

Vikram abandoned the vacuum mid-stroke, sprinted down the stairs, and peeled out of the driveway like he was auditioning for Fast & Furious: Caper Cove Edition.

"Wow." Suggie's eyes were wide. "If that's not devotion, I don't know what that is. The man just left a running vacuum cleaner for you. That's practically a marriage proposal in cleaning language."

"I don't know how comfortable I am with that," Claire said, remembering her own early days at the firm, trying to prove herself to the partners while wrestling with imposter syndrome until the hectic pace and endless pursuit of billable hours became an unsustainable rhythm. She would have to have a chat with Vikram. For now, she hoped the lab results would provide the breakthrough she needed.

"While we wait, I've got the pictures you requested." Suggie pulled her digital tablet from her bag and opened the 'fireinyourmouth folder.' "These are the photos of the crowds for each location where the troll took his pictures. If we cross-reference them and proceed by elimination, we should be able to catch him. Not many people were out the night ICE came to the

Osprey kitchen, nor when Renée posed as the Vandstam Queen in front of the trident toss pit with your father.

As Claire scrolled through the images, her finger suddenly froze. There, in the background of every single image, lurking, was a face she knew all too well.

"What is it?" Suggie leaned in, her shoulder pressing against Claire's. "You look like you've seen a ghost."

"Not a ghost," Claire whispered as she zoomed in on one of the images. "Kerant Weber. I didn't think anything of it at the time, but he's in every single one of these photos with the red hot dog cart in the background. Did he switch from sandwiches to street food?"

"Haven't you heard?" Suggie's breath carried the aroma of the gochujang sauce as she spoke. "He got blasted online by several clients who discovered he was recycling stale bread for his catering services, reheating day-old loaves in the oven for his sandwich platters. My neighbor Jenny told me you could smell the staleness beneath the butter he'd slathered on to mask it."

"Wow. He's lucky he doesn't get sued." Claire rubbed her temples, feeling a headache building. "But what does he have against me?"

"Probably blames you for his failings. Before the troll, your reputation preceded you: fresh, fancy, and healthy with a French twist. Men and their fragile egos," Suggie muttered, her dark eyes narrowing as she studied the photos. "Look at his positioning in each shot. He's always facing the action with his phone, always just far enough away to avoid notice, but close enough to—"

"To document everything," Claire finished, her mouth dry. "The ICE raid, Dad at the trident toss, Renée's performance…he wasn't just selling hot dogs. He was surveilling us."

Claire's phone buzzed. Vikram had the lab results.

Chapter Fifty-Two

Claire was dreaming of stale bread loaves chasing her when her phone pinged her awake. She squinted against the cruel, bright light of her phone screen. 2:14 a.m. What could possibly deserve a middle-of-the-night text? Vikram was usually too polite to disturb her beauty sleep unless specifically asked—which she had. The earlier lab results had revealed that the substance on the murder weapon was hand cream made of shea butter, sweet almond oil, grapefruit, and glitter. However, the toxicology report hadn't confirmed whether the residue was a match to Sierra's hand cream or not. Claire had begged him to notify her ASAP of any new development.

VIKRAM: <The cream is an exact match to Sierra's>

<the teal fiber turns out to be a human hair>

Claire sat upright in her bed, her heart beating as hard as when she waited the jury verdict on a case she defended. Many of the Vandstam crew had blue hair, artificial fiber woven into their braids, each sporting a different hue of blue. But only one had her hair dyed that distinctive teal shade.

CLAIRE: <OMG you're amazing!!! Thank you!>

Sleep completely forgotten, Claire leaped out of bed, her croissant-patterned nightgown flying as she rushed to share the news with Torres. She slammed her door open with all the grace of a caffeinated chimpanzee, then skidded to a halt at his door, and knocked. No answer.

What if he had company over? The last thing she needed was to interrupt whatever might be happening behind that door. Then again, with his early morning shift, he was probably alone and unconscious like any sensible person at this hour.

She grabbed the doorknob in her hand and started to push when the door swung open. Physics sent her stumbling forward until she face-planted directly onto Torres's bed, her dignity left somewhere in the hallway.

The ceiling light blazed like a supernova, and there stood Torres by the door, wearing nothing but an obscenely tight boxer shorts that left little to the imagination.

"If you wanted to jump in my bed," he drawled, leaning against the doorframe with a smirk, "you could at least buy me dinner first."

Chapter Fifty-Three

Later that morning, Claire stood with Suggie in the observation room, watching through the one-way glass as Sierra Thorne recounted her story to Detective Torres and Deputy Chief Ernshaw. The police file lay open on the table, filled with damaging, undeniable evidence that was sure to send her to jail—facts so irrefutable that even the best criminal attorney would find nothing to counter.

The makeup-free performer looked smaller somehow, her teal hair faded under the interrogation room's harsh light.

Sierra's attorney, a man in a tailored suit, sat beside her, his strategic silence speaking volumes. Claire recognized the tactic immediately: let the client show her emotional distress, build a foundation for passion or self-defense. It was clever. Sierra's story could easily frame Renée as the true aggressor, someone who had systematically destroyed Sierra's identity and livelihood.

Suggie slurped her third cup of coffee, the sound echoing in the small room. "I swear," she mumbled into her 'Live, Laugh, Audit' mug, "whoever invented early morning interviews should be tried for crimes against humanity."

Claire shot her friend a look. "You're kidding, right? It's literally the time when everybody's workday starts."

"Not on weekends. Weekends are for lazy mornings and binge-watching TV series. I highly recommend *Yellowjackets* by the way."

"Noted."

"Start from the beginning," Torres prompted on the other side of the glass. "Why Renée?"

"It wasn't supposed to be about her at first," Sierra said, her fingers tracing patterns on the metal table. "When she showed up at that first convention with her blue skin, I actually felt sorry for her. I was the one who encouraged her to embrace it, to join our community." She laughed bitterly. "I basically handed her the weapon she used to destroy me."

"You mean her appearance?"

"The blue skin was just the start. She studied me, copied everything. My mannerisms, my accent, even my signature poses. But she took it further. Instead of makeup and prosthetics, she went full body modifications. Gill tattoos on her neck, fin subdermal implants, bio-wire threading under her skin for that ethereal glow. She turned herself into a living, breathing Vandstam Queen no one could compete with."

Claire thought of how appearances could be both armor and weapon. The more Renée changed her exterior, the more she had obscured who she truly was—until the transformation itself became her identity. It wasn't just about looking different; it was about becoming someone else entirely.

On the other side of the one-way glass, Sierra's hands clench into fists.

"The producers loved it," Sierra continued. "Why hire someone who needed hours in makeup when they could have the real thing? I could have handled losing the role. I really could have. Until I found out about the spin-off series."

"Vandstam: The Air People," Torres said.

"Yes. I'd been developing that character for months. The aerial sequences, the wing designs. I even started taking hang gliding lessons..."

"That's why Lance's hang gliding lessons were fully booked," Suggie murmured, "Renée was preparing for the roles."

"...I discovered Renée had been secretly meeting with the producers," Sierra continued, her hands clenching into fists. "Not just giving them recommendations on the casting, but actively campaigning against me. She told them I was 'too conventional,' that the franchise needed someone who embodied the character naturally.... She was going to take that from me, too."

Torres leaned forward. "When did you find this out?"

"Two nights before she died. I confronted her about it." Sierra's voice sounded distant, as if she was reliving the moment. "I found her by the catering tent after the evening showcase. Asked her straight out if she'd been sabotaging my auditions."

Sierra's composure began to crack.

"She didn't even try to deny it. Just looked at me with those blue eyes and said, 'Sierra, you taught me everything about being a queen. But you could never teach me how to be authentic. That's something you either are or you aren't.'"

"That must have been painful to hear," Ernshaw said.

"She told me I should be grateful," Sierra's voice hardened. "That she was doing me a favor by helping me 'find my real path.' As if eighteen months of mentoring her, of opening every door I could, meant nothing. As if I was just…disposable."

Claire leaned closer to the glass. That had been the trigger, she could see it in Sierra's eyes.

"I said, 'I created you, Renée. Without me, you'd still be hiding from cameras.' And she laughed." Sierra's hands were shaking now. "She actually laughed and said, 'No, Sierra. You created an imitation. I became the real thing.'"

"Is that when you decided to hurt her?"

Sierra was quiet for a long moment. "That's when I realized she wasn't just taking my crown. She was erasing me. Making it so that everything I'd built, everything I'd worked for, would be forgotten. Like I'd never existed at all."

This was the exact moment Sierra had chosen murder over defeat. It was written in the way her shoulders straightened, the way her voice went flat and emotionless.

Sierra's voice cracked. "The franchise was about to announce the new court roster, the names of the lucky few they would endorse as official Vandstam representatives. My agent got an advance copy. I wasn't on it. No part at all. Not even as a substitute."

"So you decided to erase her instead," Ernshaw said.

"I followed her that night. I knew her routine with Ramos. When I heard Henry's spear gun go off, I thought it was perfect. He'd done my job for me. But when I found his spear on the ground..." Sierra's gaze drifted to a faraway place. "I realized the universe was giving me a second chance to fix what Renée had broken."

Ernshaw and Torres exchanged looks.

"You planned this," Ernshaw said. It wasn't a question.

In the observation room, Claire shivered despite the warmth. She had seen enough killers to recognize the moment passion transformed into obsession, when resentment curdled into hatred. Sierra had planned it perfectly. She used Grumpy Henry's shot as cover, knew the secluded beach's access points, and followed Renée. If Vikram hadn't found the one teal fiber and hand cream and Henry's security footage hadn't caught her distinctive gait, it would have been the perfect crime.

"That fleeting moment between finding the trident and deciding to use it was all the premeditation the law required. Sierra could get the maximum sentence," Claire whispered.

"The irony," Sierra said, staring at her reflection in the one-way glass, "is that she was talented enough to succeed without stealing my life. She could have created something uniquely her own. Instead, she chose to become a copy of me, of my Vandstam character. A better copy, maybe, but still just a copy."

"She might have gotten away with it," Claire finished. She thought about the way Sierra had helped them find the French movie that had inspired Ricky's murder, how she'd played the concerned friend while methodically destroying any evidence of her own crime.

"About getting away with it. Any updates about Ricky's murder?"

"Ramos's attorney filed a motion to dismiss. They're convinced some outsider did it, so they've created this elaborate profile of a strange, suspicious character. What they don't understand is that sometimes the most dangerous monsters are the ones who look just like everyone else."

Chapter Fifty-Four

The morning sunlight spilled through the thinning fog, a rare break in June's usual gloom as spectators claimed their spots on the metal bleachers. The competing surfers warmed up along the water's edge as the judges took their places, coffee and morning sandwiches in hand. The line at The Osprey was getting long, the scent of brewing coffee and grilled meat wafting up from the taco bar, which desperately needed an extra hand, but Claire had to wait for Suggie to finish her article.

"Done!" Suggie declared with triumph as her computer sounded the whoosh of sent email. "That should make the front page!" Her coverage of the murder investigation had gotten her a lot of attention from the brick-and-mortar newspapers. She turned to Claire. "You ready?"

"As much as I'll ever be!" Claire grabbed the croissant hat Suggie had brought her and led the way out the door.

Today was the day they would catch fireinyourmouth, the anonymous troll who had been harassing her online, and who they traced to the hot dog seller. Kerant Weber was about to get caught, if the trap they had crafted the night before worked. Claire took her position at The Osprey's smoothie booth and proceeded according to plan.

Catching this guy should be easy—unlike finding Ricky's killer, who was still at large. A light shiver ran along her neck and spine. Two murderers active in the same week in Caper Cove was an unsettling statistic for the small town.

Claire adjusted the ridiculous croissant hat on her head as the ocean breeze threatened to carry it away. The plush pastry bobbed against the cloudless sky, its golden-brown curves concealing one tiny camera monitoring the boardwalk and beach in front of her.

"I still think we should've gone with the shark," Suggie's voice crackled through Claire's earbud from her strategic position on the other side of the boardwalk, shaded by a palm tree.

"The croissant is so absurd it's perfect," Claire murmured, arranging fresh fruit while pretending not to notice the seagulls eyeing her hat. "No one would suspect it's actually surveillance equipment."

She caught her reflection in the ice cream freezer's glass—the croissant perched at a rakish angle, looking completely out of place among the beachgoers in their swimsuits and sunhats. @fireinyourmouth wouldn't be able to resist the opportunity to humiliate her in that hat. The hidden camera blended perfectly with the chocolate drizzle details, its lens catching the glare of sunlight off the ocean.

"Heads up," Suggie whispered. "Hot dog cart incoming. He's setting up right by the railing with a perfect vantage point of your booth."

Claire's heart raced beneath her apron, but she maintained her composure as she blended a coconut smoothie, the whir of the blender drowning out the crashing waves. Through the swirling crowds of tourists and beach visitors, she spotted him. Kerant Weber was positioning his red cart with calculated precision, his eyes hidden behind mirrored sunglasses.

"The second camera is active," Suggie confirmed, referring to the tiny lens they had placed on Claire's balcony to get an aerial view of the scene. "We've got eyes on every angle."

Claire served her customers with extra enthusiasm, making sure her croissant hat bobbed visibly as she scooped ice cream and topped smoothies with extra whipped cream. A seagull swooped particularly close to her hat, making her duck, but the camera stayed steady.

"Activity," Suggie whispered over the sound of crashing waves. "Phone's up….Got it! Time stamp 09:17:33. He just photographed you making that rainbow shave ice."

Claire maintained her cheerful demeanor as she handed change to a sunburned tourist, fighting the urge to glance at Weber. On her phone's hidden feed, she could see him pretending to check the weather while his camera was clearly focused on her booth.

"We've got everything: photos, timestamps, GPS coordinates," Suggie murmured. "Now we just have to wait for fireinyourmouth to post."

As soon as he did, he would be caught in flagrante delicto—red-handed.

They didn't have to wait long. Less than a minute later, Claire's phone pinged, the notification making her nearly drop a scoop of mint chocolate chip. @fireinyourmouth had tagged her in a post, accompanied by the photo of her in the croissant hat taken seconds ago:

Look who's trying to be cute at The Osprey! Someone tell this wannabe she's about as French as a gas station croissant and about as much a chef as she is a lawyer. Bet that hat's the closest thing to real pastry she's ever made. Pick an identity and stick with it!

#FraudChef #FailedLawyer #IdentityCrisis #PickALane #FakeAccent

Claire smiled as she read the post. The timestamp matched perfectly with their surveillance footage. They had him. The question now was what to do with all this proof. Part of her wanted to confront him, but doing so could play against her. Society always disliked women who stood their ground, especially in public. And Weber would likely play the victim. She needed to be patient and let Suggie go forward with the plan they had agreed on. Patience, she told herself. Patience. Alas, patience required the absence of a trigger.

Chapter Fifty-Five

Weber stepped away from his hot dog cart and walked up to Claire's counter to order a smoothie. Claire took his small piña-colada order with a smile, made an extra-large smoothie, kept half aside, and handed it to him.

"I know you're fireinyourmouth," she said, her eyes meeting her reflection in his mirror glasses.

"You can't prove it," Weber whispered as he took the smoothie. Then he declared loudly enough for nearby customers to hear, "Let's see if what the internet's saying about you is true, that you're just a failed lawyer playing dress-up as a French chef?" He walked away.

"Who would like a free piña-colada smoothie? I made too much and have two small ones," Claire offered to the next customers—a young couple with bride-to-be and groom-to-be caps eagerly accepted.

Weber was serving his third hot dog when his phone started buzzing uncontrollably. His sunglasses slipped down his nose as he reached for the phone and discovered the post by @AnonymousCaperCove: timestamped pictures of Weber capturing Claire with his phone and posting as @fireinyourmouth. The accompanying caption read "Local Food Vendor Exposed as Online Troll."

"Hot dogs getting cold there, buddy," Torres said, materializing beside the cart. "Interesting reading material?"

Weber's head snapped up to find half of Caper Cove staring at their phones and then at him, their expressions ranging from disgust to disappointment.

"This is harassment!" Weber's voice was high. "What about her?

Pretending to be French, stealing clients with her fancy accent!"

"My accent is from a medical condition," Claire's voice cut through the growing crowd as she approached, the croissant hat perched defiantly on her head. "Which you'd know if you had bothered to ask instead of trying to destroy my business."

The irony wasn't lost on her—how quickly people formed judgments based on something as superficial as how she spoke. Her accent had become both her vulnerability and her strength. In a world obsessed with authenticity, people's most genuine parts were often the most questioned.

Weber's complexion deepened from red to purple. "I can best her anytime! This whole French chef act—"

"Then prove it," Suggie's voice rang out as she shouldered through the crowd, phone raised to record. "Competition, live-streamed, with ingredients chosen by your followers. Unless you're afraid to face her without a keyboard to hide behind?"

The crowd's murmur grew louder, phones raised to capture the moment.

"I have nothing to prove! That smoothie of hers is disgusting!" Weber spat, hurling his drink to the ground.

"Her smoothie was delicious," the bride-to-be protested. "She gave us the same you had."

The crowd erupted in boos until Weber retreated. Within minutes, #CulinaryShowdown #cookoff were already trending, and the San Diego County News had picked up the story.

"Sometimes the best revenge is simply proving someone wrong in front of an audience," Claire said as they walked away.

Suggie typed on her phone. *#RevengeBestServedHot.*

Claire half-smiled at the hashtag, her mind drifting to the murder investigations. Renée had been the victim of "hot revenge"—Sierra's immediate reaction to losing her crown. But what about Ricky? What if Ricky was the victim of a revenge served cold?

Chapter Fifty-Six

The international surfing competition was in full swing. Athletes from around the world exchanged jerseys and gifts—French berets, Japanese kokeshi dolls, Australian boomerangs, Brazilian Havaianas flip-flops, and Moroccan tea glasses—with fellow competitors. Their friendly chatter filled the air with accented English, turning Caper Cove into an international hub. It reminded Claire of Washington, D.C., where she would enjoy the daily melody of languages spoken by foreign diplomats and World Bank employees.

Claire manned the smoothie booth through lunch. Her newly found online-born popularity had sent a tsunami of customers who requested piña-colada smoothies—the drink of choice to show support. The constant whir of the blender had become the soundtrack to her day.

"If the Guinness World Records judge were here, I bet you'd have won most smoothies made by a single person in three hours," her father said as she took a well-deserved break.

"Every customer asked me whether Weber and I are going to face off in a cook-off," she said, massaging her sore hands. "Someone started a Kickstarter for the cook-off ingredients, and it's already fully funded. Can you believe it?"

"I know. I've already pitched in." Frank said.

"Dad!" Claire's voice rose in mock outrage.

"I did too," Torres announced as he joined them under the patio shade. "Everybody at the station and the medical examiner's office did. Including your sweet Vikram."

Claire ignored the comment and directed her gaze to the beach. The afternoon sun transformed the water into a sparkling canvas. Briggs was one of the four surfers competing in the water, waiting for the next wave. His secret sister and now manager was watching him from the shore.

"And here's Briggs approaching this clean right-hander…beautiful positioning…off the bottom into the bow with so much speed and control," the surf commentator's voice boomed over the beach. "…comes flying through, oh my god, comes over the foam ball and makes it out of that tube. That's textbook surfing right there!"

Torres took a long pull from his beer bottle. "The way that guy handles himself over the foam ball makes him a pro for sure. No wonder Ramos wanted to get rid of Ricky."

"About that. You think Ramos lied about Ricky?" Claire whispered to Torres, leaning in so close she could smell the remnant of his aftershave.

"He's telling the truth," Torres said before grabbing his sandwich with both hands, a drop of tartar sauce escaping onto his thumb. "Or he was at least too relaxed to kill anyone that night. According to the club's night manager, the night of Ricky's death, Ramos ordered not one but two servings of tiramisu and a hot chocolate at midnight. When room service brought it up, he was already in his pajamas, watching Vandstam reruns." Torres said, his mouth full, crumbs catching in the stubble along his jaw. "The guy who delivered it said Ramos was so mellow he could barely keep his eyes open. Tipped him fifty bucks and told him to 'spread the love.'"

"That's very specific." Claire picked up a California roll, the seaweed wrapper crackling between her chopsticks.

"Gets better. Security footage shows him trying to swipe into the wrong room twice before figuring out he was one door down. Then at six AM, he nearly missed morning practice because he was still in such a good mood he forgot to set his alarm."

Claire raised an eyebrow. "Are we sure he wasn't…"

"Already tested. Clean for anything illegal. Just a guy who had a very good night. Not exactly the behavior of someone who just committed murder. The motel's keycard logs and cameras confirm he never left his room until morning."

"So we can rule him out?" Suggie asked, jumping into the conversation, her long-lens camera hanging from her neck.

"The DA just dropped the charges. Plus, the killer had to be pretty tall, because Ricky was hit straight in the lumbar spine with drag marks going up. Ramos's only five foot four. We need to look elsewhere."

Claire squeezed a roll with her chopsticks, the rice compacting between the wooden sticks. "We need to check the people he wronged in the past."

Torres frowned. "How far in the past?"

"As far as you can go. Maybe start with the National Driver Register. Unless his parents were able to expunge his record, there should be a trace of his criminal history, including DUIs."

The semi-finals concluded with thunderous applause as the last competitor rode her final wave to shore, the judges tallying scores while exhausted athletes gathered their boards. The competition was about to be officially adjourned until tomorrow's finals, when Ricky's parents took the stage. They requested a minute of silence for their beloved son."

"Are they for real?" Suggie asked. "Did you know the mother came to the spa, demanding the most expensive package for free, stating that as a grieving mother, that's the least people could do."

"What did your mom say?"

"That she was sorry, but that the spa was a business with overhead costs and not a charity, but she could give her free samples." Suggie's smile was sharp as she adjusted her camera strap.

Torres snorted. "Looks like psychopathy runs in the family. They also put up a one-million-dollar reward."

"That's...generous," Claire said with suspicion.

"Not quite." Deputy Chief Ernshaw said as she approached the counter, her uniform pristine despite the heat. "They want to sue Caper Cove PD because no advances have been made on the case. The mayor needs your help."

"Now?" Claire checked her watch that marked five and sprang up. "I have to go! I need to get ready for the Gidget competition." She grabbed a napkin and jotted a few words—*motion to dismiss for failure to state a claim and/or based on police's qualified immunity and/or for summary judgment, and request a stay of proceedings, claiming that ongoing litigation could compromise the active investigation*—and handed it to Ernshaw. "Here's what they should do first. I'll talk to your attorneys on Monday."

She grabbed the last sushi roll and shoved it in her mouth. Shonda Greenfield had asked her to look Vandstam-like to represent the franchise at the Gidget contest—an opportunity to gain new catering clients that Claire couldn't miss. Suggie pulled the keys from her purse.

"The Bingles want to sue us for fifty million," Ernshaw warned.

"What?" Caper Cove didn't have that type of money. She could see the Bingles dragging the litigation to waste the city's money, forcing them to settle. Caper Cove would have to file for bankruptcy if the Bingles won.

She needed to identify the killer in the next twenty-four hours or Caper Cove would face financial ruin.

Chapter Fifty-Seven

The sky glowed pink and orange as the last evening of the surfing festival drew to a close. Claire settled behind the judges' table on the competition stage, next to Walsh, who was replacing the late Ricky, and a Hollywood studio executive whose pristine white suit featured the turquoise embroidery of the Vandstam logo. The seashell-studded gavel beside her scoring sheets—a gag gift from Suggie—reminded her this was supposed to be fun. Two weeks ago, she was crafting seven-course dinners for wealthy vacationers. Now, she was judging a Gidget/Vandstam cosplay contest, her French bob replaced by a tight blue braid.

"Stop scowling," Suggie whispered. "You're supposed to be enjoying this. It's one of Caper Cove's best traditions."

Her best friend's notebook was already half-full of observations about the contestants—everything from authentic 1950s bikinis and perfect blonde flips to elaborate blue-scaled warrior costumes that would make any Viking merpeople proud.

Claire hadn't wanted this gig, but when the Vandstam casting agent explained that her French accent would bring sophistication to the contest—like Simon Cowell but pretty and kind—to judge the contest, Suggie had practically shoved her into accepting. "Think of the publicity and new clients," she'd insisted. "And you need to get out of your apartment."

The stage manager approached with a tablet of contestant information. Behind him, a teenage girl in Vandstam warrior regalia helped an elderly woman perfect her Gidget victory roll. Claire picked up her scoring pencil, surprised to find herself fighting back a smile. Maybe she would find an unexpected clue that would break open the case of Ricky's death.

"Keep your eyes peeled," she whispered to Suggie, who had started photographing the scene.

"First up, the Gidget category," the announcer's voice boomed. Twenty women of every age walked to the stage in 1950s attire, from bikinis to cropped pants with tied blouses.

The men's category came next in board shorts, t-shirts, and canvas sneakers, followed by the Vandstam category. Claire took meticulous notes, attributing points based on conformity and creativity until the last category was announced.

"Next up, the innovation category…"

Claire's attention drifted to the preparation area. After Sierra's arrest, the remaining Blue Crush team and Vandstam crew had rallied, transforming the courtyard into a mythical waterfront, their elaborate costumes catching the late afternoon light.

"Remember," the studio exec whispered, "we're looking for someone who embodies innovation, not just accuracy. We're scouting inspiration for the Vandstam spin-off, the Air Tribe."

Claire nodded, though her mind processed the few days. Sierra's confession to killing Renée, Ricky's unsolved murder, and the Bingles' upending lawsuit still nagged at her. The only missing clue was the metal pipe that had struck Ricky.

A collective gasp snapped her attention back to the stage. Lance Foster was making his entrance. His wheelchair had been transformed into something from Leonardo da Vinci's sketchbooks—elegant wooden wings extended from either side, incorporating modern carbon fiber and traditional sailcloth. The contraption gleamed with a distinctive silver paint that caught the dying sun like mercury.

"Presenting Lance Foster as the Vandstam Air Knight!"

Foster soared down the specially constructed ramp, the wind catching his wings. The crowd erupted as he executed tight turns impossible in a regular wheelchair. The silver paint flashed with each movement. Claire gasped quietly.

"Torres," she whispered into her phone, not taking her eyes off Lance's contraption. "I need you at the Gidget contest stage. Now."

By the time Lance completed his routine, Torres was there, studying the wheelchair's framework. The distinctive silver paint, the perfectly sized metal supports that could easily have been used as a weapon...

Chapter Fifty-Eight

"Lance Foster," Torres said quietly as Lance waited backstage. "We need to talk about the night Ricky died."

Lance's smile faded. He looked at Claire, then back at Torres. His shoulders straightened, a decade of buried rage finally surfacing. "Yes?"

"You were at Launch Point that night," Claire said. "Why?"

"I saw him stumbling to his car the first day of the festival," Lance's voice was tight with controlled anger. "Rich guy, expensive sports car, drunk off his ass. Just like ten years ago, when he put me in this chair. He was sixteen, showing off in daddy's car. His parents paid their way out of everything—my medical bills, the lawyers. I couldn't afford to fight it."

Torres's expression shifted with understanding. "You confronted him."

"I tried talking sense at first," Lance's laugh was bitter. "Told him to call a ride-share. You know what he said? 'Like I give a damn about other people's lives.' He didn't recognize me. Ten years, and he didn't even remember the kid whose life he destroyed."

Claire leaned forward. "You knew about his team's catfishing plot. You're the one who cancelled the meeting with the waitress."

"I wanted a face-to-face with him when he was off guard. I told him who I was. Reminded him about the settlement and the NDA his parents forced on me. He just…smirked. Said, 'Well, you got the money, right? What more do you want?' Like it made up for everything, my surfing career, my dreams, all of it." Lance's hands gripped his armrests until his knuckles went white. "I just wanted an apology. One genuine moment of remorse. Instead, he laughed. Started mocking my paragliding wheelchair, my 'pathetic' attempts at flying."

"So you charged at him," Torres said softly. "With the wing support."

Lance nodded, his eyes clear and unflinching. "I'd seen him around town, still driving drunk, still treating people's lives like they didn't matter. I realized he'd never change. He'd keep hurting people, keep buying his way out of consequences. So I ended it." He looked at his silver-painted wings. "The irony is, these actually work. I really can fly now. More than he ever could."

Torres handcuffed Lance and read him his rights, the handcuffs looking stark against the elaborate costume. Unlike Aurora, who vanished when threatened, Lance had stayed and fought—no matter how long it took. Suddenly, Aurora's disappearance felt different. She hadn't fled teenage drama. She'd escaped something real, something dangerous.

The crowd had fallen silent, phones raised, but Claire's focus was on Lance's face—no relief, but grim satisfaction, as if he had finally balanced some cosmic scale.

"Wait," she called as Torres began to lead Lance away. She turned to the judges. "Before he goes, I think we should announce our decision."

The movie executive, Amy Walsh, and Shonda Greenfield exchanged uncomfortable glances, then handed their sheet to the stage manager.

"The winner of the innovation category," the stage manager announced, his voice carrying across the stunned crowd, for his groundbreaking fusion of adaptive technology and Vandstam mythology...Lance Foster."

A confused murmur rippled through the spectators.

"Sometimes innovation comes from our darkest places, but that doesn't make the achievement any less real," Claire whispered to Suggie, who was recording the scene. Her shoulders relaxed. Caper Cove would be free from the Bingles' lawsuit.

As Torres led Lance away, Claire caught snippets of conversation from the crowd—about justice and vengeance and the weight of old wounds as if the tragedy they witnessed was just a tiny pebble on one's road.

The remaining contestants resumed their performances, but Claire's thoughts went to her missing sister and whether she should return to

Washington, D.C., now that she was safe from any threat. Her healing was complete, besides her lingering French accent, for which some decided to give her a hard time, like Weber and his online harassment. Maybe she should agree to the cooking challenge. Crushing his audacity publicly might be the best way to shut down his behavior and regain the clients she lost. But was Weber/Fireinyourmouth arrogant enough to take her on?

Chapter Fifty-Nine

The last rays of sunset painted Vikram's kitchen in gold as Claire arrived, a bottle of cider in hand. After Lance Foster's arrest, the quiet domesticity of his home—her childhood home—felt like stepping into another dimension.

"Perfect timing," Vikram called from the stove, where steam rose from a pan filled with vibrant green spinach. "I made palak paneer. The first Indian recipe we made together, remember?"

Claire inhaled the rich aroma of ginger, cumin, and cilantro. "It smells incredible," she said, placing the bottle on the counter. "What babysitter could forget a ten-year-old math genius who loved to cook?"

Vikram smiled, stirring wilting spinach. " You were so patient, showing me how to toast the spices just right. Remember how I kept burning the cumin?"

"Your mother warned me about that— your kitchen smelled like smoke for days," Claire laughed, leaning against the island. It was surreal seeing this grown man, confident in his movements, around the kitchen, and reconciling him with the gap-toothed kid who'd once needed a step stool to reach the counter.

"Those cooking lessons got me through med school," he said, adding paneer cubes to the spinach. "You always said palak paneer was the perfect dish to forget the world's craziness. Something about the creamy cheese and earthy spinach just resets your brain." Vikram paused, his wooden spoon suspended over the pan. "You know, I never told you why I really bought this house."

Claire looked up from her cider, surprised. "I assumed it was a good investment."

"It was, but that wasn't the real reason." He glanced toward the kitchen window. "After your family left, this place sat empty for two years. When I finished my residency, Frank was ready to sell, and I...." He shrugged, suddenly looking more like the shy ten-year-old she remembered. "I guess I wanted to take care of it. To keep it safe."

Claire felt her throat tighten, unprepared for the weight of shared memory in his voice.

"I left your bedroom and Aurora's room exactly as they were," he continued. "I told myself it was because I didn't need the space, but honestly? I couldn't bring myself to change them. It felt like erasing something important."

The vulnerability in his confession hit Claire like a physical force. This accomplished professional was still, in some ways, the earnest boy who'd wanted to fix everything he could reach. She settled at the counter, noticing how he'd preserved her mother's ceramic fruit bowl in the breakfast nook, and how the kitchen had transformed from her parents' 1980s design to a modern space. Everything familiar and unfamiliar at once, like the man himself.

"So, are you going to face off with Weber in a cook-off?" he asked.

Claire shook her head. "I don't think so. I'm not one to throw down the gauntlet."

"You should do it. Weber needs to be taught a lesson." Vikram's eyes flashed with unexpected intensity. "That man's ego could fill the morgue twice over."

"That's certainly true, but I'm not sure I could challenge him without losing my respectability as an attorney," she said. If she couldn't make a living as a caterer, returning to law was her only option. "Let's talk about something else, like how grateful I am you offered this impromptu dinner..."

"Well, you said you'd come over once the investigation was over... I heard about Lance's arrest," Vikram said softly. "Must have been intense, finding the killer after all this time."

"It was unexpected," Claire admitted, accepting the cider he offered. "I never imagined someone could carry that much anger for years."

"Some wounds never heal. Speaking of which, how are you doing with everything? The trolling, the murders, the FBI calling…"

Claire took a long sip of her drink. "Truthfully? I feel like I'm standing at a crossroads. Washington beckons, but Caper Cove has started to feel like home again." She paused, studying his face. "Thank you, by the way. For helping with the lab tests, even when it puts your job at risk."

"I'd do it again," he said simply, transferring the palak paneer to a serving dish. "Besides, it worked out. We found our killer."

"Two killers," Claire corrected. "And one internet troll. That's quite a record for a small beach town."

After dinner, Vikram led her upstairs to her perfectly preserved bedroom, a teenage time capsule. The air felt thick with memories of late nights studying, of crying over Aurora's disappearance, of plotting escape routes from Caper Cove with Suggie.

"And Aurora's room?" she whispered.

"The same," Vikram replied. "Just across the bathroom you shared. Take your time, I'll be downstairs if you need anything."

Claire nodded, but instead of going to Aurora's room, she found herself drawn to their shared bathroom. Something had been nagging at her since learning about Sierra's methodical planning—how she'd studied every detail of Renée's life before destroying it. It reminded her of something Aurora used to say: "The best hiding places are the ones people see every day but never really look at." Standing in the bathroom doorway, Claire remembered how Aurora had been secretive in the weeks before she disappeared. She'd catch her sister coming out of the bathroom at odd hours, not using it but just…lingering. And Aurora had been obsessed with their childhood spy novels, always talking about secret codes and hidden messages.

Claire knelt before the small linen cabinet, running her hands along its edges. Aurora had been fascinated by the cabinet's construction when their father installed it—she'd watched him work for hours, asking questions about the joints and backing. If Aurora had wanted to hide something where only she would think to look…. Her fingers found the slight seam in the wood that she now remembered Aurora pointing out years ago, calling it "sloppy workmanship." Claire pressed firmly until a soft click sounded.

The false back of the shelf swung inward, revealing a hidden compartment. "For important things," Aurora had said. "Things that need to stay hidden until the right time." They'd used it to hide Haribo Tagada candies bought at the gourmet store and binged on behind their parents' backs. Growing up with a physician mother, candies weren't allowed in the house. The space was empty now, but something caught her eye—a folded paper tucked into the hinge at the back.

With trembling fingers, Claire extracted it, unfolding what appeared to be a page torn from a book. She recognized it immediately. It was from "The Lonely Spy," their favorite childhood book about a teenage sleuth. A small paragraph was circled in red pen: "I must go away to keep everyone safe. Don't look for me. I'm choosing this. Tell no one. Someday, maybe, I'll find my way back." A single handwritten letter stood in the margin—A.

The note blurred as tears filled her eyes, but she couldn't stop staring at that single letter—A. Aurora's signature flourish, the way she'd always signed her name with an exaggerated curve.

Claire sank onto the edge of the bathtub, the paper shaking in her hands. All these years, they had believed Aurora had been kidnapped or killed. The investigation had gone cold. Her parents' marriage had shattered under the weight of grief and blame.

This note changed everything.

Chapter Sixty

The fog had lifted early, welcoming a bright midmorning sun, a rare treat for the surfing enthusiasts who attended the festival. Athletes were surfing the last heat of the competition. The atmosphere was more relaxed but bittersweet. The side pool where Lance Foster taught adaptive surfing was now empty. Claire leaned against the boardwalk rail, her gaze lost on the morning horizon, still processing the discovery of the night before, unable to focus on the final competition.

"Delphine Vauché again showing off her agility and fearless style…" the commentator's voice echoed through the speakers.

"You okay, kiddo?" Frank asked.

"I'm okay," Claire replied, withholding the fact that her sister might be alive, struggling to look him in the eye. Sharing with him her discovery would either give him hope that might be false or destroy him all over again. What if Aurora was still in danger? What if telling Frank put her at risk? As much as she wanted to share her hope with her father, she couldn't reveal anything until she investigated further. "I just wish justice worked better, you know…Ricky might not have been such a bully and might still be alive if his parents hadn't constantly bailed him out."

"People's pride often gets in the way of parental judgment and tough love. Many are more concerned about the effects of their children's mistakes on their own reputations than on the long-term consequences for their children's lives."

"I'm happy you're officially cleared, though. Reputations are harder to build than to destroy."

"Not here in Caper Cove. When your friends and community truly know you, they'll always have your back. Like you and Suggie," he said, motioning at her best friend, who was capturing the athletes with her camera. "Two peas in a very driven pod."

Claire smiled. "About that, do you mind if she moves into the apartment's third bedroom? Daniel might be back early, and they don't have a place of their own."

"Sweetie, consider the apartment yours. Invite whoever you wish, just don't forget to inform Torres about potential new roommates. The second bathroom should be functional on Wednesday." Frank gave her a one-armed hug. "I've got to go, and so do you. The cook-off is in less than three hours."

"What cook-off?"

"The cook-off between you and Weber. The account SharpWave announced it earlier."

Tension filled Claire's forehead. "I'm not going to be forced into a challenge. I have nothing to prove."

Frank threw her a grimacing glance. "You sure about that? You don't want Weber to win by forfeit."

Claire chewed on her lips. Her dad was right. Because of that stupid troll, her catering bookings for the next two months had all been cancelled, leaving her virtually unemployed. She expected her catering for Shonda Greenfield and the Gidget contest would bring her new clients, but it was too early to tell. She needed an income—one that preferably didn't require her to work for her dad.

"When and where is that cook-off?" she asked.

"Today, five p.m., at the Osprey. Right after the festival's closing ceremony."

"So it's really happening then."

"Yep. Alexandra Frenet, the French surfing champion, confirmed it with me. I was about to close for the day, right after lunch. But I don't mind keeping it open to watch my daughter kick that jerk's butt."

"Do I need to prepare? What are the parameters…the competition guidelines?"

"Nobody knows. @SharpWave will post instructions at four."

Claire shook her head. "This is insane...."

"It's also juicy, prime news content," Suggie remarked as she joined her side. "The perfect balance between news and tabloid."

Claire shook her head. "If that can help your career, I'm happy to help."

Everything was getting back to normal. The killers were apprehended, her father was officially cleared of any suspicion of wrongdoing, and her bully was outed. Now, how does someone prepare for a secret-ingredient cook-off?

Chapter Sixty-One

The beachfront part of The Osprey had never felt more like a gladiator arena. Two pop-up tents had been erected to protect the food from the seagulls, two competition-grade grills gleamed under the afternoon sun, and the normally cozy space had been transformed with additional prep stations and cameras to accommodate the upcoming showdown. #Culinaryshowdown was trending number one in Southern California, and the livestream hadn't even started.

"Five minutes!" Suggie called out, adjusting her headset. She had somehow convinced the San Diego County News to sponsor the event, turning what started as a personal vendetta into legitimate entertainment. "You ready?"

Claire tied her apron with steady hands, surveying the outdoor kitchen setup. After everything—surviving an explosion, solving murders, facing down trolls—a grilling competition felt almost peaceful. Almost.

"Ingredients are sealed in these coolers," Torres announced, gesturing to two identical containers positioned between the grills. "Chosen by public vote and verified by an independent chef." He shot Claire a quick wink. "No peeking."

A black SUV pulled up to the beach access path, and Kerant Weber strutted across the sand, wearing a pristine white chef's coat that still had creases from its package. His hot dog cart was conspicuously absent.

"Last chance to back out," he sneered, though Claire noticed his hands shaking slightly as he tied on his apron, the ocean breeze immediately tugging at the strings.

"Funny. I was about to say the same thing."

The beachfront was packed with spectators – locals, tourists, and what seemed like half of the Caper Cove police force gathered around the competition area. Frank stood near the front, beaming with paternal pride. Even Vikram had escaped his morgue duties to witness the showdown, though he was carefully avoiding Torres's territorial glares.

"Going live in three…two…." Suggie counted down, her phone raised to capture everything.

Then a taxi pulled up to the beach access path. The camera turned around, revealing a familiar figure in desert camo. Daniel, still dusty from deployment, stood in the afternoon sun.

Suggie froze, her face going from confusion to disbelief.

"Daniel?" Suggie whispered, before breaking into a run. They collided in an embrace, and when Daniel swept her into a kiss, her phone clattered to the ground. The crowd erupted in cheers as husband and wife reunited, while Claire teared up for her friend's happiness.

"Sorry I'm late," Daniel grinned, steadying Suggie. "But I couldn't miss this."

"If we're done with the romantic interruptions, some of us have reputations to defend," Weber called out, his face flushed with impatience.

"Then let's begin." Torres stepped forward, his badge catching the sunlight. You'll have exactly two hours to create a complete three-course meal using *all* the ingredients provided. "And remember," he added, raising his voice to be heard over the crowd, "You'll be cooking for thirty people tonight—judges, special guests, and randomly selected audience members. So plan accordingly."

Claire and Weber took their positions at opposite cooking stations

"Judges will score on creativity, technique, and taste. And in the spirit of community involvement, the audience will also get to vote! Their collective opinion will count as one additional judge's score," a member of the audience added. "Winner takes all."

Claire and Weber took their positions at opposite cooking stations. Each area had a grill, but Claire was pleased to see additional equipment, including a Dutch oven and portable burners. The sealed coolers sat between them like gauntlets thrown down in challenge.

"Open your coolers…now!"

Claire lifted her lid and almost laughed. Inside was the most bizarre combination of ingredients she'd ever seen: durian fruit, blue corn tortillas, lavender, ghost peppers, and…escargot. The internet had outdone itself.

"Begin!"

Chapter Sixty-Two

Claire's former confidence in the courtroom fighting for her clients' lives didn't translate well when facing a grill—she couldn't prepare or remove the dangerously biased jurors. But both situations were comparable enough, she thought, pumping herself up. She would have to improvise without clear instructions, like when she was blindsided by a prosecutor withholding crucial evidence. She was familiar with dealing with the chaos and frustration of the unknown. And she was a chef, no matter what people wanted to believe or told her that she was not. Because she'd decided, and this was enough. She took a deep breath and glanced at her competitor.

Weber's face fell as he surveyed the ingredients. Reheating pre-made food wouldn't work here. This required actual skill.

"I am a chef and I am a lawyer," she repeated out loud for all to hear. "I don't have to choose between them any more than I have to choose between breathing and having a heartbeat."

She closed her eyes and breathed in the scent of charcoal and sea salt, recalling the words of her culinary and legal mentors: "Master the fundamentals, then make them your own," and "Cooking is the art of transforming obstacles into opportunities. Just like life itself."

For the next two hours, she worked with the same methodical precision she'd once used to dismantle a prosecutor's case. Every technique was deliberate, every choice strategic. She wasn't just cooking—she was making an argument. An argument that she could be exactly who she chose to be. The beachfront was a blur of motion and fragrant smoke. The crowd's excited murmurs and occasional gasps mixed with the local radio music and the sizzle of ingredients hitting the hot grill. She set up the Dutch oven for steaming, knowing it would be perfect for the delicate escargot. The durian's custard-like flesh, when properly treated, could become a savory sauce. The ghost peppers would cut through the richness, and the blue corn tortillas could be transformed into delicate chips.

Beads of sweat trickled down her back as she worked, the heat from the grill combining with the afternoon sun. Her fingers moved deftly, chopping ingredients and herbs. Meanwhile, Weber was struggling. His movements were frantic, unpracticed. When he knocked over his third tray, the resulting crash made everyone wince.

"Time's up!" Torres called. "Step away from your stations!"

The judges' panel—the festival organizer, the head of the Caper Cove restaurateur association, and the Swim and Racquet Club's head chef—approached the first table. The thirty plates for the audience members were already being distributed, each person receiving a small portion to taste and evaluate. Weber's rubber-tough escargot rested on a tortilla with a slice of durian.

Then came Claire's three-course meal: blue corn tostadas with Dutch oven-steamed escargot in herb butter, durian-glazed grilled fish with lavender-infused rice, and caramelized pineapple with ghost pepper choco-late sauce. Her techniques skillfully blended grilling with steaming, show-casing her versatility. The architecture was French, but the soul was pure California fusion cuisine. The judges sampled each dish, their expressions shifting from polite interest with Weber's creation to undisguised pleasure with Claire's offerings. In the background, audience members were casting their votes via an online survey.

The judges' deliberation was brief. "The winner is," the festival organizer announced, his voice carrying over the sound of crashing waves, "Claire Fontaine!"

"And I should note," Torres added with a grin, "that the audience vote was unanimously in Claire's favor as well!"

The beachfront erupted in cheers. Weber slumped against his grill, defeat written on his face and tense body.

"I believe you owe my friend an apology," Suggie said, her phone recording everything while Daniel's arm stayed wrapped around her waist.

Weber straightened, his face red. "I…I'm sorry. For saying you had to be one thing or another. You made it look so easy, being…everything you are. While I…. " He gestured at his failed dishes and then at himself. "I couldn't even be one thing well."

"Being yourself isn't easy," Claire said softly. "Neither is letting others be themselves. But it's possible." She extended her hand. "I'm Claire. I'm a lawyer, a chef, an American with a French accent, and probably a dozen other things I haven't figured out yet. And that's okay."

He shook it, managing a weak smile. "I'm Kerant. I'm…a guy who makes decent hot dogs but terrible life choices. Working on the second part."

"We all are," Claire replied.

* * *

Later, as the crowd celebrated at The Osprey, Claire found herself on the beach with Torres, watching the sunset paint the ocean gold.

"Not bad for a former lawyer," he said, handing her a piña colada smoothie. The paper cup was cool against her fingers, the cool fruity aroma a nice change from two hours in front of a hot, spicy grill.

"I'm not sure about 'former,'" she said. She hadn't told everyone how much she missed practicing law. Fighting to save people's lives from wrongful convictions and unjust punishments was what she was all about. Yet, she could also make a difference here—protecting her dad and growing old by her best friend's side—but she would need regular clients.

"As long as you keep cooking," Torres said. "The department would riot if we lost our favorite chef."

Nearby, Suggie and Daniel swayed together on the beach, their silhouettes merging and separating against the crimson sky, while Frank held court at the bar, already turning the day's events into local legend.

Claire lifted her smoothie in a toast. "To new chapters?"

Torres bumped his coffee cup against her cup. "To new chapters."

The sun sank lower, casting long shadows across the sand, but Claire wasn't watching the sunset anymore. She was wondering how she would proceed next in her search for her sister, but right now she needed to savor the moment.

The murder cases had been solved, the troll vanquished, and the cooking equipment was being packed away as the stars began to appear. Claire Fontaine, chef and occasional detective, she thought, wiggling her toes in the sand.

"Do you work tomorrow?" she asked.

Torres swiveled toward her. "Why? You have something in mind?"

"I was thinking of lending the apartment to Suggie and Daniel. Giving them full privacy for like twenty-four hours. You know…since he just returned from deployment."

"Sure, but we're not allowed to sleep on the beach and all the hotels must be booked because of the competition."

"I have a place," she said. "Follow me."

Chapter Sixty-Three

The sun was setting when Claire led Torres across Suggie's backyard, their footsteps silent on the grass. The massive oak's silhouette towered above them, its branches stretching toward the appearing stars.

"You're seriously inviting me to a kid's treehouse," Torres said, his voice heavy in skepticism.

Claire laughed and aimed her flashlight at the wooden ladder. "Not quite. After you, Detective."

Torres eyed the weathered rungs dubiously. "You sure it's solid?"

"If you fall, I'll catch you," Claire promised with a serious tone.

"Oorah for a fellow Marine," Torres groaned as he started up the ladder, each rung creaking beneath his weight.

As Claire climbed through the treehouse's trap door, she found Torres standing perfectly still, taking in the recreation of her college dorm room. The Taylor Lautner and Lady Gaga posters, the twin beds with matching comforters, and the small kitchenette with stools. The gentle hum of a mini-fridge provided the only sound.

"This is…" Torres turned slowly. "Impressive and slightly disturbing."

Claire switched on a string of fairy lights that cast a warm glow across the space. "That's Suggie and Daniel's work. The NYU dorm recreation was Suggie's way of holding onto that time when everything seemed possible."

"Before the real world hit?" Torres asked, touching a framed concert ticket with unexpected gentleness.

"Something like that." She gestured to one of the beds. "There are clean sheets in that trunk. The bathroom situation is…primitive. There's a camping toilet behind that curtain, and we'll have to use the garden hose to rinse off in the morning."

Torres laughed. "Still better than some places I've been stationed at."

An easy silence settled between them as Torres examined the photographs pinned to a corkboard—younger versions of Claire and Suggie grinning from various locations around New York City.

"Congratulations on your culinary victory, by the way," Torres said, settling onto the other bed. "Weber's face when you served that durian fish—"

"It was the escargots on blue corn chips that really broke him," Claire said, with a satisfied smile.

The distant sound of waves crashing against the shore filled the comfortable silence that followed. Claire hugged her knees to her chest, suddenly aware of how strange yet natural it felt to be here with Torres.

"I never thanked you," she said finally.

Torres raised an eyebrow. "For vacating our apartment so Daniel could have a proper homecoming?"

"For allowing me to help with the investigation."

Torres leaned back against the wall, his expression unreadable in the dim light. "I'm not sure I had a choice."

Claire studied him—the way the string lights softened his features, how different he looked without the constant alertness that characterized him at work. Here, surrounded by the artifacts of her past, he seemed more human somehow. Less Detective Torres, more just…Ben.

"Can I ask you something?" she said, picking at a loose thread on the comforter.

"If it's about the shower thing, I maintain that your French soap smells better than mine."

"It's not about the soap." Claire took a deep breath. "If someone disappeared a long time ago, and the trail had gone cold…where would you start looking again?"

Torres straightened, all traces of playfulness vanishing from his expression. "This is about your sister?"

Claire nodded, not trusting her voice. "The cases we solved reminded me of Aurora," she said as they settled into the treehouse. "Renée transformed herself to escape who she'd been. Lance waited ten years for justice. Aurora…Aurora found a third option. She disappeared to stay alive but left herself a way back."

"Records that weren't digitized twenty years ago would be accessible now. Witness statements, old phone records, even weather reports from that day." He paused. "But cold cases…they're cold for a reason."

"I know." She pivoted, meeting his gaze. "But what if I told you I found something in my old bathroom at Vikram's house? Something my father never saw."

Torres leaned forward, elbows on his knees. "I'm listening."

She told him about the hidden compartment in the linen closet and the torn page from 'The Lonely Spy'. "It was our favorite book growing up. There was a circled paragraph: 'I must go away to keep everyone safe. Don't look for me. I'm choosing this. Tell no one. Someday, maybe, I'll find my way back.' There was a handwritten letter A in the margin."

Torres sat up straighter. "She left voluntarily?"

"All these years, we thought she was taken. My parents' marriage fell apart over it." Claire's voice cracked. "But she chose to leave. The question is why, and who was she protecting?"

"You'd need to track down original case files, find out if they kept evidence that could be tested now."

"I know that too."

"Your dad—"

"He can't know until I'm sure," Claire insisted. "I can't put him through that roller coaster again."

Torres nodded, understanding in his eyes. "Okay." He reached across the space between them, his hand covering hers. "Where do we start?"

The word "we" hung in the air between them.

She looked at their hands, his fingers warm and steady against hers, and felt something shift, like puzzle pieces finally falling into place.

"You don't have to—"

"I know I don't," Torres interrupted. "I want to."

Outside, an owl called into the darkness, its voice echoing across the quiet neighborhood. The treehouse creaked gently in the breeze.

"I'm not staying in Caper Cove forever," Claire whispered.

"I know that too." Torres's hand remained steady on hers.

"D.C. is home. My work is there. My life is there."

"And yet, here you are." He gestured around the treehouse. "In a pretty convincing recreation of your past, talking about investigating your sister's disappearance."

"That's different."

"Is it?" Torres's eyes held hers. "You're a lot of things, Claire Fontaine. Criminal defense attorney with a French accent syndrome. Caterer extraordinaire who can make durian fruit palatable. Murder solver who wears ridiculous hats to catch internet trolls."

Claire laughed despite herself. "Weber tried to make me pick just one."

"And you told him where to stick it. Literally." Torres's eyes held hers. "You're not a person who fits in one box, Claire. That's what makes you… you."

"That used to scare me."

"And now?"

Claire considered this. "Now I think maybe the point isn't to fit in a box. Maybe it's to build a life big enough for all the pieces of yourself."

"Your point?"

"My point is, maybe home isn't a place. Maybe it's where you feel like yourself, whatever version of yourself you want to be."

He squeezed her hand once, then released it. "Now, if we're going to solve a decades-old case, we'll need coffee. Please tell me this elaborate time capsule includes a coffee maker."

Claire pointed to the kitchenette. "French press only."

"Of course it is," Torres said with a groan, but he was smiling as he stood up. "You handle that. I'll call in a favor with a buddy at the California State Police."

As he pulled out his phone, a strange lightness filled her chest. Not the weightlessness of letting go, but the buoyancy of possibility. Whatever came next, whether in D.C. or Caper Cove, or somewhere yet undetermined, she wouldn't be facing it alone.

Acknowledgments

Special thanks to Verena Rose for acquiring Threads of Deception, book one the Suddenly French Mystery series; to Shawn Reilly Simmons and Deborah Well of Level Best Books for continuing the series. My heartfelt gratitude to the Pitch Wars mentees class of 2015 and Sisters in Crime members for their support and camaraderie throughout the writing journey, especially Alison Miller, critique partner extraordinaire. To Jonathan Maberry and his Writers Coffeehouse meetings, for stressing that writing is as much a business as it is an art; to Kate Jackson and Lauren Silberman for their guidance in the world of published mystery writers. A big thank you to my readers who have helped me get to where I am today. With love and thank you to my sons, Aiden and Neil, for their unwavering belief in me, and to my husband, Tony, for reading all my manuscripts. With love and gratitude to all.

About the Author

Elle Jauffret is a French-born American lawyer, former criminal attorney for the California Attorney General's Office, and culinary enthusiast. She graduated from Université Côte d'Azur Law School (France) and the George Washington University Law School (USA) and is an active member of Sisters in Crime, Mystery Writers of America, and International Thriller Writers. An Agatha Award nominee, PenCraft Award recipient, and Claymore Award finalist, Elle volunteers as a write-in host for Sisters in Crime and regularly appears as a panelist, moderator, and guest speaker at conferences across the country (including WonderCon, Comic-Con, San Diego Writers Festival, and Southern California Writers' Conference). She has chaired the Pediatric Literacy Program at the Walter Reed National Military Medical Center (aka Bethesda Naval Hospital), promoting children's literacy among the military community. Elle is an avid consumer of mystery and adventure stories in all forms, especially escape rooms. She lives in Southern California with her family, along the coast of San Diego County, which serves as the backdrop for her Suddenly French Mystery series.

You can find her at https://ellejauffret.com or on social media @ellejauffret.

AUTHOR WEBSITE:
  https://ellejauffret.com/

SOCIAL MEDIA HANDLES:
  https://www.instagram.com/ellejauffret/
  https://www.facebook.com/elle.jauffret
  https://www.threads.net/@ellejauffret
  https://bsky.app/profile/ellejauffret.bsky.social

Also by Elle Jauffret

Threads of Deception (2024)